NO WAY OUT

NO WAY OUT

a novel

CHRISTINE KERSEY

Covenant Communications, Inc.

Published by Covenant Communications, Inc.
American Fork, Utah

This is a work of fiction. The characters, names, incidents, places, and dialogue are products
of the author's imagination, and are not to be construed as real.

Printed in United States
First Printing: July 2005

11 10 09 08 07 06 05   10 9 8 7 6 5 4 3 2 1

ISBN 1-59156-845-5

*I would like to dedicate this book
to my husband Dave and our four children—
Ryan, Valerie, Michael, and Laura.
They've always supported me in my quest to
write and become published.*

ACKNOWLEDGMENTS

Many people were kind enough to give me input as I labored with this story. My sister, Annette Fruit, has always been supportive and encouraging and one of my best readers. My parents, Bob and Suzanne White, have always encouraged me to follow my dreams. Several people assisted me by reading my drafts and giving suggestions. I would particularly like to mention Howard and Marie Wattleworth. As an accountant, Howard provided relevant input to this novel. I would also like to thank Special Agent Gary Price for his input on how the FBI might respond to certain situations.

I received invaluable help from my editor at Covenant, Angela Eschler. My writers' group has also been helpful in critiquing my work, and I appreciate their support and encouragement.

Although many people gave me suggestions regarding this book, ultimately I decided what to include and what not to include, and any mistakes are mine alone.

CHAPTER ONE

Eric Breuner gazed at his sleeping wife one last time before creeping down the stairs and out the front door. He took only one change of clothes; he would pick up a few other things later.

The sick feeling in his stomach intensified as he backed his Jeep out of the garage and the pressure of doing what was required mixed with distress over Abby and what her reaction would be. When he visualized his wife and what he was about to put her through, he nearly turned back. Pounding the steering wheel in miserable frustration, Eric squeezed his eyes closed.

He pressed the accelerator, knowing the only solution was to get this whole mess over with as quickly as he could. He only wished it had been possible to explain to Abby what was about to happen. That wasn't an option, but just the same, he deeply regretted that his wife was going to have to suffer. His heart ached at the thought of his sweet Abby, pregnant and all alone.

How can I do this?

He pulled over to the side of the road, contemplating once again whether this was really necessary. One glance at the documents on the passenger seat convinced him it was.

After the initial discovery, the situation had rapidly gotten out of control. He had hoped he would be able to deal with his situation without leaving, but after what had happened the day before, it was obvious that leaving was the only option. Even so, last night he had tossed and turned until the decision was final.

Despite the fact that he wanted to let Abby know what was going on, he was convinced they would all be better off if she didn't know anything. Not only that, he knew if he tried to explain, she would never allow him to go. He hoped she would someday be able to understand why he had made this choice. And that she would be able to forgive him.

Resigned to the inevitability of his task, Eric put the Jeep into gear and pulled back onto the road. A few minutes later he realized he needed to double-check the map for directions to his destination. He pulled over again and opened the glove box, digging through the contents.

"Where'd it go?" he said out loud. He reached his hand under his own seat and felt a thick bundle. "There it is." He pulled it out and blinked at the un-expected items. "What the—?"

He nervously read the note and thumbed through the other items.

Good thing I found these. If the police had found them first my situation would be disastrous.

Now he knew with certainty that leaving was the right thing to do. He also knew that as long as he was driving this vehicle he could be tracked. But going back home wasn't an option. He thought for a moment, then turned another direction. He left the Jeep where he hoped it wouldn't be found for a while and hurried down the street to the nearest bus stop.

Once he reached his destination, he found a pay phone. Rather than speak to Abby he wanted to leave a message; he knew she would be taking the girls to school about now. He picked up the phone, dropped in some change, and dialed. At the sound of the ringing on the other end, he quickly hung up, suddenly not sure what to say. He heard the coins slide into the cup at the bottom of the phone.

How can I apologize for something she doesn't know about? How can I let her know I love her but that this is unavoidable?

Eric collected the change from the dispenser and dropped it in again. He let out a sigh and dialed his home number.

"Hello, you've reached the home of the Breuner family," the message began in Abby's smooth voice. "We can't come to the phone right now, so please leave a message and we'll call you back."

Eric's heart pounded as he listened to his wife's voice. He took a deep breath before leaving her a simple message.

* * *

"Abby Breuner," the nurse called out.

Abby set the parenting magazine back on the table and followed the nurse into the examination room. After the nurse left, Abby looked at the monitor that would soon hold the image of her unborn child.

Eric should be here, she thought with irritation.

She recalled the message he'd left on the answering machine that morning. Even though he had apologized for not coming with her, she was annoyed he hadn't made this appointment his top priority.

"Good morning, Mrs. Breuner." A tall woman wearing a white lab coat walked into the room. "I'm Marcia. I'll be giving you your ultrasound."

"Good morning," Abby said as she handed the woman the blank videotape. She climbed onto the examination table and lay back on the pillow. The cool gel on her stomach made her start, but as she looked at the screen her discomfort was quickly forgotten.

Mesmerized by the moving figure before her, she stared at the screen. The picture was so clear that she was speechless for a moment. As the technician pointed out the baby's head, Abby could actually make out the shape of a miniature nose. She could see four fingers and a thumb on each tiny hand, and five toes on each exquisitely shaped foot.

As Marcia pointed out her baby's beating heart, Abby gasped in wonder at the miracle of it all.

"Do you want to know the baby's gender?" Marcia asked.

"Well, I . . . I don't know. I wanted to know before, but now I'm not sure." She bit her inner lip, wondering if she should find out.

Marcia nodded. "If you'd like, I can write it down on a piece of paper and you can decide later."

That seemed like a good compromise to Abby, and she agreed.

"I'll just stop the recording here, and if you'll look the other way I'll see whether you're having a boy or a girl."

A few moments later Abby watched in fascination as the technician folded the green piece of paper with the secret information into the shape of a tiny bird.

At the look of pleasure on Abby's face, Marcia explained, "It's origami. You'd be surprised at the number of people who can't decide if they want to know their baby's gender. I thought it might be fun to do more than just write it down on a piece of paper and hand it over." She laughed quietly. "This little bird is my specialty."

Abby took it from her. "It's beautiful."

"Thank you," Marcia said, smiling. "That one's usually a big hit."

Before Abby left the room, the technician gave her several still photos of the ultrasound along with the video. Abby glanced at the photos and saw that the pictures were as clear as they had been on the monitor.

A short time later Abby stared at herself in the doctor's bathroom mirror, wondering if her face radiated the happiness she felt. She pushed her shoulder-length brown hair behind her ears and leaned in closer to apply pale-colored lipstick, noticing her green eyes had a brilliance to them that hadn't been there earlier. Certain it was from the inner joy she was feeling, she smiled to herself. Then, popping the lid back onto her lipstick, she straightened her maternity blouse and left the bathroom, hoping she wouldn't be late for work.

Nadine, her supervisor at the county library, didn't like it when employees took time off from work to take care of personal business. Fortunately, Abby was usually able to make appointments on her own time.

As Abby walked out of the doctor's office, she looked up at the sunny California sky and thought it looked bluer than when she'd arrived. Rose-scented air drifted toward her as a smile lit up her face. She felt all was right with the world on this splendid late-April morning.

However, Abby's mood diminished a little as she pulled into the library parking lot. Just as she had feared, she was ten minutes late for work. Hoping Nadine wouldn't notice her late arrival, she went to the back to put her things away before getting started. Abby grabbed the stack of books waiting to be checked in and began scanning them into the computer. After only a few minutes she heard a voice behind her.

"Oh, there you are, Abby. I was beginning to wonder if you were coming today."

Abby put a smile on her face before turning toward Nadine. "I'm sorry. My appointment took longer than I expected. I'll stay an extra ten minutes this afternoon."

"Very well," Nadine said, a tight smile on her face. "When you're finished checking in the books, you can start shelving in the nonfiction section."

Nadine's forced smile reminded Abby that she was hoping to quit soon. Even though she loved the library and enjoyed working there, she wanted to be a full-time mom again. She and Eric had only begun talking about the possibility, but she knew he was worried about being able to make ends meet if she quit. The year before, when Susannah had started first grade, she had started working part-time. But soon she wouldn't even have time for that.

As Abby scanned in the books, she thought about the bills she and Eric had racked up in their quest to become pregnant with this baby. Their insurance hadn't covered the fertility treatments, so they had taken out a home equity loan and then had nearly maxed out their credit cards to pay for the procedures. After only two attempts, they couldn't afford any more tries and had given up.

Pulling the last pile of books in front of her, Abby glanced around for more that needed checking in. Mary, her friend and coworker, came in dragging a cart behind her.

"Hey there, Abby," Mary said, smiling. Her voice dropped to a whisper. "Nadine was looking for you."

Abby rolled her eyes. "I know. We've already spoken. You'd think I was an hour late instead of ten minutes."

Mary gave her a sympathetic glance. "Well, here are more books for you." She pushed the cart closer to Abby. "I'm going to start shelving the children's books."

"See ya," Abby called after her, grabbing an armful of books and setting them on the counter. It was nice to have someone she could commiserate with.

Oh, well, she thought as she set to work. *I won't be working here forever. I'll just enjoy my job while it lasts.*

The baby kicked a few times in agreement, and Abby rubbed her abdomen, love for her unborn child filling her heart.

It was a miracle she was pregnant at all. After getting pregnant so easily with her first two children, it had come as a shock when after two years of trying she still hadn't been able to conceive. That was when the fertility treatments began. When the money ran out, she and Eric figured that was it for them—two beautiful girls. She'd tried to accept that but longed for more children. Then, when she least expected it, she became pregnant without any medical help at all.

"Abby."

She nearly jumped at the sound, then whirled around to see who had called her name.

"You were daydreaming." No smile graced Nadine's narrow face.

Redness flooded her cheeks at the rebuke, and she had unpleasant memories of being scolded by her mother. "I'm sorry. It won't happen again."

"See that it doesn't. The books are beginning to pile up already." Nadine spun on her low heels and walked away.

She noticed Nadine had brought in two more carts of books to check in and shelve. She worked through her embarrassment for two hours until it was time for her lunch break. Before leaving, she checked the area where new books were held to see if the book she'd requested had arrived. She loved to read, and one of the perks of her job was being privy to the arrival of new books.

"Yes!" she said to herself as she pulled the book from the shelf. After checking it out she walked to her car, ready to go home for lunch. Eric was supposed to meet her there so they could watch the video of the ultrasound together. Amazingly, Nadine hadn't said anything when Abby had requested a long lunch.

Maybe she felt guilty for scolding me earlier, she thought as she pulled into her garage, leaving enough room for Eric to park his Jeep.

The first thing she did was put the video of the morning's ultrasound into the VCR. Her heart lifted in delight at the sight of her unborn child. At the conclusion of the video she remembered the delicate bird the technician had made for her and retrieved it from her purse.

Pleased it had not been damaged after sitting in her purse all morning, she could hardly wait until Eric came home for lunch so they could open it together. She set it high on the bookshelf where it wouldn't be misplaced, then stood daydreaming for a moment.

* * *

Abby was getting worried. She looked at her watch again. Her usually prompt husband was thirty minutes late. She paced the room, feeling the restless motions of her baby, as if it too were worried.

He knows I only have a limited amount of time. He would have called if he couldn't make it.

She remembered their disagreement the night before. Although she had wanted him to come to her doctor's appointment, this lunch date had been their compromise.

Abby stopped pacing and walked into the kitchen, convinced Eric would have called by now if something had come up. She picked up the phone and dialed his cell number. His voice mail came on. She waited for the beep before leaving a message.

"Hi, it's me. Just wondering where you are." She tried to hide her irritation. "I'm at home. Did you forget our lunch date? I have the ultrasound for you to see, and if you want to know if it's a boy or a girl you'd better get home soon. I don't know what we're having, but I have a surprise for you if you want to know. Please call me back."

Eric, of all the days to not answer your phone, today is the worst. Abby looked at the little green origami bird. *I want you here so we can find out together if we're having a boy or a girl.*

Wondering if someone at Eric's work might know where he was, she picked up the phone again and dialed.

"Central Valley Construction," a cheery voice answered.

"Accounting department, please," she said, trying to keep her voice pleasant.

When she reached the right department she identified herself and asked for her husband.

"One moment," the voice told her.

Abby tapped her fingers on the counter and glanced at the clock.

The woman came back on the line. "I'm sorry. He's at lunch. Do you want to leave a message?"

"Can you tell me how long ago he left?" She was glad to know he was on his way.

"One moment, please. I'll see if I can find out."

Abby let out a sigh, wondering if Eric would walk in the front door before the secretary came back on the phone.

"Mrs. Breuner?"

"Yes, I'm still here."

"I came in late this morning, and I haven't actually seen him yet. I'm afraid I don't know when he left, but I would expect him back anytime. Would you like to leave a message on his voice mail?"

Glancing toward the door to watch for his arrival, Abby shook her head. "No. He's probably on his way now."

She hung up the phone and walked to the front window, looking in the direction Eric normally came from. No one was on the street. Abby checked her watch and saw that her lunch break was rapidly ending.

CHAPTER TWO

Abby waited another ten minutes before eating lunch without Eric. Angry with him for not showing up or calling, she could hardly taste her chicken salad sandwich.

Who does he think he is? He's not the only one with a schedule to keep. Does he place so little value on my time and my job that he can't bother to let me know he had something more important to do than meet me for lunch?

Shaking her head in anger, she decided she would have a talk with him that night. If he couldn't remember she had a job to get back to, maybe he was ready for her to quit. That was fine with her, but in the meantime, she did have a job and she got back in time to run into Nadine.

"Did you have a nice lunch?" her supervisor asked, a surprisingly pleasant smile on her face.

Abby wasn't about to admit her lunch had been a total failure. "It was fine, thanks."

"Of course, you're staying an extra half hour to make up for the long lunch. That, plus the ten minutes you already promised, right?"

She opened her mouth to protest, but Nadine turned and walked away before she could say a word. A short while later, as she sat on a chair and arranged the books on the shelving cart in the proper order, she thought about the rest of her afternoon. That's when panic momentarily hit. She usually got home at least half an hour before her daughters walked home from school—now they would arrive home before she did.

Catherine Spencer, Abby thought in relief. *I'll call my visiting teacher. She has a third-grader in Tiffany's class. I'm sure she wouldn't mind letting the girls come to her house until I get there.*

No one answered at Catherine's house. Leaving a message, Abby groaned and hung up the phone. She wondered if her job was worth it, and she vowed to talk to Eric that evening. At the thought of her husband, she bristled. *If he had called to let me know he wouldn't be able to make our lunch date, I could have come right back to work and I wouldn't be late getting home this afternoon.* Trying to put aside her anger and annoyance, Abby shelved the nonfiction books from her shelving cart.

Later that afternoon, Abby checked her watch and realized it was decision time. Catherine had not called back, and school would be getting out in a few minutes. Abby was supposed to stay at work for another twenty-five minutes, but if she did her daughters would come home to a locked and empty house.

I should have arranged for this type of situation a long time ago, she chastised herself. Putting away the half-finished shelving cart, she set off to find Nadine. She found Mary first. "Have you seen Nadine?" she asked her coworker.

"She left early today," Mary said, an eyebrow arched in comment.

Letting out a breath of disdain, Abby shook her head. "It figures. Well, that makes my decision easier. I'm cutting out of here early too."

"Ooh, are you sure?" Mary asked.

"I need to get home before my girls do. I don't have a choice. Besides," she said, her mouth turned down in a frown, "what's she going to do, fire me?"

"Uh, I wouldn't put it past her," Mary said. "I think that's her favorite part of the job."

Abby laughed out loud, drawing a sharp look from one of the librarians. She covered her mouth with her hand, then waved silently to Mary and went to get her things before heading home.

Susannah and Tiffany were sitting on the porch when she arrived. They jumped up and ran to their mother after she pulled into the garage. Abby immediately noticed that seven-year-old Susannah's eyes were red, as if she'd been crying. Nine-year-old Tiffany seemed calm, however.

"Mommy, mommy. Where were you?" Susannah cried, fresh tears coursing down her cheeks.

They couldn't have been waiting for more than five minutes, but Abby knew five minutes could feel like an eternity to a young child. As she gazed at Susannah's tear-streaked face, Abby's anger at Eric for throwing off her whole day was rekindled.

She pulled her daughters into her arms and hugged them. "I'm sorry I'm late, sweethearts. I got here as soon as I could." Abby was glad she hadn't stayed any longer; there was no telling what kind of state she would have found Susannah in.

"I tried to tell her you'd be here in a minute, Mom," Tiffany said, pulling back from her mother and shooting a look in her sister's direction. "But she wouldn't listen."

"Thank you, Tiff." Abby let Susannah go as well and stood up. "Let's go inside and have a treat. How does that sound?"

Susannah perked up and ran into the house.

After Abby fixed them a plate of cookies, she went into the office to check for messages. She hoped Eric had called to explain his behavior.

The button was blinking. Abby hit PLAY and listened as Eric's voice filled the room. "I . . . I guess I just missed you. I wanted to tell you that I love you and . . . I'm sorry." Abby immediately realized it was the message from that morning. In her haste to be on time to her appointment, she'd forgotten to erase it.

Before her anger could revive, another message began playing. It was Eric's coworker, Timothy Meher.

"Eric, this is Tim. Call me at home when you get this message."

She called Eric's office, a whole list of questions flooding her mind. Carly, the secretary, informed her she hadn't heard from Eric yet and had no idea where he was.

"Are you sure he didn't have an appointment today or something?" Abby asked, a slight feeling of alarm beginning to replace her earlier irritation. She could hear the woman typing on her keyboard.

"No, it doesn't look like he had anything scheduled. I'm sorry, Mrs. Breuner."

"Do you know if he came in this morning?" she asked as different scenarios raced through her fertile imagination.

"I'm not sure. I could ask around and call you back. Would that help?"

Grateful for her suggestion, Abby felt calmer. "That would be great."

Abby tried to busy herself in the office while she waited for the phone to ring. After a few minutes she went to see what Tiffany and Susannah were up to. Seeing they were nearly done with their snack, Abby asked them to get started on homework.

"I need help, Mom," Tiffany said, pulling out her daily folder.

Trying to put aside her worries about Eric, Abby walked over to her older daughter and looked over the assignment. It was a multiplication worksheet. "What do you want me to help you with, sweetie? Do you want me to get the flashcards so you can practice?"

Tiffany groaned. "No, I want you to help me figure these out."

"I'll tell you what. Do all the ones you know, then we'll see where you are, okay?"

"Okay," she agreed, obviously not happy with her mother's answer. Nonetheless, she bent over her paper, concentrating intently.

The shrill ring of the phone broke the quiet. Tiffany jumped from her chair and raced to the phone before Abby had a chance to get it.

"Hello?" Tiffany said, apparently hopeful it would be one of her friends so she could get a break from her dreaded homework. "She's right here." Tiffany frowned and held out the phone to her mother. "It's for you. She says her name's Carly or something."

"I'll take it in the office. Please hang it up in a second." She hurried to pick up the office extension. "This is Abby."

"Mrs. Breuner, this is Carly at Central Valley Construction."

"Yes," she said, as she heard the click of the other phone being hung up.

"I'm afraid no one has seen Eric today. In fact, he had a meeting this morning and didn't show up."

Abby shook her head, trying to clear her mind, wondering if she'd heard Carly correctly. "Are you sure he never came in?" Her stomach suddenly felt like it was full of wasps trying to force their way up her throat.

"It appears that way, yes," Carly said.

"That can't be right," she whispered.

"I beg your pardon?" Carly asked.

"Nothing. Thank you for your help. Good-bye." Abby slowly hung up the phone, puzzled at what was happening. Eric was an accountant and rarely left the office. She wondered if Tim, one of the other accountants, had any answers.

She called the office again. Carly told her Tim wasn't there and she didn't know if he would be in the next day. She regretfully refused to give Abby his home number, saying it was against company policy.

"Look, my husband is missing," Abby said, guilt for her previous anger at her husband compressing her chest. "Tim left a message earlier asking Eric to call him at home. I don't have his home number and I need to talk to him. Please give me his number."

"Mrs. Breuner, I'm sorry, but I could lose my job. They're really strict about this." Carly paused. "Have you tried the phone book?"

"No," Abby said, trying to control her now-shaking voice.

"I'm sorry."

Abby hung up the phone and grabbed the phone book, thankful to have something concrete to do.

Setting the phone book on the desk, she sat down and began thumbing through the *Ms* until she came to the place where *Timothy Meher* should be. He wasn't listed.

Though she would have liked to hide out in her bedroom and think through what was happening, she remembered she had two children in the next room who were depending on her to make their world okay. She smoothed back her hair and calmly walked into the kitchen, trying to hide her very real feelings of apprehension.

Apparently she looked like her usual self because Tiffany smiled and asked, "Are we going to have a baby brother?"

A sharp pain flared in her heart as she thought of Eric and his desire to have a baby boy. She kept her composure as she answered her daughter's question. "I don't know yet, honey." She didn't mention the little origami bird, not wanting to explain they were waiting for Eric before opening it. At the thought, her mind jumped to horrible conclusions and she couldn't seem to stop herself from assuming the worst.

Abby spoke to the girls in a quiet voice. "If you want to take a break from homework, you may watch TV if you'd like."

The girls cheered and raced into the adjoining family room, thrilled at the unusual privilege. Then they began arguing over which program to watch. The sound of them fighting stretched Abby's already taut nerves to the breaking point, and she took several deep breaths to keep from screaming at them to quiet down. Just as she was about to yell at them, they settled on a program and were soon peacefully watching TV.

The phone rang and Abby snatched it from its cradle. "Hello?"

"Abby, this is Tim Meher."

"Oh! I'm so glad you called. I'm really starting to worry." Abby was relieved to finally speak to someone who might have answers.

"Carly called and said you needed to talk to me. What's going on? Is Eric there?"

"No. That's why I wanted to talk to you. Have you seen him today?"

"No, I haven't. But it's urgent that I speak to him as soon as possible."

It's urgent that I speak to him as soon as possible too, she thought as she closed her eyes. Opening them again, she focused on the new plant her visiting teacher had given her on her last visit, a time when her worries were few.

Bringing her mind back to the distressing conversation, Abby forced her voice to remain calm. "I haven't heard from him since this morning. That's why I wanted to talk to you." She shifted her gaze to the clock. It was a quarter past four. "He was supposed to come home for lunch today, but he never showed up or called. Is it possible he went on an errand for someone there?" Abby unconsciously held her breath as she waited for Tim's reply.

"Anything's possible I suppose. But I seriously doubt he's on an errand. Besides, I asked around earlier and no one had seen him."

She exhaled abruptly. "Well, as far as I know, he went to work this morning."

"I wish I could help you, Abby. Like I said, it's very important that I speak to him right away." He paused.

"I don't mean to alarm you, but have you tried calling the police to see if there have been any accidents?"

"No," she whispered in a shaky voice.

"Well, you might want to give that a try." He paused, then asked, "Is there anything I can do?"

"I don't know." She fought her racing thoughts. "I don't think so. Thanks for asking."

"Will you keep me posted?"

"Yes." Abby tried to control the panic that welled up inside her. "Can I get your home number?"

He gave it to her and they hung up.

Tim's suggestion of an accident was more than she could bear. "Girls," she called out over the blare of the television.

They turned to look at her.

Abby stared back for a moment, the weight of her concern paralyzing her.

"What, Mom?" Tiffany asked as Susannah turned back to the program they were watching.

"I'll be up in my room if you need me."

"Okay."

Going to the entry hall, Abby couldn't avoid noticing the family photograph hanging on the wall. The photo had been taken the previous November right there in the living room. Surrounding Eric were his three girls, as he liked to call Abby and their daughters. His blond hair was cut short, and his blue eyes sparkled as if he had a surprise he was about to share. His broad shoulders made a backdrop for Abby's head as she leaned against him, the girls on either side.

Seeing his handsome face smiling down at her, she felt his absence more sharply and the sense of dread became stronger. She tried to push the feeling away as she trudged up the stairs, turning right on the landing. As she entered her bedroom she felt calmer, the design of the room doing its intended job. This room was her sanctuary, and she always came here to relax at the end of the day.

Nestled in a small alcove under a shuttered window were a love seat and a small end table. A cordless phone sat in the middle of the oak and glass table. The alcove was where Abby enjoyed relaxing with a good book.

Even now, under the stress she felt, she found herself automatically walking over to the love seat, sinking into its soft fullness and leaning back against the cushions. She allowed herself to close her eyes for a moment and felt her baby kick.

The motions of her unborn child reminded her of all the responsibilities she had, and she felt her stress level edge up a notch. She opened her eyes and picked up the phone, staring at it as she realized she didn't know where to start. She set the phone down and leaned back, forcing herself to relax.

A moment later, the phone rang.

She jumped at the sudden noise, her heart racing. Then a tiny smile lifted the corners of her mouth as she picked it up, imagining Eric on the other end, chagrined and apologetic.

"Hello?" she said, feeling a cheerfulness that had been lacking all afternoon.

Silence greeted her.

"Hello?" she repeated, her smile fading.

Still no response.

"Who's there?" She gripped the phone with both hands as she listened to what sounded like muffled breathing on the other end. "Eric? Is that you?"

She heard a click and knew the caller had hung up. She stared at the silent device, alarm and uncertainty beginning to grow within her.

As she thought about Eric and the trials they had experienced in their marriage, a familiar fear mixed with the worry she had already been experiencing. Abby stood and began pacing, stopping at her bedroom window and gazing toward the street, hoping against hope that Eric would pull into their driveway and put all her concerns to rest.

Maybe I should call the police like Tim suggested. She immediately dismissed the idea, not yet ready to believe her husband could be hurt. *Besides, if the police knew Eric was in an accident, wouldn't the police call me?* Staring into the empty street, she felt completely alone.

Maybe I could call the bishop, she thought as she watched a car travel past her house. "But what could he do?" she asked the empty room. "He doesn't know any more than I do." Turning from the window, Abby's gaze stopped on the set of scriptures sitting next to her bedside.

Heavenly Father. A brief feeling of tranquility washed over her at the thought. *He can help me. He knows what's happening.*

She knelt next to her bed, pausing as she considered what to say. Bowing her head, she waited quietly, trying to invite the Spirit. She began her prayer by thanking her Heavenly Father for her blessings, listing them one by one. Then, feeling the warmth of the Spirit, she asked Heavenly Father to watch over Eric. She prayed to feel calm and to know what to do. Waiting several minutes for a feeling of peace, she felt only anxiety and closed the prayer.

She lay on the bed, trying to push away the sense of unease. Then, as she thought about an incident about six years earlier, she became more worried.

Could he be in some kind of trouble?

The noise of the girls bounding up the stairs broke Abby's troubled meditation. The sound faded as the girls went toward their own rooms.

Restlessness pushed Abby off the bed, and after a moment she found herself in her bathroom standing in front of the medicine cabinet. As she pulled the door open, her gaze was drawn to Eric's things. His shaving cream and razor were there as well as his cologne.

She reached in and touched the cologne, hesitating for only a moment before pulling it out and unscrewing the cap. Tilting it toward her nose, she breathed in the musky scent. As she smelled the fragrance he had worn ever since they'd met, emotions and memories inter-mingled. She thought back to the secret Eric had shared with her soon after they had started dating, then replaced the cap and set the bottle back on the shelf, not wanting to consider that just now.

CHAPTER THREE

"Where's Daddy?" Susannah asked at the dinner table that evening.

Abby bit her lip. "I'm not sure, but he'll probably be home soon. Now eat your dinner."

Susannah accepted the answer without question, and Abby looked over at nine-year-old Tiffany to see her reaction. Tiffany seemed unconcerned and Abby realized with relief that she was hiding her anxiety better than she thought. She tried to fill the silence with questions about the girls' school and friends. They eagerly talked about their day, and she only had to half listen to their conversation as the other half of her mind thought about Eric and where he could be.

Adrenaline rushed through her veins as different scenarios flashed across her mind. The baby must have felt it too, because Abby could feel her little one moving around more than normal.

Glancing at her watch, Abby saw it was six forty-five.

"Mom? How come you're not eating?" Tiffany asked as she pointed at Abby's plate. "You're not going to get any dessert."

"What?" She looked at her older daughter, trying to smile back at the joke.

Susannah joined in. "Yeah, Mommy. No dessert for you."

Abby pushed back from the table and carried her plate and glass to the sink. She set the dirty dishes inside and leaned against the counter, staring unseeingly at the charming room that was the center of her home. Then her gaze darted around the room, trying to find something to focus on, something to help her figure out what to do next.

"Who wants to go out for ice cream?" she suddenly asked, turning to face her daughters.

The girls squealed with delight.

As she backed the minivan out of the garage, Abby hoped that when they returned Eric would somehow be waiting for them. And though it was possible Eric might call or come home while they went for ice cream, Abby could not stand being in the house any longer. She had to get out.

Driving through town, Abby couldn't stop herself from looking at every car they passed and down every side street in hopes of spotting Eric's car. It was after she swerved into the lane next to hers and heard a horn blare that she realized the whole purpose of going out for ice cream was an excuse to look for Eric.

She didn't care. She continued looking, and when she saw the flashing lights of a police car and a tow truck to the right, she turned sharply down the street to investigate.

"Wheeeee!" Susannah cried from the backseat. "Do it again, Mommy."

Abby ignored her and drove slowly by to see who was involved in the accident. In the intersection, three police cars formed a makeshift barricade around the damaged vehicles. One of the cars was being loaded onto a flatbed truck. It wasn't Eric's. The other car was still in the center of the protective barrier and Abby couldn't see what kind of car it was, but she could make out the color. It was blue. Eric's Jeep was red.

Tremendous relief swept over her when she realized neither of the cars was Eric's. At the same time, her heart constricted in fear and sadness.

What if it had been Eric? What would we do without him?

She forced the thought from her mind as she continued past the accident and drove to the shopping center.

Absently watching her daughters lick their ice-cream cones, Abby's mind flashed to the conversation she'd had with Eric soon after they'd begun dating—and the subsequent incident in their marriage. Not yet able to consider his returning to that lifestyle, she used all of her self-discipline to push it to the back of her mind.

After several minutes of waiting for her daughters to finish their ice cream, Abby felt an urgency to get home to see if there had been any contact from Eric.

"Are you girls almost done? We need to get back home."

"Is Daddy there?" Susannah asked, her eyes bright with anticipation.

Abby tried to put a reassuring smile on her face. "I don't know, sweetheart. I hope so. Hurry, so we can go see."

Within a few minutes they finished their cones and climbed into the minivan. This time Abby avoided looking at other cars on the road, staring straight ahead until they reached their driveway.

As the garage door slid open, she immediately saw the empty space where Eric's Jeep should have been. Her heart sank as the hope he would somehow be home by now was smashed. Then her spirits lifted at the thought of a message on the answering machine.

She hurried the girls into the house and went straight into the office to check for any messages. Though the light wasn't blinking, Abby punched the PLAY button, just to hear the message from that morning, just to hear Eric's voice.

"I . . . I guess I just missed you. I wanted to tell you that I love you and . . . I'm sorry."

As she listened to the now-familiar words, she wondered if she had misunderstood the intent of the message earlier that day. She had assumed he was apologizing for not accompanying her to the doctor's appointment. Now she began to believe it was something altogether different.

Confusion and worry coiled together in her mind. She didn't understand what was happening.

She went upstairs to help the girls get ready for bed. "Let's have family prayer," she said.

"Mom, why isn't Dad having prayers with us?" Susannah asked as she knelt next to her mother. "He always has prayers with us."

Abby looked from Susannah to Tiffany. "I'm not sure when he'll be home."

"How come, Mom?" Susannah asked.

Stress made Abby's tone sharper than usual. "I don't know, okay?"

Both girls stared at their mother.

"I'm sorry," Abby said, putting a warm smile on her face. "Let's say the prayer now. Tiffany, will you say it?"

Abby hesitated before adding, "Would you please ask Heavenly Father to help Daddy come home soon?"

Tiffany looked at her mother, her eyes questioning.

After the prayer was said and the girls were tucked in, Abby wandered down the stairs. It was getting late, and she feared Eric would not be coming home at all that night.

Just like before. She shook her head. *I thought that was behind us.*

She considered calling her mother or sister but immediately dismissed the idea, not ready to confirm their low opinion of her husband.

Walking slowly around the house, Abby locked the front door, activated the burglar alarm, and closed all the blinds. As she reached for the book she had gotten from the library earlier that day, she saw the green origami bird on the bookshelf and vowed she wouldn't open it until Eric was there with her.

Unexpected tears filled her eyes as the reality that her husband was missing seeped into her very soul. Abby sank to the floor and leaned against the bookshelf, tears rolling down her face. All kinds of images raced through her mind, and now that she didn't have to put up a brave front for her daughters, she let the pictures flow freely.

Eric, what have you done? Could I have helped you? Why did you leave?

Brushing the tears from her cheeks, she slowly stood and trudged toward the staircase, not bothering to turn off the lights.

Dropping her clothes in a heap on the bedroom floor, she crawled under the covers on Eric's side of the bed and pulled the blankets up tight against her chin.

The baby began its nightly ritual of kicking, and Abby rubbed her belly to comfort herself as much as to comfort her baby.

During the night Abby woke up several times from nightmares she couldn't recall, each time reaching over to receive reassurance from Eric and jolting awake when she remembered he wasn't there.

CHAPTER FOUR

It had been twenty-four hours since Abby's world had shifted. Now, as she lay in bed waiting for her alarm clock to tell her it was okay to give up on sleep, she decided it was time to do something about Eric's absence.

As she gazed at the ceiling, a new day stretched in front of her—a day that could end well if Eric came home, or badly if she didn't hear anything. Tossing back the covers, she rolled out of bed and headed to the shower, where the hot needles woke her up completely and soothed her clammy skin. Once she dried off and pulled on her robe, she used her towel to wipe the steam from the mirror, then stared at her face. The heat of the water had turned her cheeks into blazes of pink. She knew that wouldn't last. The circles under her eyes had been steam-shrunk into submission, and her wet brown hair dripped paths of water down the back of her robe.

Wrapping the towel around her head, she padded into the walk-in closet and stared at Eric's clothing. On impulse, she rifled through the carefully arranged rows of shirts and pants to see if anything was missing. She wasn't certain, but there did seem to be a few items absent. She grabbed a handful of his shirts and pulled them off their hangers, burying her face in the fabric. Eric's scent filled her nostrils, and she closed her eyes, picturing his grinning face.

How could you leave without telling me anything? What's going on?

Carefully hanging Eric's shirts back up, Abby stared at his clothes again. Then overwhelming anger at her husband coursed through her, and she wrenched half the shirts and all of the pants from their hangers in a vain attempt to purge the helplessness and rage.

Abby stopped mid-pull and slowly sank to the floor, drawing her legs as close to her chest as her pregnant stomach would allow and laying her cheek against her knees.

Where are you? her mind shrieked. *Why haven't you contacted me? Don't you care about me? Don't you care about our children?*

Abby stared at the pile of clothes on the floor as she thought about that day, eleven years before, when Eric had confided in her.

They had both been in college, Eric a junior and Abby a freshman, when they met in a biology class. After they had been dating for four months, Eric had asked her to come with him to the park. They were walking hand in hand when Eric pulled her onto a nearby bench.

"Abby, I have something very important to tell you."

Thinking he might be about to propose, Abby sat silently on the bench, watching the man she was falling in love with.

"You have no idea how hard this is for me." Eric looked directly into her eyes as she smiled her encouragement. "Last year, I finally faced up to something."

A sinking feeling started in Abby's heart as she realized this conversation was about to take an unexpected turn.

Eric took her hands in his. "You must know how much I've grown to care about you these last couple of months." He smiled, his whole face lighting up. "I never thought I'd feel this way about anyone." The smile faded. "But if this relationship is going to go anywhere, I think you have the right to know something about me that . . ." His gaze dropped to his lap. "That might make you want to forget you ever knew me."

Abby's pulsed quickened as she waited to hear what he was about to reveal.

"When I was in high school I gave in to a temptation I never thought I'd be faced with. I started smoking pot." He concentrated on his hands before going on. "Then I began snorting cocaine. I even began dealing it." He lifted his gaze to meet Abby's.

She stared at him, shocked by his admission.

"And to make matters worse I got arrested. Even though I wasn't convicted, it was horrible. Not only that, I started failing most of my classes and I stopped going to church." He stared at his hands. "I did some awful things to pay for the coke." He looked back up at Abby, an ashamed expression on his face.

"Last year," he continued, "when someone I knew died of an overdose, I finally realized I could be next. That's when I quit. Believe me, it was the hardest thing I've ever had to go through, but I did it. I met with my bishop and repented fully. It was a long process I never plan on having to repeat." He stopped and looked steadily at Abby.

"Why did you try it?" She wanted to understand him.

Eric closed his eyes briefly, then looked at Abby. "Looking back, I can see I was trying to escape the problems I was having with my father. Hanging out with certain people didn't help. In fact, that was one of the things my Dad was always bugging me about. He wanted me to change who I spent time with. He wanted me to hang out with the guys from my ward, but I never felt like I had anything in common with them. I wanted to fit in with some guys from school, and part of being accepted was using the drugs. I went along with it. I have to admit I liked it. It seemed to make my troubles fade away." He looked at Abby as his voice softened. "I know it sounds lame now, but I just wanted to fit in."

Abby was quiet. Finally she said, "I know how it feels to want to be loved." A lump formed in her throat as she thought back to her own childhood.

His face brightened. "Thank you for listening. I knew you'd understand—"

Abby stopped him. "I need to think about this for a while. I feel like I know you and can trust you, and I care about you a lot, but this is a pretty big deal."

Eric was quiet, but he nodded.

In the end she'd decided to trust him. Now, sitting in her walk-in closet and staring at the mess she'd made on the floor, Abby thought about Eric's drug problem.

Could he have had a relapse? Am I foolish to believe he's changed? They say once you're addicted it's something you have to battle for the rest of your life. But after that last time, he promised me he was really done with drugs now . . .

Then the doubts started crawling in, and she had to squeeze her eyes closed to make them go away.

When she felt in control of her thoughts, she stood, ignoring the pile of Eric's clothes, and with calmness she didn't feel, grabbed some of her own clothes and walked out of the closet.

As difficult as it was, for the girls' sake she had to get control of her emotions. She plodded over to the love seat in her little alcove and sank down onto the full cushions, staying there until she felt composed.

Once she was ready to meet the day, she wandered down the stairs and punched the code into the burglar alarm to turn it off, then paused, thinking how even this small thing made her think of Eric. They had chosen the code together.

It was recently, after they had been living in this house for five and a half years, that Eric had suddenly decided they needed a burglar alarm. After the man had installed it, she and Eric had come up with their own code. They had toyed with the idea of using the digits of the year they had married. Though it was corny, Eric had loved the idea. But in the end they had settled on Tiffany's birth year, thinking it would be easier for her to remember the code—if they decided to teach their daughter how to use the system at all at only nine years old. Now, after turning the alarm off, she couldn't help but reflect on the suddenness with which Eric had decided they needed to buy one. She was glad he had, though.

She flipped off the porch light and opened the front door.

The late-April morning felt wonderful. She smiled briefly as she looked at the pansies blooming in her flower garden and ignored the weeds. Stepping onto the front porch she saw the cat's empty bowl. She picked it up and brought it to the kitchen, where she scooped out the day's portion of food.

As Abby set the bowl back on the porch, the sound of a bell on a collar caught her attention. Pumpkin, their orange tabby, scampered up to be scratched. Abby obliged, then walked down the driveway to retrieve the paper, looking up and down the street at the neighbors' houses. She envied their normal lives.

Silently praying Eric hadn't had another relapse, she spread the newspaper on the counter and searched for any mention of an accident with an unknown victim. She found nothing.

She didn't know if she should be relieved or not. *Is it better for him to be hurt rather than using drugs again?* The thought seized her already-troubled mind, and she scolded herself for losing faith in her husband. Then, thinking about the promises he'd made more than once, she wondered if he was trustworthy. Abby went into the family room and lay on the couch, exhausted from the events of the last twenty-four hours. She wanted to rest for a few minutes before it was time to wake the girls for school.

Instead, she woke to the sound of the television. She sat up on the couch and saw Tiffany and Susannah engrossed in a morning cartoon, still wearing their pajamas. Abby looked at her watch and jumped up.

"Girls! School starts in twenty minutes."

Looking at their mother in surprise, they sprang into action, running upstairs to get dressed while Abby went into the kitchen to pour them bowls of cereal.

After dropping them off at school, Abby drove back home and noticed the sink was full of dirty dishes. In contrast to the day before, when she had tackled the job with energy, today the task seemed overwhelming, and she still had to go to work later that morning.

Pushing thoughts of work aside, she realized she couldn't put off doing something about Eric's disappearance any longer. The uncertainty was crushing her.

Whether he was intentionally missing or not, he could be hurt. So she started by calling the local hospitals. The second one she called said they had a John Doe in the emergency room matching Eric's general description. They wouldn't tell her what his injuries were but suggested she come down to see if it was her husband.

After hanging up the phone, Abby felt saliva gathering in her mouth. It was a signal that she was about to throw up. Pressing her hand against her lips, she hurried into the bathroom and flung up the toilet seat, hanging her head, waiting. She was grateful when nothing happened.

She gently closed the lid and sat down on it.

It's probably not him, she tried convincing herself. *I'm sure it's someone else. I'll check to be certain, but I'm sure it's not him.*

Once she felt in control, she rushed out to the car and raced to the hospital. Parking her car haphazardly, she hurried into the emergency room. Frustrating Abby's haste was a line at the counter. She tried to get someone's attention as nurses strode by. Everyone ignored her until a man in a white jacket noticed her pregnant condition.

"I'm Dr. Edson, ma'am. Can I help you with something?"

She looked at him with appreciation. "Yes. I think my husband might be here."

He looked puzzled. "You don't know?"

"He's missing and I think he might be here."

"Oh." He paused, then asked gently, "Our John Doe?"

"Yes. Can I see him?"

She followed the doctor down the hall toward an examination room. He stopped outside the curtained area. "He came in this morning and he's in pretty bad shape. If he's your husband, the police will want to talk to you. Do you want to call someone to be with you?"

"No, no," she said quickly, anxious to see if it was Eric.

The doctor looked at her with uncertainty. "Okay. If you're sure."

Abby breathed in sharply as he pulled back the curtain. The man on the bed had several wires attached to him and an oxygen mask on his face. It was hard to make out his features with all the swelling. Walking softly to the bedside, she gazed down at the unconscious man.

"It's not him," she said with a mixture of relief and frustration.

The doctor nodded as Abby turned and left the room.

CHAPTER FIVE

Eric dumped his meager belongings onto the motel bed, searching for the key to his safe-deposit box. Beads of sweat broke out on his upper lip as he felt around the sides of the now-empty duffel bag.

Where is it?

His head throbbed as he yanked at the fabric-covered cardboard that lined the bottom of the bag, pulled it all the way out, and tossed it aside. A sick feeling swelled within his gut as his hand frantically felt the corners of the bag.

There.

The relief was so strong he nearly gagged. He lifted the small, shiny key and held it in front of him. Closing his eyes, he gripped it in his hand. The root of all his troubles lay in that safe-deposit box, and he wanted to go to the bank and make sure the contents were the way he'd left them, just to reassure himself.

It would be helpful if I had my Jeep.

Eric shook his head. He would have to rent a vehicle, which worried him. He didn't like the idea of leaving a paper trail.

Though frustrated to be away from his family, Eric knew it was the only solution. He had a plan, but it would take time. He needed to do some investigating, and he needed to make sure those involved weren't watching. And now that he'd had a day away from the turmoil, he'd been able to think things through.

He'd spent the previous day working on his disguise and mapping out his plan. Now, gazing in the mirror at his new look, he pulled the baseball cap low on his black-dyed hair and scratched at the mustache he'd applied. To himself he looked odd, but his only concern was that he would no longer be recognizable to those who knew him.

Would Abby know me?

He shook his head, despair washing over him as he considered the consequences if he didn't do this right.

He shoved the key into his pocket and left the room.

* * *

Abby didn't know where to direct her attention when it turned out Eric wasn't at the hospital. Knowing she needed to keep up her strength, she wandered into the kitchen to fix herself a snack of crackers and milk while she thought about what to do. If Eric hadn't been in an accident, she could only assume that he had left on purpose.

As she lifted the first cracker to her lips, the phone rang. She dropped the cracker back onto the plate and snatched the phone off the hook, half terrified and half hoping it would be one of the other hospitals calling to admit a mistake, that they did have someone there fitting Eric's description.

"Hello?"

The voice on the other end was brusque. "I'd like to speak to Eric Breuner."

She didn't recognize the man's voice. "Who is this?"

Silence.

"Hello?" she said.

"Never mind," he said.

"Wait. Please, what is this in regards to?"

The caller had hung up.

Abby drifted over to the family photo. "Where are you, Eric?" she whispered.

What is going on? Was that someone from his past? Someone who used drugs with him? Someone who dealt drugs with him? Is that why he left, to reestablish his drug-dealing contacts?

The thought terrified her. Instead of dwelling on that horrifying scenario, she tried to think of all the people Eric was currently involved with. He didn't have a lot going on in his life. Besides his family, he had his Church calling and he had work. He was on the activities committee at church, but Abby didn't think anyone on the committee would refuse to identify himself on the telephone.

I guess it could have been work related.

Eric had worked as an accountant at Central Valley Construction for three years, and he seemed to like the people there, especially Timothy Meher. Eric had invited him over for dinner once, although he hadn't come. Abby only saw Tim once a year, at the Christmas party Central Valley Construction threw for their employees.

Abby decided to try talking to Tim again, to see if he had any idea where Eric could be.

"Abby," he said when he came on the line. "I was going to call you today. Have you heard from Eric?"

"No, I haven't. Do you have any idea what's going on?"

"I'm really sorry, Abby. Eric hasn't been in touch with me either. But would you be able to stop by here today?"

"I guess so, but I couldn't stay long. I have to get to work."

"That's fine," Tim said. "I just need to talk to you for a minute."

"All right. I'll be there as soon as I can."

Abby hung up the phone, wondering what it was Tim wanted to talk to her about. She hoped he could tell her something that might help her understand where Eric was.

A few minutes later she headed to the minivan. Though it was possible Eric was off using drugs and not hurt, she decided to stop by the police department and file a missing-person's report.

The sound of several people talking at once battered her as she opened the door to the local police precinct. She walked right up to the desk sergeant. He gave her a bored look as she told him she wanted to file a missing-person's report.

"You'll have to talk to the Missing Person's Bureau."

Her boldness faded as she followed the directions the desk sergeant had given her and found herself sitting across a desk from the Missing-Person's officer.

Officer Holland smiled grimly as he asked his questions. "What is the name of the missing person?"

"My husband, Eric Breuner." Abby felt herself blush as the officer glanced at her before typing the information into the computer in front of him.

He looked back at her. "The age of the missing person?"

"He's thirty-three."

The officer dutifully typed that in. Then he asked Abby several more questions about when she had last seen Eric and what he looked like.

At the last question she pulled out a picture and handed it to the officer. He glanced at it before setting it aside.

"Now, you say someone called to speak to your husband earlier but wouldn't tell you who they were?"

She nodded, not sure if she should feel humiliated or upset by this experience. It was as if her life was being looked at under a magnifying glass. "Yes. And then he hung up."

Holland scowled as he typed that in.

"Has your husband ever taken off before?" he asked.

"No," she said.

"And you say his car is also missing?"

Abby nodded.

He asked her for the license plate number, which she gave him, and then asked, "Was there any indication that something was wrong? Any reason you can think of that he would leave?" He hesitated. "Another woman, perhaps?"

Shocked at the suggestion, Abby didn't know how to reply at first. "It couldn't have been another woman. I know that for sure."

Officer Holland looked doubtful. "Okay. Anything else?"

"Well, he did leave a message yesterday morning saying he was sorry."

"Sorry for what exactly?"

"Nothing in particular. He just said he loved me and he was sorry."

Clearly surprised by this bit of information, Holland gazed at Abby for a moment. "It sounds to me like your husband left of his own accord. You realize we can't do anything if an adult chooses to leave on his own."

Abby closed her eyes briefly, fighting back the gathering tears. "So you're saying you'll do nothing?"

Holland smiled, apparently feeling pity for Abby. "I'm really sorry, ma'am. We just don't have the manpower to look for missing people unless there's some sign of foul play."

Abby sighed as her shoulders slumped. Thoroughly embarrassed at this point, she thanked the officer and left the building.

Climbing into the minivan, she thought about Eric's recent behavior, trying to find anything to explain his absence. It occurred to her that he had been acting a little different lately. He seemed to be more stressed than usual, too. For the past couple of weeks, when he had come home from work he'd gone straight into the office and closed the door.

Reflecting on those nights, she wondered what it was that had occupied his attention. As she pulled into a parking space at Central Valley Construction and turned off the engine, she sat in the van, thinking about Eric and what he could be hiding from her.

I thought we weren't keeping secrets from each other anymore. At least, I wasn't keeping any secrets.

On her way to Tim's office she walked past Eric's office. The door was tightly closed. She suppressed the urge to open the door and instead walked toward Carly, the secretary shared by the accountants.

"Go right in, Mrs. Breuner. He's expecting you."

"Thank you," Abby replied softly, already feeling intimidated and wondering why Tim had asked her to come.

Abby gently opened the door and walked into the unfamiliar office. Because he was the senior accountant, Tim's office was larger than Eric's and better furnished. Tall bookshelves lined one wall, and several pieces of expensive-looking artwork decorated the walls.

Tim was on the phone as Abby approached his desk. His back was to her, and she timidly stood by the door. She noticed his full head of hair, and when he turned, she saw that his body was trim and his bearing confident. She also noticed he had a thin upper lip with a fuller bottom lip, making him look as if he had a perpetual pout.

When he saw her, he quickly ended his conversation and came around to where she was standing. He held out his hand, and she shook it with more confidence than she was feeling.

"Good to see you, Abby. Please sit down." He motioned toward one of two chairs facing his desk. Abby was surprised to see him sit on the chair adjacent to hers rather than the one behind his desk.

"So, Abby, how are you doing?"

"I would be doing better if I knew where Eric was."

"Yes." He touched his mouth before speaking again. "I hate to ask at a time like this, but by any chance, did Eric leave anything for me at your house?"

"Like what?"

"It's a file for a client. It might be in an envelope or even a box."

Abby thought about it. "I don't think so. I'd have to look around his office at home. But I don't remember seeing anything addressed to you."

They both turned at the sound of a knock on Tim's open door.

"I'm sorry. I didn't realize you were with someone," the man at the door said.

Tim stood and walked to the door. "Brock, you know Abby Breuner, I believe."

Abby watched as Brock Mendez, Tim and Eric's manager, turned to her.

"Oh, yes, of course. How is Eric? Is he sick? He's been gone since yesterday."

Abby stood and faced Brock, her thoughts racing to explain Eric's absence in hopes of saving his job. But before she could get the words out, Tim said, "He'll be gone a few days. But I'm sure everything's under control with his workload."

Abby closed her mouth, not sure what to say.

"Okay, then," Brock said to Tim, then added, "let me know when you have a free minute." With that he walked away.

"Thanks for covering for Eric," Abby said, a relieved smile on her face.

"Not a problem." He sat behind his desk and motioned for Abby to sit as well. "Eric's a good guy. I enjoy working with him and I'd hate to lose him. I'll have to tell Brock if he doesn't show up in the next day or so, but I can at least soften the news by making my confidence in Eric clear."

Abby nodded, then said, "On my way here I stopped by the police station and filed a missing-person's report." She thought she saw concern flicker across Tim's face, but his response was positive.

"Good. What did they say?"

She frowned. "They aren't going to do anything. They basically said they don't waste time on adults unless they have evidence of foul play."

"Is that right?" He stared beyond Abby for a moment before looking at her and standing. "I'm sure everything will turn out all right. It's probably just a premature midlife crisis or something." Tim smiled reassuringly. "Keep in touch, won't you? And if you find anything for me, let me know."

"Uh, yeah, okay." Taking that as her cue to leave, Abby stood too. "Thanks again for covering for him. I really appreciate it," she said, even as she wondered why Tim had asked her in. Surely he could've asked about that file over the phone.

He smiled briefly before escorting her to the door of his office.

A short time later Abby pulled into the parking lot at the library, her mind full of questions. Topping them all was whether she should go to work today. What if Eric tried to call and she wasn't home?

Yes, another voice whispered in her head, *but what if he never comes home and you don't have a job to support your family?* That thought frightened her enough to get her out of the minivan and inside the library.

My shift is only a few hours today. I can do it.

With that assurance in her mind, she was able to face the books that had been deposited overnight.

Forty-five minutes after arriving, as she alphabetized the books on the cart in front of her in preparation for shelving, Nadine walked in. Abby cringed, waiting to be reprimanded for leaving early the day before. Instead, Nadine greeted her, picked up a pile of books, and left the room. Abby exhaled in relief, her pounding heart slowing to a normal rate. Yesterday the idea of getting fired hadn't seemed like a big deal. Today it would be devastating.

She thought about Tim and his willingness to cover for Eric. *That was nice of him. I hope he's not taking too much of a risk by doing that,* she thought, wondering again why he'd asked her to drop by. *Perhaps he was really concerned about Eric, or at least about that file he'd mentioned.* For the rest of the morning Abby kept a low profile, trying to keep out of Nadine's way. No one seemed to notice her strange behavior. No one except Mary.

"What's the matter?" Mary asked when she found Abby hunkered down in the biography section.

Abby had been deep in thought, wondering where Eric could be and what he might be doing. She was startled to find Mary standing there and wondered how long she had been watching her. Standing slowly, she forced a smile. "Hi, Mary. How are you?"

Mary's brows pulled together. "I'm fine. But it's you I'm worried about. You've been acting strange all morning. Is something wrong?"

"No, not at all," Abby said, shaking her head, her mouth forming a fake smile. "I'm just tired. What's up? Do you have more biographies for me?"

Mary's face relaxed. "No. I wanted to know if you'd had lunch yet. I thought we could eat together."

"Oh." Abby realized she was starving, but was worried about being around other people. She didn't feel strong enough to hold herself together. Then she suddenly felt angry with Eric for putting her in such a difficult situation. *I would be mortified if anyone thought that my husband left me for another woman or was involved in something illegal. And even if people don't think that, they'll be talking about it constantly and asking for updates . . .*

"Abby?"

Abby looked back at Mary, realizing she hadn't answered her request to go to lunch, and pushed the smile back onto her lips. "Thanks, but I've already eaten." Her stomach grumbled in response to the lie.

"Oh, okay," Mary said as she turned to go. "I'm going to go out and grab something. I'll see you in a little while."

"Bye." Now that her thoughts were on food, she felt famished. She briefly considered skipping lunch, but her kicking baby reminded her that would be a mistake. As she thought about the sack lunch waiting in the refrigerator in the break room, she knew she would have to be stealthy in eating. If Mary found out she had lied about already having eaten . . .

She quickly completed shelving the biographies on her cart before hurrying to the break room to have her lunch. As she pushed the door open, she was surprised to see Nadine on the phone, her back to the door. "Okay, Mom," she was saying. "I'll see what I can do. Make sure to take your medicine. I'll be home later this afternoon."

Abby hesitated before entering, then walked over to the refrigerator and took her lunch from the shelf before spreading the sandwich, fruit, and chips out on the table in front of her.

Nadine turned around at the noise. "I'll see you later, Mom. Good-bye."

"Is everything all right?" Abby asked. She knew Nadine took care of her sick mother.

"Yes, thank you. But I'd rather not discuss my private life at work. I like to keep them separate." She gave Abby a meaningful glance.

"I understand," Abby said, knowing Nadine wouldn't want to hear about Eric, even if she was willing to tell.

Nadine smiled briefly before leaving the room, and Abby turned back to her lunch. As she finished eating her sandwich, the door opened.

Abby's appetite vanished as Mary walked in.

"What's going on here?" Mary demanded playfully, a fast-food bag in hand.

"What do you mean?" Abby said, guilt now mixing with the worry she had been feeling earlier.

Mary strode over to the table and pulled out a chair, setting her food down as she spoke. "I invite you to lunch, you claim you've already eaten, then here you are eating all by yourself. Don't you find that strange?"

Abby looked down at the proof of Mary's argument laid out in front of her. She didn't know what to say. "I'm sorry?" she tried, looking back at Mary.

"Something's wrong. I can tell. Now, are you going to tell me what it is or do I have to badger you for a while?"

She couldn't help but smile at her friend's persistence. She knew Mary cared about her, even if she didn't know when to leave things alone. "I'm sorry, but I don't want to talk about it," she said as she gathered up the remains of her lunch.

"Oh no. You're not getting away that easily." Mary grabbed Abby's arm, forcing her to stop what she was doing and look Mary in the eye.

Abby tried to smile with confidence, hoping Mary wouldn't ask more. "I've got to get back to work," Abby said as she gently lifted Mary's hand from her arm.

"Look, Abby, I know something's wrong. And I know you need someone to talk to." She paused as she sat at the table and picked up her hamburger. "You will tell me when you're ready to talk, won't you?"

Abby pushed away from the table and set the rest of her lunch back in the refrigerator. "I'm sorry I lied to you. Please don't be angry." She flashed an apologetic smile before walking out the door.

Abby was able to get through the final hour of her shift without Mary confronting her, and was grateful when she was able to go home. As she pulled into the garage, her gaze was drawn to the conspicuously empty spot where Eric usually parked his Jeep. She got out of the van, closed the door, and walked over to Eric's tool bench, looking at his neatly lined-up tools.

She shook her head in disbelief that Eric was gone. After all they had been through, she had believed they no longer kept secrets from each other. All she could do was hope he would somehow contact her and let her know he was okay. Even more, she hoped he would come home.

As Abby walked into the empty house, she remembered Tim's missing file. It also occurred to her that she might find some clue, some answer, among Eric's things in the office. She was glad her shift had been so short today. It gave her some extra time before her girls got out of school. She went directly down the hall to the office where Eric had spent so much time lately. Pausing in the open doorway, she pictured the last time Eric sat at the desk.

It had been his last night at home. He'd gone straight from his place at the dinner table into the office. Later that evening, after Abby had put the girls to bed, she had come back downstairs to find the door to the office closed and no noise coming from inside. She had knocked quietly, and he had invited her in. She had walked over to him and knelt on the floor next to his chair, stroking his back as he looked down at her. He had smiled at her, looking more tired than Abby could remember seeing him.

Now she slowly made her way over to the desk chair and brushed her fingers against the back of the seat, imagining Eric sitting there. After a moment she looked around, feeling foolish for her actions. No one was there of course, and she pulled out the large leather chair and settled into it. She ran her hands along the armrests, getting used to the feel of the chair. Abby hadn't spent much time using the office; it was usually Eric's domain.

She stroked the highly polished wood of the desktop, a dark mahogany, and thought about all the time Eric had sat in front of this desk. It had been an expensive purchase, but that was before all their medical bills had piled up. Eric had always been proud of this desk.

Her gaze ran over the items Eric had considered important enough to occupy the top of his immaculate desk. She smiled as she looked at a smaller version of the family photo that was hanging in the entry hall. In the opposite corner was the phone and answering machine. But her eye was drawn to the large flat-panel monitor set on the center of the desk.

Abby had minimal computer skills—she had always left that to Eric. Though she realized she might have to eventually attempt to search things on the computer, for now she wanted to stick to familiar things, things she could actually hold in her hands.

Leaning back in the chair, she looked at the desk, not sure where to start. There were three drawers on either side and one in the middle.

Before opening any of them Abby looked around again, hopeful Eric would suddenly appear and tell her it had all been a bad joke. Frowning at her wishful thinking, she yanked open the drawer directly above her knees. Though she hadn't been expecting to find anything important, she was disappointed that all she found were neatly lined-up pencils and pens, a stapler, Scotch tape, stamps, and address labels. They were all carefully arranged in an organizer, the paper clips and pushpins set in the little square sections. She pushed the drawer closed.

The top right-hand drawer was next. A stack of folders was piled one on top of another. She pulled the small stack out and spread it on the desk. Across the top of each was Eric's distinctive printing listing the general contents of the folder.

She pulled the top folder closer and read Eric's writing. It said "UNPAID BILLS." She opened it and flipped through the pile of opened envelopes. Nothing out of the ordinary in there. She set them aside and moved on to the next folder. That one was marked "RECEIPTS." She skimmed through them but didn't find anything new. The last folder was marked "THINGS TO DO." She opened it up and saw it was an old list. She shoved the folders back into the drawer and slammed it closed.

Heaving a sigh of frustration, Abby stood and stretched the kinks out of her back, gazing out the window into the backyard. The swings stood empty and the grass needed mowing. Then, walking into the kitchen, she poured herself a large glass of ice water and brought it back into the office.

She sighed again as she reached for the next drawer on the right. It slid open easily, revealing Eric's address book. She lifted out the brown leather book and sipped her water as she flipped through the first two pages. On the third page she saw a name she hadn't seen in a while. *Harry Breuner.* Abby stared at the name for several moments, wondering if she should call Eric's father. She knew the two of them had not spoken in a long time. They had argued about something several years ago, something Eric had never shared with her, although she had her suspicions what it was about. Unresolved bitterness remained between them.

What if Eric contacted his father? Maybe he would know something about Eric's whereabouts.

She tentatively lifted the phone, almost afraid to speak to Harry and upset it wasn't under happier circumstances.

Wanting to get it over with, she quickly punched in the number and listened as the phone rang several times. When she was about to hang up, a gruff voice answered, "Hello."

Abby hesitated for a fraction of a second. "Harry?"

"Yes. Who is this?"

She gripped the phone tighter, her hands beginning to feel damp. "It's Abby. Eric's wife."

The gruff voice softened. "Abby. It's been a long time."

"Yes, Harry. It has." Another pause. "How have you been?"

"Not so good, if you really want to know."

"I'm sorry to hear that," she said, wondering what was happening in his life, but not able to deal with someone else's problems just then.

"How's that husband of yours treating you?"

"Um . . . fine. Just fine." It was obvious Harry had no idea Eric was missing, and she wasn't sure she was ready to tell him yet.

"And how're my two beautiful granddaughters?" he asked quietly.

Sadness filled her heart as she thought of how long it had been since Harry had seen Tiffany and Susannah. Her voice wavered slightly when she answered. "They're fine. They love school and their friends."

"So. Why are you calling after all this time, Abby?"

"I . . . I wanted to let you know you'll be having another grandchild later this year."

"Well, that's wonderful." He was quiet for a minute. "Will I be able to see this one?"

"Yes. Absolutely." She decided right then that no matter what, she would make sure Harry had the opportunity to get to know his grandchildren.

"Well, that's great. You have no idea how much that means to me. Thank you, Abby." Harry cleared his throat. "Now, I've got to go, but we'll talk another time, okay? You take care now, you hear?"

"Yes, I will. You too. Good-bye, Harry."

Abby gently set the phone back in its cradle, disappointed the call hadn't led anywhere, but with a warm feeling in her heart at the pleasure she'd heard in Harry's voice.

Perhaps it will be a step in helping Eric reconcile with his father, she thought, trying to look at the positive side of the situation. She looked through the rest of the address book but didn't find anyone else to call.

She lifted the cold glass of water and pressed the icy surface against her cheeks, trying to cool her warm skin. Setting the glass back on its coaster, she bent over to open the bottom drawer. When she pulled, nothing happened. She gave it another yank. It was locked. She swiveled the chair to the left and tried all three drawers there. They opened easily. But now she was only interested in the contents of the locked drawer.

CHAPTER SIX

Abby had searched the office for a key. She'd found a small one, but it didn't fit the lock.

Frustrated, she'd tossed the key into the middle drawer, then leaned back in the chair and tried to think of another way to get the drawer open, preferably without causing too much damage. In her mind's eye she saw Eric's organized tool bench.

She went out to the garage and stood in front of the tool bench, her gaze darting from one tool to the next. None of them seemed suitable for the job at hand. She pulled open drawers until she found a group of small screwdrivers arranged by size, then grabbed the two smallest ones and brought them back into the office.

She inserted the smaller screwdriver into the lock and wiggled it back and forth. It didn't work. She tried the other screwdriver. No success. The scratches around the lock opening were still unnoticeable. She went back out to the garage to see what else she could find.

Again Abby quickly looked over the items hanging on pegs. It took only a moment for her to notice the crowbar. She knew Eric would be angry if she damaged his desk.

What can he expect, taking off the way he has? she thought. Tossing the useless screwdrivers onto the top of his workbench, she grabbed the crowbar and headed back into the house.

She jammed one end of the crowbar into the slight space between the side of the drawer and the desk. Then, grunting with effort, she pushed against the crowbar. She had to stop and wipe the sweat from her face before continuing. The locked drawer finally budged, and Abby was able to push the crowbar in deeper before resuming her tug-of-war with the desk.

The ringing of the phone startled her and she screamed, letting go of the crowbar. She was annoyed to be interrupted in her quest to open the drawer, especially since it was starting to give.

"Hello?"

"Hi, Abby. It's Michelle Penrose."

"Oh, hi, Michelle," Abby said, trying to sound pleased to hear from the Enrichment leader.

"I wanted to call and see if you needed any help with your scrapbooking class tonight."

Abby's eyes shot open. With all that had happened in the last two days, she had completely forgotten about the commitment she'd made to teach at the monthly Relief Society meeting. She didn't know if she was up to it, but knew she couldn't back out at the last minute. At least a dozen sisters had signed up for the class and had already paid for their materials. "Is . . . uh . . . could you help me find a babysitter?"

"Oh, yes. Is your husband out of town?"

"Uh . . . yeah," Abby said, not about to explain what was happening.

"Okay, then. I'll call you with a babysitter's name and number and see you at six thirty to set up?"

"Sure. I'll be there."

Abby hung up the phone and closed her eyes, overwhelmed by her commitments on top of her worry for her husband.

I need to focus on one thing at a time. I can manage if I do that.

With that, she turned her attention back to the desk and the task of prying open the drawer.

Picking up the crowbar, she jammed it into the small opening, pushing with all her strength and sweating with effort. When the drawer popped open, Abby had to catch herself on the desk chair to keep from toppling onto the floor. She steadied herself and leaned in to look at the contents.

At first she didn't see anything, but after closer examination she noticed a lone twenty-dollar bill tucked into one corner. She extracted it and inspected it closely. It looked genuine. Shaking her head in confusion, she wondered why Eric would lock a single twenty-dollar bill in the desk drawer. She put it in her pocket and closed the drawer, no closer to answers than when she had begun.

She sank back onto the chair, exhausted. Then, crossing her arms over her bulging middle, she hung her head in despair and let the droplets of sweat drip down her forehead. The ringing of the phone brought her out of her dejection.

"Hello?" she answered wearily.

"Mrs. Breuner?"

"This is she," Abby said, trying to sound cheerful.

"This is Sally Carter at Betterman Elementary."

"Yes?"

"We have your daughter Tiffany here, and she's not feeling well. Would you come pick her up, please?"

"Yes. I'll be right over."
Now what?

* * *

He watched the minivan back out of the driveway and turn the corner and wondered why the woman wasn't at work. He'd been under the impression that no one would be home. Still, she was gone now, and it was his chance to do what he came to do. As he quietly shut the door to his dark blue sedan and strode confidently across the street, he knew he might only have a few minutes before she returned. He hoped she'd been in too much of a hurry to bother setting the burglar alarm. He glanced around once before ringing the front doorbell, then tried the knob. He didn't expect an answer and there wasn't one, and the door was locked, of course.

He walked purposefully away from the front door and, pausing as he reached the driveway, reached into his coat pocket and pulled out a pair of black leather gloves. He tugged them on as he continued past the garage door and over to the back gate. He saw the string hanging limply and pulled it taut. The gate gave way instantly. Gently closing it behind him, he looked around at the silent backyard.

He noted with a smirk that the back lawn needed mowing. He reached out and touched the doorknob leading to the garage, then reached into his bag and pulled out the right equipment.

After fiddling with the lock, he put the items back in the bag. His fingers gripped the knob and he twisted it to the right. He smiled as the door opened smoothly, but started when he heard a bell tinkling nearby. Realizing it was just a cat, he glared at the animal as it rubbed against his legs. Pushing it roughly away with his foot, he almost laughed out loud as it mewed in protest.

After the brightness of the sun outside, the interior of the garage was near pitch black. He plunged in and was rewarded by tripping over something he couldn't see. He caught his balance before hitting the floor, then stood in place until his eyes had adjusted sufficiently to the dim garage. He looked at the object near his feet to discover what had made him lose his footing. It was the cat's litter box. There were bits of kitty litter all around the box. He momentarily panicked as he realized he didn't know if the litter had been there before he kicked it or if the floor had been clean.

He swore under his breath and for several seconds was undecided about what to do, then elected to deal with it after he had completed his errand. The door from the garage to the house was conveniently unlocked, and he let himself in. He smiled at how stupidly naïve some people were. He was relieved no alarms had gone off when he entered, either. Today was his lucky day, he thought as he began his errand.

He had barely left the office when the doorbell rang. He froze, then thought he heard tapping on a far window. What if a neighbor had seen him? He panicked and decided he'd have to go in the upstairs rooms another day. The only good thing about this little visit was that he'd found a spare key to the house. He walked swiftly back to the garage door, ducking low as he passed windows. Then he let himself into the garage, past the backyard, and out through the gate, watching the front yard until all was clear.

* * *

When Abby pulled up to the school just a few blocks from her home, she could see the children at recess. As she walked to the doors of the office she saw Tiffany's teacher, Mr. Phillips, walking toward her.

Other than at parent-teacher conference, she hadn't really spoken with him. She knew he was single; Tiffany and her friends had mentioned that several times while giggling over him. Most of the third-grade girls had a crush on Mr. Phillips, and Abby could see why.

He seemed an average height, about five feet ten, Abby guessed, and he had wavy brown hair and deep blue eyes. If she were to guess his occupation, she would think more in terms of fashion model than elementary schoolteacher.

He held his hand out to Abby as he approached and she took it, feeling the strength in his grip. They stood near the office as they spoke.

"I understand Tiffany's not feeling well," Abby said.

"Yes." A sympathetic smile curved his lips. "She complained of a stomachache, and the nurse said she had a fever."

Abby nodded as she listened. "Thank you for taking care of her."

"No problem, Mrs. Breuner."

"She's in there?" Abby pointed toward the closed office door.

"Yes." He held out some papers. "I brought some assignments for her to do if she feels better."

"Thank you."

Tiffany was sitting on a chair, her face flushed. She walked slowly over to her mother and put her arms around Abby's waist. Abby knelt in front of her daughter and laid her hand against her forehead. It was warm. "Hi, sweetheart. How are you feeling?"

"Not good, Mom. Can I go home?"

"Of course. Let's go home and tuck you into bed."

Tiffany smiled faintly as she nodded.

Abby pulled the van into the garage and wearily climbed out. She walked around to the passenger side and helped Tiffany out. Tiffany leaned against her as they made their way to the house door. Something crunched under their feet as they crossed the garage, and Abby looked down to see Pumpkin's kitty litter scattered across the floor. She shook her head in irritation. She had swept up the same mess only the day before.

"Pumpkin's getting messier and messier," she said absently.

Tiffany only nodded.

After giving Tiffany a fever reducer and settling her in bed for a nap, Abby made arrangements for Susannah to go home with a friend after school, then sat on the couch in the family room and thought how just twenty-four hours before she'd been waiting for Eric to come home so they could view the video of her ultrasound. She closed her eyes in disbelief at how things could change so drastically in such a short period.

She didn't want to think about that for a while. Instead, she wanted to think of happy things. She walked over to the television and looked through the videos in the cabinet. She found one from the previous Christmas and put it in the VCR.

Tears filled her eyes as she watched the video. Eric was stringing the lights onto the Christmas tree, with

Tiffany and Susannah helping him. The camcorder had been set on a tripod so the whole family could be in the film.

Mesmerized, Abby stared at the scene unfolding before her. She watched herself walk over to Eric and saw him take a thinner Abby into his arms and give her a passionate kiss. The girls wrinkled their noses as they watched their parents' display of affection.

She remembered how happy they had been the day they trimmed the tree, and she had believed they were happy together now. She couldn't understand why Eric would leave her like this.

She clicked the video off, angry again with Eric for his selfish behavior. Trying to get her mind off that thought, she decided to check on Tiffany. Abby tiptoed into her room and saw she had fallen asleep, her favorite doll lying on the pillow next to her. Abby's heart brimmed with love at the sight of her daughter sleeping peacefully. She didn't know what she would do if one of her children failed to come home like Eric had. The thought sent chills up her spine.

Bending over Tiffany's sleeping form, Abby laid her hand against her forehead and was relieved to find that the fever had vanished. She tucked the covers around her daughter's chin and left the room, softly closing the door behind her.

Once in the office again, Abby left the door open in case Tiffany called out to her. Before resuming her search of the drawers, she looked around for a file addressed to Tim. She didn't find anything. Then she sat in front of the desk and looked through the rest of the drawers. The top-left one was a simple catchall. She quickly flipped through the pile of letters, the girls' report cards, and store catalogs. Nothing interesting.

She closed the top drawer and pulled out the middle one. It was the paperwork from the purchase of their home. Abby didn't bother taking it out, knowing pretty much what it contained.

Instead, she reached for the bottom drawer, raising her eyebrows in surprise at the stack of pictures she found there. She didn't remember putting them in there. She pulled them out and spread them on the desktop. As she flipped through the stack, she relived the memories associated with each one.

The sound of soft footsteps startled her.

"Mom?"

"Tiffany. You scared me half to death," Abby said, swiveling in her daughter's direction. "Are you feeling better? That was a short nap." Awkwardly, she pulled her nine-year-old daughter onto her lap.

Tiffany laughed. "Mom, I'm too big to sit on your lap."

Abby smiled. "I know. How are you feeling?"

"Good."

She was relieved to hear that. "Mr. Phillips gave me some work for you to do if you feel up to it."

Tiffany jumped off of her mother's lap. "Okay."

The surprise must have shown on Abby's face because Tiffany immediately toned down her response. "I mean . . . I guess."

"I'm glad you want to please Mr. Phillips by doing your work, but you don't have to do it right now."

"It's okay, Mom. I feel fine now."

Tiffany's gaze wandered over the top of the desk where the pictures were laid out.

"I hope I see Dad tonight," Tiffany said, a smile on her face. "I want to tell him I passed my multiplication test."

"That's wonderful, Tiff. I guess studying paid off, didn't it?" Abby said, trying to distract her daughter from the subject of her father.

"Do you think Dad will be home earlier tonight, Mom?" Tiffany persisted.

"I don't know, sweetie. Now, let me get those papers Mr. Phillips gave me."

Looking uncertain, Tiffany followed her mother out of the office.

CHAPTER SEVEN

Eric had only been alone one day but already he hated the solitude. Recalling the message Abby left on his cell phone the previous day, he desperately wanted to communicate with her, let her know it wasn't what she thought—at least not what he assumed she thought. He figured she would conclude he'd gone back to using drugs.

Unfortunately, it was much worse than that.

Instead of dwelling on Abby, he pictured the items in his safe-deposit box. He'd gone to the bank that morning to make sure everything was there. Everything was as he'd left it.

As he glanced around the library, he thought about all that had happened and what the consequences would be if he didn't do this right. Shaking his head in frustration, he leaned over the keyboard and continued searching on the Internet, grateful no one at this branch knew Abby or him. At least he hoped they didn't. He pulled the cap lower on his forehead and hunched his shoulders, trying to make himself invisible.

It was difficult to concentrate on what he needed to do when all he could think about was his wife and what she was going through. Sometimes he thought she would have been better off with someone else. He knew he was selfish; if he wasn't, he would never have allowed her to fall in love with him. He knew she could do better than him. *But I love her so much. I can't imagine my life without her. But what kind of example am I setting for my children—running when things get tough?*

He stared at the monitor, trying to focus his thoughts. *Plausible deniability.* He had to keep remembering that phrase. If Abby were confronted by anyone about anything he had done, her denial had to be believable. He was confident it would be. She knew nothing.

He pulled up the search engine and began typing.

* * *

That evening, after leaving the girls with the babysitter, Abby had rushed over to the church to set up for her scrapbooking class. Now, two hours later, Abby looked at her watch with relief. It was time to go home. As she packed up her materials, she saw Arlene Williams, the Relief Society president, walk into the classroom.

"Thanks again for teaching the scrapbooking class, Abby."

"No problem," she said, thinking about the Tylenol she would need to take for her pounding headache. "I hope the sisters learned something new."

"Oh, I think they learned a lot. I saw some of the pages they put together and they looked great." Arlene hesitated. "Abby?"

Abby turned, feeling desperate to get home. "Yes?"

"Is everything okay? I had a couple of sisters comment that you seemed out of sorts."

During her time in the ward, Abby hadn't gotten to know Arlene very well, but she had always seemed caring and sincere. Still, Abby wasn't ready to share her worries yet. "I'm just tired. You know how pregnancy can be."

Arlene smiled. "I do. I was about your age when I had my last one. I was pretty much exhausted all the time." Helping Abby box up the last of the supplies Arlene said, "Please let me or Catherine know if you need anything. We'd be happy to bring in a meal if you need it."

"That's nice of you to offer, but I'm okay."

"Your husband must be really dependable. A real help around the house."

Abby froze for a second before recovering her composure. "Yeah, he's great." She was able to hold herself together long enough for Arlene to turn and walk from the room before the tears began sliding down her face.

She drove home, wondering what surprise might be awaiting her there.

Staying in the driver's seat in her garage for several moments, she wiped her wet cheeks with a tissue before going in to face her children and their babysitter. The moment she opened the door to the house, her children were upon her.

"Mom, Mom!" Susannah shouted, making Abby's head throb harder. "Kelly let us do finger painting."

Abby looked over at the fourteen-year-old babysitter, then back to her daughter. "Well, that sounds like fun."

Glancing at the kitchen counters and at the table and not seeing any splotches of paint, she decided not to comment. "We need to take Kelly home." She turned toward the sitter. "Are you ready?"

As they drove the short distance to Kelly's house, Abby bit her lip before speaking quietly so the girls wouldn't hear from the backseat. "Did anyone call, Kelly?"

"Just one person."

Abby's heart fluttered. "Who was it?"

"I don't know. He wouldn't leave a message."

"Did you recognize his voice?" she asked, wanting to ask if it sounded like Eric.

"No. Should I have?" Kelly glanced at Abby, a confused look on her face.

Abby realized the ridiculousness of the question and tried to laugh it off. "No, of course not. I was just wondering." Disappointment pinched her heart. "Well, I appreciate you babysitting tonight."

"Sure, no problem, Sister Breuner."

* * *

After Tiffany and Susannah had been tucked into bed, Abby strode into the kitchen and picked up the phone. It was time to call her mother and sister to let them know what was going on. As much as she didn't want anyone to know her secret fears, her family—dysfunctional as it was—was her main safety net. However, calling her family was something she had hoped to avoid. Especially the call to her mother.

Her mother, Barbara Kincaid, had been opposed to Eric and Abby's marriage from the start. Barbara had felt Eric wasn't good enough for Abby and had made sure he knew it too.

After Eric had made his confession when they were dating, Abby had made the mistake of recording it in her journal. Her snoopy younger sister, Jennifer, had read the entry and told their mother about Eric's past.

Barbara Kincaid couldn't fathom her daughter marrying someone with such a shady past. Immediately confronting Abby, she commanded her to stop seeing Eric. Of course that had only pushed Abby into Eric's arms. Still, doubting whether her continued dating of Eric was to spite her mother or because she really loved him, Abby went to her father, Martin Kincaid, and confided her concerns about her growing relationship with Eric.

Martin had always been understanding, and he and Abby were close. After she poured out her soul to him, he counseled her to listen to her heart. When Eric proposed a few months later, she did listen to her heart and to the Holy Ghost, and she accepted Eric's proposal. They were sealed in the Oakland Temple four months later.

Though Barbara attended the ceremony, there had been tension between Abby and her mother ever since, not that she and Abby had ever gotten along very well. Barbara had always made her strong opinions known to all, including her opposition to Abby's marriage. Consequently, Abby had consistently avoided her mother during the years since her wedding.

As Abby picked up the phone to call her mother now, she hoped her mother would somehow be there for her, although she braced herself for what her mother might say. Abby never could guess what her mother's mood might be. No one ever could. She'd often thought her father must have been a saint to put up with Barbara all those years.

The phone rang several times before the voice of her mother came on the line.

"What do you mean he's missing?" Barbara said angrily after Abby explained what was happening.

Abby held the phone away from her ear to distance herself from her mother's wrath. Apparently she was not in one of her better moods this evening. Abby tried to be patient. "I told you, Mother, he didn't come home last night and I don't know where he is."

"I knew he was no good. Didn't I try to tell you he was no good?"

Abby bit her lip to keep back the angry response. "Mother, please. I'm worried. Can't you at least try to understand that?"

"He's probably gone back to those drugs. I told you those drugs would be a problem."

Abby tried to muffle a sigh and said in a quiet voice, "I'll let you know if I hear anything. Good-bye, Mother."

She hung up the phone to the sound of her mother's tirade about what a rotten husband Eric had always been. It had been a mistake to call her mother, she realized. If she was looking for any support, she was looking in the wrong place. She felt more alone than ever. It seemed as if there was no one to comfort her or help her. She didn't want to worry Eric's father, and she couldn't count on her own mother. Eric was an only child, and his mother had been killed in a car accident when Eric was a teenager.

Abby wandered into the adjoining family room, sat on the couch, and stared into space. She thought about when she and her sister were young; they would fight over whether Jennifer was Mom's favorite until they were both in tears. Then their father would come and pull them both into his arms and tell them he and their mother loved them both very much. Abby had believed *he* loved her but wasn't as sure about her mother's feelings. That was one of the reasons she had been so devastated when her father had died eight years before.

Her gaze took in the room before her, and she smiled sadly, remembering the letter she had received soon after her father's funeral. He had written it a short time before he died, as if he had known his time on earth would soon be over. He had told her how much he had always loved her and what a wonderful mother she was to Tiffany, who was only a year old at the time.

But now he was gone. Resigning herself to the only reassurance available, Abby picked up her scriptures and opened to her favorite passage, Doctrine and Covenants 121:7–8. She read aloud: "My son, peace be unto thy soul; thine adversity and thine afflictions shall be but a small moment; And then, if thou endure it well, God shall exalt thee on high; thou shalt triumph over all thy foes."

Peace filled her heart at the message. She silently prayed she could get through this trial. And then, feeling an overwhelming trust in her Heavenly Father, she knelt next to the couch and thanked Him for His love and kindness.

She finally stood. Knowing she had this avenue of assistance made all the difference. She knew she could get through anything with divine help, and her prayer gave her the courage to call her younger sister and perhaps get the moral support she needed.

Abby thought about her sister and wondered what her reaction would be. Jennifer was three years younger than Abby and had always been much more willing to do their mother's bidding than Abby had been. As a result, Barbara had more openly favored Jennifer, which made it difficult at times for the two girls to be friends. Even now, with Jennifer married and a mother herself, the sisters did not have much contact. It made Abby sad, and she tried to be fair with her own girls so they would never have to feel the pull of competition over their mother's love.

The last time Abby had talked to Jennifer was to tell her about the pregnancy. Jennifer had expressed happiness for Abby, but they hadn't communicated much since. Jennifer lived many miles south of Abby, in Los Angeles, and had only been to the Breuners' house twice since they had moved in. Both of those visits had also involved their mother, which had ruined any opportunity for the sisters to become better friends.

Not knowing what kind of response she would receive, Abby picked up the phone anyway. Jennifer answered it on the second ring.

"Hello?" She sounded out of breath.

"Jennifer? It's Abby."

"What a nice surprise."

"Do . . . do you have a minute?" Abby was afraid she was interrupting something. Jennifer always seemed to be on the go.

"Yeah, sure. We just got back from a play at the kids' school. Why? What's up?"

Abby hesitated, not sure if she wanted to tell her sister, with her model family, what had happened in her less-than-perfect one. She bit her lip in indecision. "Ummm. I have a small problem."

Jennifer laughed. "What? You don't know what to name your baby?"

If only it were that, she thought and tried to swallow the tears that threatened to displace her forced calmness. Her throat hurt from the large knot forming there. "Eric's missing, Jennifer. I don't know where he is."

"Oh, Abby. How awful. What happened?"

For the third time that day Abby explained what had occurred.

"I can come up and stay with you. Would that help?"

That was not what she had been expecting, and tears rimmed her eyes. "What about your kids?"

"Rick can take care of them. He's been talking about taking time off. This would be the excuse he needs."

"Oh, Jennifer, it would be great to have you here. When would you be able to come up?"

"I'll call the airlines right now and see what's open tomorrow. Is that soon enough?"

"Yes. But I have to go to work at eleven in the morning. Do you think you can get to the airport by nine thirty? That will give me enough time to pick you up and still get to work on time."

"What do you mean you have to work? How can you go to work when your husband's missing?"

"It's not that I want to go to work, Jennifer. But what choice do I have?"

"Can you take tomorrow off?" Jennifer asked.

"No, I can't. I already got on my supervisor's bad side when I came in late the other day."

"She can't be that coldhearted. She can't expect you to carry on like everything's normal when your husband is missing," Jennifer said.

Abby shook her head. "She doesn't know, and I don't want her to know. In fact I don't want anyone to know."

"Why on earth not? If more people know, the chances are better he'll be found."

Abby hesitated. On the one hand, she needed moral support from someone who already knew her flaws and wouldn't judge her too harshly. On the other hand, she didn't need someone to constantly second-guess her.

The need for help outweighed her other concerns, and she asked Jennifer to just support her decisions. Jennifer must have sensed Abby's mood and she agreed, promising to call back.

As she waited for Jennifer to call back, she was jerked out of her thoughts by the shrill ringing of the telephone. She picked it up before it could ring a second time and was greeted by the deep voice of Mr. Phillips.

"I was calling to see how Tiffany is feeling."

Abby was surprised he cared enough to call. "She's much better. Thank you." She paused. "Do you always call your students to see how they're feeling?"

"Uh, no," he said, sounding as if the question had caught him off guard. "Not always. She just seemed to become sick so quickly. I was worried a new virus might be starting the rounds in my classroom."

"Oh. I guess I can understand that. But don't worry. Tiffany's fine now. She should be back tomorrow."

"Well, that's good. I wonder why her sickness was so sudden, then? Is she under any stress at home . . . or . . . she mentioned something about her father being gone, and I didn't know if your family needed help."

Abby froze at his words. His phone call suddenly struck her as very odd, but before she could determine whether he was seeking gossip or if his motives were truly philanthropic, her other line beeped. "I'm sorry, that's my other line. I'm afraid Tiffany is just a daddy's girl, so she misses him overly much while he's out of town on business. But thank you for your concern."

Mr. Phillips apologized for asking a personal question and assured her he only meant to help.

Abby accepted his words, remembering that he was from a small town and probably just meant the call as a sincere expression of concern.

The other line was Jennifer calling to tell Abby her flight plans, and after hanging up, Abby yawned loudly, suddenly exhausted. She went to the stairs, stopping in the entry hall to look at the picture of Eric hanging there. Any good feelings that had come from talking to Jennifer instantly vanished as she gazed at the picture of her handsome husband staring back down at her, the ever-present grin on his face.

She plodded up the stairs and checked on the girls before going into her own room. Her shoulders felt weighed down with worry and concern. After putting on her nightgown she slipped into bed and fell asleep almost immediately.

* * *

Sometime during the night Abby woke up with a start, certain someone was in the room with her. Paralyzed by fear, she tried to convince herself no one could possibly be in the house because the alarm would have sounded. Her eye caught movement in the mirror. Abby nearly screamed, then realized she had left the window open. The fluttering curtains swayed in the night breeze, reflected as dark silhouettes passing across the vanity mirror. She shut the window, but wondered if she had remembered to set the alarm. Hurrying downstairs, she realized she hadn't and quickly did so. Assuring herself she must have been dreaming, she nonetheless felt grateful the dream had spurred her awake and sent her to the alarm. When she climbed back into bed, she drifted off to sleep very relieved.

CHAPTER EIGHT

The phone woke Abby early the next morning. She grabbed it to quiet the shrill sound.

"Hello?" she mumbled in a sleep-filled voice.

A young child's voice asked, "Daddy?"

Abby's eyes snapped open. "Hello?"

"Daddy?" he said again.

"Who is this? What's your name, honey?" Abby asked gently.

"Alex Breuner," the boy said. There was a noise in the background, and a woman's voice filtered through. Then the phone was hung up.

Abby dropped the phone as her heart raced. *What did it mean? Was it a simple coincidence? Was it related to the hang-ups she'd answered earlier?*

* * *

"Why is Auntie Jennifer coming, Mommy?" Susannah asked, excitement making her voice louder than normal.

Tiffany gave her sister a withering glance. "She's just coming to visit Mom." Tiffany looked over at Abby, her spoon poised above her cereal bowl. "Right, Mom?"

Abby was surprised at the look of worry on her older daughter's face. She wondered how much Tiffany was aware of, and after what Mr. Phillips had reported, Abby had finally told the girls their father had gone out of town for a few days, which was true as far as she knew. They had been disappointed but hadn't complained. Now Abby looked over at Tiffany and tried to give her a reassuring smile. "Yes, Tiffany. I haven't seen Jennifer in a long time. Don't you think sisters should visit each other once in a while?"

The girls nodded solemnly.

Abby went on. "I hope the two of you can be good friends when you grow up. Maybe you'll be neighbors."

Tiffany and Susannah looked at each other across the table before continuing to shovel cereal into their mouths.

"Are you girls almost done? We need to get going. Jennifer's flight comes in later this morning, and I want to get your room ready for her, Tiffany."

Tiffany's lips turned down into a pout and her voice came close to a whine. "Do I have to stay in Susannah's room?"

Susannah looked hurt by the question. "I cleaned it up, Tiffany. I even made room on my dresser for you to put your stuff."

Tiffany favored her younger sister with a tiny smile. "Okay, I guess."

Abby smiled in relief; her girls were on the right track.

* * *

Abby waved to the girls as they walked to their respective classes. She was glad Tiffany was well enough to go back to school. She had too much to do to have to worry about a sick child.

First, she drove to the police department to see if they had any word on Eric. The same officer was sitting behind the desk, papers spread out around him. He glanced up as Abby approached, no glimmer of recognition in his eyes.

Abby smiled nervously, afraid to hear what he might say.

"I don't have any information for you, ma'am," he said after she gave him Eric's name.

"Are you sure?" she asked, certain they must have something.

"Unfortunately, your case isn't very high on the list of priorities here." He paused. "I'm sorry."

As she walked out the doors of the police station, she wondered how her life had come to this point.

The drive to the airport took over an hour and gave Abby time to think. The radio played quietly in the background as she thought about Eric and about her relationship with her sister.

She glanced in the rearview mirror to change lanes, not noticing that the same vehicle had been several car lengths behind her since leaving home.

* * *

Short-term parking at the San Jose airport was nearly full, and Abby had to park a distance from the terminal. She resigned herself to the long walk and tried to enjoy the sunny morning. When she finally reached the doors to the airport, she was breathing hard and in need of something to quench her thirst.

First she checked the flight board to see if her sister's flight was on time. The board claimed it was. Abby consulted her watch and saw she had about five minutes before the flight arrived. She took her time walking to the drinking fountain, then wandered over to the area where she was allowed to wait. There were several tables and chairs scattered around the vicinity. They were mostly empty, and she sat in one near the door Jennifer would eventually come through.

Abby glanced at her watch. Just then a group of people walked in her direction. Standing in anticipation of her sister's arrival, Abby pulled her purse onto her shoulder. As she walked toward the group, someone bumped into her. She turned around, but no one was there.

Then someone tapped her shoulder. She turned to see Jennifer standing there, a broad smile on her face. They embraced briefly. Abby was surprised yet pleased by Jennifer's apparent joy in seeing her, and she was comforted by the warm hug she received.

"Are you ready to go?" Abby asked, noticing the suitcase Jennifer had set on the floor. "Do you have any other luggage?"

"Actually, yes," Jennifer said. "I wasn't sure how long I'd be here so I came prepared for an extended visit."

Abby embraced her younger sister again. "I'm so glad you came," she said, drawing in a ragged breath. "I've been going crazy these last couple of days."

Jennifer pulled back and smiled affectionately at Abby. "I can't imagine what you've been going through."

They moved toward the luggage area, Jennifer pulling her carry-on bag behind her.

"What did Rick say when you told him what was going on?" Abby asked.

Jennifer glanced in her direction, then quickly looked away. "He didn't say much." She paused. "Hey, how's my new little niece or nephew doing?"

Abby smiled, despite the feeling that Jennifer wasn't being completely truthful. She gently touched her abdomen. "The baby's doing great," she began as they headed toward the car. "In fact, I went to the doctor the other day and had an ultrasound." They talked about the baby and their children until they reached the house. Then the subject that had been on both their minds finally found voice as Abby showed her sister into the family room.

"Tell me what you've done so far," Jennifer prodded after sitting on the couch.

Abby sat across from Jennifer. In a monotone she recited what had happened with the police. "I don't have much hope they'll help me out. They don't seem at all concerned."

"Do you want me to call them?" Jennifer offered.

"If you want to. But I doubt it would do any good."

Jennifer seemed surprised by Abby's pessimism, but she smiled and went into the kitchen to look for the phone book. When Jennifer turned back to say she couldn't find it and to ask for the phone number, Abby was staring blankly at a spot on the wall. "I need the number, Abby," she repeated.

Abby jumped, startled. "What? What did you say?"

Jennifer repeated the request.

"I'll have to go upstairs to get it. It's in my room by the phone," Abby said.

"I'll get it," Jennifer offered.

Abby nodded, then sighed, frustrated at her inability to focus.

* * *

Tess Michaels opened her front door, curious at who was knocking so loudly.

"Are you Tess Michaels?"

"Yes. Can I help you?" Tess asked, wondering what the man at her door wanted.

He showed her a badge. "FBI, ma'am. I'm Agent Webster and we'd like to ask you a favor."

"Okay," Tess said, wondering what kind of favor she could possibly offer the FBI.

"We understand you work with a Mr. Eric Breuner, your neighbor just up the street?" At Tess's nod, he continued. "When you're home, we'd like you to keep an eye on the Breuners' house. We'd also like you to talk with his wife—see if you can find out some information for us on anything unusual that's been happening at their house."

Shocked at the request, Tess simply stared at the man.

He handed her a card. "I'd like you to email me anytime you see Mrs. Breuner leave her home or if you see her husband, Eric."

"If I see her husband? I don't understand. Why don't you just go over there and talk to him yourself?"

"Mr. Breuner hasn't been available, and we'd like to speak with him if he comes home."

Tess wondered where Eric had been and why the FBI would want to speak with him. She glanced at the card before looking back at Agent Webster. "I work part-time, but I'll do what I can."

He smiled. "We appreciate it."

* * *

Abby wondered what was taking Jennifer so long to get the phone number. It was right on the table. She was about to get up and find out when Jennifer came down the stairs. Jennifer looked upset, and Abby almost asked her about it, but then Jennifer smiled encouragingly and picked up the phone. Jennifer's confidence gave Abby some hope, and she waited on the couch as Jennifer made the call. But her hope was short-lived. She could tell there was no news before Jennifer had hung up.

"I'm sorry. They don't have any new information," Jennifer said. "But apparently it's not unusual for people to take off and not tell their families where they're going." Jennifer looked thoughtful for a moment. "Abby?"

"What?"

Jennifer was silent, apparently considering how to ask her question.

Abby feared what her sister's question was going to be. Could Eric be using drugs again? Could he have left her?

"Look, Jennifer. I'm going to be late for work if I don't get going here." Abby stood and picked up her purse. "Can this conversation wait until later?"

Jennifer's eyebrows briefly drew together. "Do you think you should be going to work at a time like this?"

Worry and annoyance pulled at Abby's patience. "At a time like what? When I can't depend on my husband to provide an income, or when I might get fired if I miss any more work?"

Defensiveness clouded Jennifer's face. "I came here to help you. If you would prefer that I not be here, let me know."

Abby set her purse down on the counter and walked over to her sister. "I'm sorry. I do want you here. Really, I do." She put her arms around Jennifer's rigid body, trying to convey a feeling of appreciation she hoped was genuine.

Jennifer finally placed her arms around Abby as well. "I know you have a lot on your plate. I'll try to be more understanding."

Abby pulled back. "Are you sure you'll be all right here while I'm gone? It should only be four hours."

"Don't worry about me." Jennifer glanced toward the messy kitchen. "I'm sure I'll find some way to be of use."

Abby's gaze followed her sister's, guilt immediately surfacing. "I didn't ask you to come here to be my maid, you know."

"I know that. I want to help you. And if it helps for me to clean up so you can concentrate on more important things, then that's what I'll do."

"Is this what it's like to have a wife?" Abby asked, a grin on her face as the tension dissipated.

Jennifer laughed. "I guess it is. Unless she's fortunate enough to have a husband who actually shares the load. That's *one* thing I love about Rick. He still helps with the dishes at least."

Abby's laughter died in her throat. Her sister's tone was unreadable, but the words themselves caught her attention. Eric scarcely ever helped around the house. "Well, I'd better run. I don't want to keep my wonderful supervisor waiting," she said, wondering if she'd ever have the ease of Jennifer's life or if Eric would become a husband as dependable as her sister's.

CHAPTER NINE

Eric closed the gas cap and climbed into the rental car. As he drove back to the motel, he thought about how he had followed Abby to the airport that morning. *She must be stressed to have called her sister,* he decided. Eric only hoped she would find the note he had dropped in her purse when he'd bumped into her at the airport.

Being near her without being able to touch her had been agony. He was desperate to let her know he was okay and that he hadn't betrayed her. He hoped she would have faith in him. *Like you've given her any reason to have faith in you. You should have left well enough alone.*

But he knew that wasn't possible. It wasn't in his nature. And now all the mistakes he'd made were coming back to haunt him.

* * *

"I found the Jeep."

"That's great," the second man said, the phone pressed to his ear. "I know exactly how we can use it."

"Just one problem, though. I don't have a key."

The second man smiled. "Fortunately for you, I do have a key. I found a spare set when I made my little visit."

"What do you want me to do?"

"Keep it hidden for now. I'll let you know what I want done with it when the time is right."

* * *

When Abby got home from work, she was pleasantly surprised to find an immaculate house waiting for her and chocolate-chip cookies baking in the oven. She tossed her purse on the kitchen counter and went to find Jennifer.

She found her sister in the laundry room, ironing the shirts that had been sitting in a pile for over three weeks. "Thank you, Jennifer. You're a miracle worker."

Jennifer smiled. "You know, if you'd hang up these shirts as soon as they came out of the dryer, they wouldn't be nearly so wrinkled."

Abby's gratitude dimmed at the suggestion. It was like her mother had come to visit right along with her sister. Not wanting the comment to mar her appreciation for all her sister was doing, Abby ignored the remark. "Those cookies smell delicious. Chocolate chip are my favorite."

"Mine too," Jennifer said as she hung up the last shirt and turned off the iron. "I think the batch in the oven should be about ready."

While Abby and Jennifer were dipping the hot, gooey cookies into tall glasses of milk, Tiffany and Susannah walked through the front door.

"Mom, where are you?" Susannah shouted.

"In the kitchen, honey," Abby said, wiping her mouth with a napkin.

The girls walked into the room and stopped, staring at their mother and aunt. Susannah began giggling. "You guys look funny."

"What's so funny about two grown women having cookies and milk?" Jennifer asked, a big smile on her face.

"Hi, Aunt Jennifer," Tiffany said, not moving from where she had stopped. "Mom," Tiffany said, turning toward Abby, "may I have some cookies?"

"Don't you want to give your aunt a hug?" Abby asked, embarrassed by her daughter's rudeness.

"It's okay," Jennifer quickly said. "They don't know me very well."

"I will," Susannah said, a happy expression on her face. She ran over to Jennifer and threw her arms around her.

"Oh, Susannah," Jennifer said, drawing her close. "You make me miss my Emily."

"When can I play with her?" Susannah asked, pulling back from Jennifer.

"I'm sorry, Susannah. I wasn't able to bring her with me this time. But I hope you girls can get together soon."

Abby watched the disappointment spread over Susannah's face. "I'll tell you what," she said. "After you have your snack, we can go over to the park and play for a while. How does that sound?"

"Does that mean I don't have to do my homework right away?" Tiffany asked.

Abby couldn't help but smile. "Yes. You can do it when we get back."

* * *

A short time later the four of them walked to the neighborhood park. It was a beautiful day and it felt great to get out of the house. There were many people lying on the grass, pushing children on swings, or visiting with neighbors. While Jennifer and Abby spread a blanket on the grass, the girls ran over to the play area to join their friends.

Abby observed those around her behind the dark mirror of her sunglasses. There were few men there as it was still only afternoon, but watching them with their children made Abby miss Eric more keenly. She knew she would have to eventually tell the girls why they hadn't spoken to their father. It wasn't right to leave them thinking he was out of town.

Abby turned toward Jennifer, who was watching her nieces on the swings. "What should I tell them, Jennifer?"

Jennifer continued to stare at Tiffany and Susannah. "Do you think they have any idea Eric's missing?" She turned her head in Abby's direction, waiting for a reply.

Abby shrugged her shoulders. "I don't know. I mean, tonight will be the third night he's been gone, and they haven't spoken to him. They're probably starting to suspect something isn't quite right."

Jennifer nodded. "Yeah, I'm pretty sure they must be wondering."

Abby let out a heavy sigh, resigned to telling them something, although she didn't want to scare them.

"Hey there, Abby."

She looked up, startled to see her neighbor—and Eric's coworker—Tess Michaels. After introducing her sister, Abby invited Tess to join them, although she didn't really feel like company—especially company that might ask after her husband's whereabouts.

"So Jennifer, what brings you up to our neck of the woods?" Tess asked as she sat on the blanket.

Jennifer glanced quickly at Abby, then answered with a broad smile, "I'm just visiting my sister."

Tess nodded in reply, then turned toward Abby. "I haven't seen Eric around lately. Where's he been?" she asked in a voice that always sounded coy, as if she were waiting for an unsuspecting male to come around the corner any minute.

You get right down to business, Abby thought in frustration, her worst fears realized in the bat of an eye— *Tess's heavily made-up eye.* "He's on a trip for work," she answered, feeling like she needed the words printed on a T-shirt so she wouldn't have to keep lying.

"Oh. I hadn't heard he was scheduled for a trip. Where'd he go?" Tess asked.

All of her sarcasm aside, Abby actually felt quite uncomfortable lying, but she wasn't about to tell Tess that Eric was missing. She must have hesitated too long, because Tess gave her a strange look.

"You *do* know where he is, don't you, Abby?"

Jennifer jumped into the conversation. "Of course she knows where he is. She's just not feeling well today."

Both pairs of eyes turned her way, and Abby was glad she had worn the sunglasses. "He went back east." She hoped that would satisfy Tess's curiosity.

"Whereabouts?" her neighbor pressed in a tone of disinterest, though Abby wondered if the tone was forced.

Out of the corner of her eye, Abby noticed Jennifer fidgeting and wondered what her sister was thinking.

She decided it would be best to give Tess an answer of some kind to get her off this particular line of questioning.

"He's in New York." Her tone was rather clipped, but she really wanted to end the conversation.

Tess nodded and stood. "Well, I've got to get home. Nice meeting you, Jennifer." She looked directly at Abby. "When you talk to Eric, tell him I said hi."

Abby and Jennifer watched her walk away, her narrow hips swinging from side to side.

"I don't like that woman," Jennifer announced.

"She's okay. I don't think she has many friends, though," Abby said.

"Why's that?"

"She's kind of a flirt. And it doesn't seem to matter if the man is attached."

"Oh. Well, I guess I can see why women don't want to be friendly with her."

Abby nodded. "I should probably try to be nicer to her." She watched her girls swing higher and higher and allowed herself to feel a brief moment of joy before lying back on the blanket. A short time later they folded up the blanket and headed home.

"Okay, girls. Time for homework," Abby announced once they had gotten a drink of water and settled down.

Susannah got right to work, but Tiffany was less than enthusiastic.

"Abby, why don't you go lie down for a while. I'll help them with their homework," Jennifer offered.

"Are you sure?" she asked, greatly relieved to have the break.

"That's what I'm here for," Jennifer said, smiling.

Abby went to her room and lay on her bed, staring at the ceiling as she thought about Eric and past events in their marriage. Most of her memories were good ones, but the few times she and Eric had had difficulties, the challenges they endured had been severe. There were the infertility problems of course, and all the accompanying debt, but that was something they'd faced together.

Then there was that other time, when Eric had gone on a two-day fishing trip.

"It's awfully quiet," Abby murmured suddenly, sitting up on the bed. A moment later she went down the stairs. Walking into the kitchen, she found Tiffany and Susannah occupied with homework, Jennifer hovering over their shoulders.

Jennifer turned at Abby's approach, motioning for her to go into the living room where they could talk.

"How are you feeling?" Jennifer asked.

"Better, I guess," Abby said, pushing aside her uncertainties. "And thank you for helping the girls with their homework."

"It was a pleasure. My kids never get right to work like that. I almost dread telling them to do their homework."

Abby was surprised. She had assumed Jennifer's children were perfect students, with a mother so on top of things.

Jennifer was silent for a moment, apparently thinking about something else. Then she looked carefully at Abby. "There's something I think you should see. I didn't tell you before because you were having such a hard time, and I was hoping Eric would call and straighten everything out . . ."

Abby's radar immediately kicked on, fear coursing through her at what she knew could only be bad news. "What is it?"

"Well, I feel bad about the way I discovered it. I . . . I looked through drawers when I went to get that phone number from your room. I was trying to help . . . you seemed so listless . . ."

"Okay. What is it? You're scaring me." Abby no longer cared how Jennifer found whatever it was.

"Follow me," Jennifer instructed.

She watched as Jennifer walked toward the stairs, stopping at the bottom to make sure Abby was following her. They walked up the stairs together and into the master bedroom.

"What's going on?" Abby asked, apprehension hitting her in quick bursts.

Jennifer stopped in front of the dresser and silently pointed to the bottom drawer.

Staring at the dresser, Abby tried to calm herself and focus. As she did, she noticed that the top of the dresser needed dusting. It was an even coating of dust, however, and only obvious if you were looking for it. She evidently hadn't noticed it. She wondered what else in her life she had failed to notice—like things going wrong in her marriage.

"Abby?"

Abby glanced at her sister before kneeling on the floor in front of the dresser. She hesitated for a moment, then gazed up at Jennifer, who was chewing on her lower lip. She reached out and touched the drawer handles, gripping and squeezing them, afraid of what she was going to find. Trying to convince herself it couldn't be as bad as she imagined, she held the handles firmly and slowly pulled out the drawer. She didn't see anything unusual until her gaze rested on a library book tucked along one side. She rocked back on her heels as she read the title.

How to Vanish and Never Be Found.

It was the last thing she had expected to find, and she almost wished Jennifer hadn't shown it to her. Abby reached in and gently lifted it from the drawer, standing as she stared at the cover, then turned to the first page. She quickly flipped through the book, then gasped suddenly at an item pressed between the pages. The book fell to the floor as she recoiled in horror, the item she'd discovered floating to the carpet.

Forcing herself to remain calm, she reached down and retrieved the wallet-size photograph. She studied the people in the picture, blinking several times, trying to understand what her mind refused to believe.

In the picture were a man, a woman, and a young boy. Abby felt tears start as she stared at the man. "Eric," she whispered, as Jennifer put her hand on Abby's shoulder. As she stared at the family in the picture she thought her heart would break. She squeezed her eyes closed, hoping she would see something different when she opened them again. Forcing her eyes open, she gazed at the picture of Eric and knew there was no denying his identity.

The blond woman was in profile, but she looked quite pretty. The woman gazed adoringly at the man at her side—at Eric. He stared back at her, a smile on his face. Sitting between them was a towheaded boy. Abby guessed he was about three.

She remembered the phone call she'd received just that morning. The one with the little boy asking for

"Daddy." Could it have been the little boy in the picture? The thought made Abby sick.

He loves me, she thought. *He wouldn't do that to us.*

The photo of the little family seemed to mock her—the way the couple gazed lovingly at each other, the little boy who looked just like his parents, the fact that the photo was found in a book about disappearing . . . It was too much for Abby.

She let the picture slip from her hand as she sunk to her knees. She allowed the tears to flow freely. She'd never imagined Eric betraying her in this way. It was bad enough that he might have gone back to using drugs, but this was a whole new level of betrayal.

She barely croaked out, "Jennifer?"

"Yes? Can I get you something?" Jennifer said, worry on her face.

"Water?"

Jennifer hurried into the bathroom and filled a small glass with cold tap water. She walked swiftly back to Abby and pressed the cup to her lips before helping her to the love seat under the window.

Abby smiled gratefully at her younger sister.

"Is there anything else I can get you?"

"Can you watch the girls? I need time alone."

"Of course." Jennifer quietly left the room.

Abby watched her go. As soon as Jennifer was out of the room she was instantly forgotten as Abby turned her mind to Eric. Her thoughts were spinning. *Why on earth would he want to vanish? Doesn't he love me anymore? Isn't he excited about the child we're expecting? Will I ever see him again? Who were the people in that photo? Why . . . ?*

The phone rang next to her, but she ignored it, not in any condition to take a call. It stopped after two rings. She assumed Jennifer had answered it. Any flame of hope it could be Eric had been thoroughly extinguished.

Then a new emotion took over. Anger. *How dare he leave me like this? How does he expect me to take care of our children?*

Her job paid a pittance. They had no savings. Fear merged with the anger, and Abby's stomach sent her running for the bathroom. After she threw up, Abby sat for a long time. She knew it was time to tell the girls something about their father, but what?

She pushed herself off the floor and wandered over to the closet she shared with Eric. *Used to share,* she corrected herself as she stood in a confused stupor. His clothes were still on the floor where she had thrown them the day before. Numbly, she picked them up, folded them into neat squares, and left them in a stack in the corner. She stared at the pile, her eyes burning with tears.

Leaving the closet, she walked over to the dresser and opened Eric's top drawer, gazing at the things inside. Surprisingly, a cold anger took over and she couldn't cry. She pulled her mind together and assessed his belongings. Everything was as he usually kept it. It suddenly occurred to her that if he had been planning on leaving he should have taken some of his belongings.

Or is he planning on buying a whole new wardrobe? And how is he financing this little expedition? she thought with sarcasm. But then panic crowded out any feelings of anger as Abby considered the idea that Eric had cleaned out what little was available in their bank accounts. Hurrying down the stairs to the office, Abby didn't think to ask Jennifer who had called. She closed the office door behind her and went directly to the filing cabinet. Pulling out the drawer that held the bank statements, she perused the balance numbers but noted they were for the previous month. The current month's statements had yet to arrive.

She carried the page over to the desk and laid it on the desktop, settling herself into the soft leather chair and pulling out a pad of paper and a pen. She wrote down the balance amounts, then, reading farther down the page, noticed a website the bank had. She wondered if Eric had arranged for them to do online banking.

Pressing the button to turn on the computer, Abby hoped he'd signed up for the feature. It would make her job much easier. She waited while the computer booted up, then opened the browser and watched the home page appear. It was Eric's Hotmail account. It looked like he had mail. The computer appeared to remember his password, so she went ahead and logged in.

She clicked on the MAIL tab and saw three new messages. Abby clicked on the first one. It was a newsletter. She perused it and quickly determined it was sports related. That was deleted. The next one looked interesting, but it turned out to be an offer to make loads of money. *Delete.* She clicked on the last one, expecting nothing. Her heart pounded.

I want the package returned immediately, she read.

Abby's eyebrows drew together in puzzlement. She noticed the sender's email address was simply a series of numbers. It was meaningless to her. She wondered if the message could have something to do with a drug delivery. It certainly seemed unrelated to the photograph in the book.

Feeling profound sadness, Abby closed her eyes and breathed deeply, trying to collect herself. In all the scenarios she had imagined, Eric dealing drugs again had been her biggest fear. But she no longer knew what she should be the most afraid of. *What could I have done to help you? Are you hurt? Do you really have another family? Did a drug deal go bad and you've been injured?* The thought made her feel sick. She didn't know if she'd ever feel well again.

"Abby?" Jennifer's voice came from the hallway.

"I'm in here," Abby called out. Then, afraid Jennifer would see the awful message, Abby closed it and turned toward the door.

Jennifer crossed the room quickly and took her sister in a firm hug. Abby burst into tears, then began sobbing. The sisters simply held each other as the minutes ticked by.

Jennifer finally broke the silence. She spoke gently. "I hadn't realized you'd come downstairs. I . . . uh . . ." Jennifer seemed to sense that Abby wasn't ready to talk yet. "I want you to know that I haven't . . . accepted what we found. There are plenty of possible explanations. Things aren't always what they look like at first. And I support you in whatever you want to do, no matter what happens."

Abby thanked her, not ready to decide anything either.

"Anyway," Jennifer continued, "I wanted to let you know . . . a man called looking for Eric."

Abby sat up straighter, sniffing and holding back more tears. "Did you get his name?"

"Yes. He said it was Tim Meher."

At the questioning look on Jennifer's face, Abby said, "Someone Eric works with."

"Oh. Well, he wanted to know if you had heard from Eric. He said he needed to talk to him."

Abby shook her head, sarcasm emboldening her words. "Yeah, well, I'd like to talk to Eric myself." She almost laughed at how surreal her world had become. Then she felt tears threatening. She put her hand over her mouth, willing the tears to stay inside.

Jennifer waited with her, and when Abby had calmed a little, she said, "Heavenly Father will help you get through this. So let's see if we can't start solving this mystery. Now, what were you doing in here?"

Abby knew Jennifer was right. She had to pull herself together, even if only in preparation to protect and guide her family. Trying not to let the feelings of anger and despair overcome her, Abby pointed to a chair in the corner. "Pull that up. Maybe you can help me find my bank balance."

A moment later they were looking at the bank's web page. There were two lines that had to be filled out: one for a Social Security number, the other for a password. Abby's shoulders slumped in failure. She had no idea what the password was, and this one wasn't automatically filled in by the computer.

"Do you know his Social Security number?" Jennifer asked.

"Not offhand, but I'm sure I can find it." Abby paused, embarrassed to tell her sister she didn't know the password.

"What about the password?" Jennifer asked softly. "Did he ever tell you what it was?"

Abby turned to face her sister. "Stupid me. He tried to show me, but I wasn't interested."

Jennifer reached out and rubbed her sister's shoulders. "That's okay. Don't feel bad. We'll figure it out. If we can't you can always call your bank."

Abby felt the warm concern radiating from her sister. "Jennifer, why did it take something awful like this to bring us together?"

"I don't know. Maybe Mom had something to do with it," Jennifer said, a knowing smile on her face.

Abby actually chuckled, grateful for the distraction. "Naw. Not our mother."

They looked at each other and burst out laughing. It felt wonderful.

"What do you think she would say if she knew we were here without her?" Abby asked.

"Yeah, with us talking about her. I think that's her greatest fear—that we'll get together and talk about what a pain she can be." Jennifer shook her head. "Poor thing. Doesn't she realize we love her, even if she is difficult?"

Abby didn't say anything for a moment. "I'm glad at least one of us appreciates her."

"What do you mean?"

"Sometimes the only thing I can feel toward her is anger and annoyance. I mean, she has no concept of other people's feelings. Like last night, right before I called you, I called her and told her Eric was missing. Do you think she showed any sympathy?" Abby shook her head in answer to her own question. "All she could say was that she'd warned me he was no good." The memory made her angry, but then Abby stopped, wondering if her mother was right. After all, her mother had merely assumed Eric had gone off to use drugs, and after the disturbing discoveries today, she couldn't say her mother was too far off the mark—maybe even too conservative in her judgments. Abby looked at Jennifer sadly, tears threatening again.

"What?" Jennifer asked.

"I'm just wondering if maybe Mom is right."

"Don't you go thinking that," Jennifer scolded. "When has Mom ever been right?"

Abby tried to smile in agreement, but she couldn't shake the sensation that Eric was in serious trouble and that she didn't even know her husband. She shoved that aside and focused on the task at hand. "The Social Security number," Abby said, standing and walking to the file cabinet.

She looked for the previous year's tax return. Once she found it, she flipped to the first page. *There it is!* She carried the paper over to the desk and set it down, then typed the number into the space and hit the TAB key. The password was next. Abby looked over at Jennifer, a helpless smile on her face. "Now what?"

"Have you looked through the other bank statements? Maybe he wrote down the password when he signed up for the online banking."

Abby's eyes brightened at the idea. Pushing back from the desk, she went to the cabinet again and found the bank account file. At the desk, she and Jennifer studied it page by page.

On the bottom of one of the pages they saw it. *Moneyman* was written in Eric's handwriting. The sisters looked at each other and grinned. Abby immediately turned her attention to the keyboard and typed in the word.

The computer screen filled with numbers. There was the deposit of Eric's last paycheck and a list of all the checks that had been written and cleared. Nothing unusual. No large withdrawals. The balance amount was not much different than their current statement indicated. Somehow this discovery buoyed her spirits. Maybe she could trust her husband.

"Okay. He didn't clean us out," Abby said with relief.

"Did you think he had?"

"After I looked through that book you found, the thought crossed my mind." Abby paused. "I wonder how he's paying for this."

Jennifer shrugged her shoulders.

Abby looked over at Jennifer, and her sister's love made the tears start again. "Thanks for all your help," she choked. Frustration now motivated her tears. She just didn't know what to think. "I'm exhausted," she said between sniffs.

"You need to take care of yourself and that baby. Go sleep off some of this stress. I'll keep an eye on the girls."

Abby smiled gratefully and nodded. "Thank you, Jennifer."

They walked out of the office together, Abby shutting the door behind them.

* * *

Crawling under the fluffy comforter, Abby hugged Eric's pillow and thought about the email message addressed to her husband. *Maybe I shouldn't jump to conclusions. It might have nothing to do with drugs, or . . . with anything else we found,* she considered as she drifted into an exhausted slumber.

A while later she woke up and noticed it was dark outside. Looking at the clock, she saw it was past 8:00 P.M. Abby wondered if Jennifer had already put the girls to bed. She stretched out the kinks in her back and felt her baby moving around restlessly.

She rubbed her abdomen. "It's okay, baby. Don't you worry about a thing. Momma's going to take care of you." As she said it, she realized that someone would need to take care of *her.* She knelt by her bed and prayed for a long time. When she finally felt enough resolve to face the challenges ahead, she stood and considered her girls.

She thought for a moment, trying to come up with an excuse to give her daughters for their father's absence. After pulling on her robe, Abby left her bedroom and walked down the hall toward Susannah's room. Susannah was in her bed, and Tiffany was in a red sleeping bag on the floor. They were still awake and smiled at their mother as she knelt down between them.

"I'm glad I caught you before you fell asleep." Abby looked back and forth between them.

They didn't say anything as they looked at her with sleepy eyes.

"Did you say your prayers?" Abby asked.

"Yes, Mom," Tiffany answered for both of them. "But we didn't have a family prayer."

A grim smile on her face, Abby folded her arms. "Okay. We'll do it now."

When they were kneeling together, Abby began the prayer. When she was nearly done, she asked Heavenly Father to bring Eric home to them safely. She had to pause halfway through to keep from crying. After closing the prayer, she glanced at her daughters and saw their questioning faces. "You've probably been wondering when Daddy is going to come home," she began.

They nodded.

"Aunt Jennifer said he went away for his work," Susannah said.

Abby tried to keep control of her emotions, taking a deep breath before continuing. "The truth is, I'm not sure where he is."

Tiffany sat up straighter on her sleeping bag. "What do you mean?"

Abby couldn't stop the tears from filling her eyes.

Susannah began crying as she patted Abby on the back. "It's okay, Mommy. We're still here."

"I know, sweetheart. And I love you both very much." Abby reached over and hugged each girl. "And I'm sure that wherever your father is, he misses you and loves you very much too."

"But when's Daddy going to be home?" Tiffany persisted.

Abby pressed her lips together as she tried to gain control of herself. She shook her head from side to side. "I wish I knew, honey. But I don't." Abby looked Tiffany in the eyes. "Daddy hasn't called to tell me." Abby hoped they wouldn't have more questions. She didn't think she had the energy to answer them. "Now get back in bed and try to sleep. You both have school tomorrow." Abby watched Susannah crawl under her covers. Then she smiled down at Tiffany, who showed no signs of sleeping.

"Mom?" Tiffany asked. "Why would Daddy do that? Doesn't he love us anymore?"

She stroked Tiffany's cheek. "I don't know why he's done this, but I do know he loves you very much. I'm sure of it."

Tiffany didn't look convinced as she turned on her side and closed her eyes.

Abby left the room and went down the stairs.

Jennifer's back was turned as Abby came toward the family room, and she had the phone pressed against her ear. "I know, Rick. I wonder the same thing, but what can I do?"

Abby stopped in the doorway.

"Yeah, she was pretty shocked about the book and picture . . . I don't know . . . Okay. I love you too. Bye."

Abby waited a moment before she walked into the room. Jennifer seemed surprised to see her.

"Hey. You're awake." Her smile showed nothing but kindness. "Are you feeling any better?"

"A little," Abby said. "I talked to the girls." As she thought about Tiffany's question about their father loving them, her heart tightened with sadness. "They're pretty confused. They think their Daddy doesn't love us." Abby's voice broke as she said the words, then it fell to a whisper. "I'm beginning to wonder the same thing."

Jennifer rushed over to Abby, who was now slumped in the depths of the couch cushions. She sat beside her sister, stroking her back.

"I don't know what to say," Jennifer began. "Why would he do this? Do you have any idea?"

Abby looked at the floor. "I really don't know. I thought things were going well. I mean, sure, we had problems like every other couple I know, but nothing that would send him running away."

Jennifer forced Abby to look at her. "What kind of problems were you having? I mean, exactly."

Abby felt ill at ease sharing such personal things, even with her sister. "I'm not comfortable talking about it."

"I can understand that. But it might give us an idea of what's going on in Eric's mind."

Abby stood abruptly. "I'm really hungry. What'd you guys eat for dinner?" She moved into the kitchen, opening the refrigerator and cupboards.

Jennifer wasn't far behind. "We had soup and salad. Sit down and I'll heat some soup for you."

Abby didn't answer as she sat at the table and laid her head on her arms. When Jennifer set the steaming bowl of soup in front of her, she looked up and smiled gratefully.

"It's hot," Jennifer said, sliding into the chair opposite Abby. "While it's cooling, why don't you fill me in on what's been going on with you and Eric?"

Abby smiled. "You don't take no for an answer, do you?"

Jennifer grinned back.

"Okay. You win." Abby stood and began pacing the short length of the kitchen. She stopped and looked at Jennifer, who nodded encouragement. "Well, you know how long it took us to become pregnant with this one," she said, caressing her belly.

"I remember you telling me you didn't think you'd ever get pregnant."

Abby nodded in agreement. "We almost gave up. The expense of the in vitro fertilization procedures ate up our savings, and we started getting cash advances on our credit cards to cover the cost."

"Didn't your insurance cover it?"

"Not really. They only covered a small percentage of it. We had to come up with the rest ourselves. But somehow Eric always managed to come up with the money we needed."

"I thought Mom told me you got pregnant naturally."

"Yes. After spending nearly every cent we had and then some."

"What does this have to do with Eric's disappearance?" Jennifer asked.

Sighing, Abby stopped pacing and sat down across from Jennifer. "I guess I might have pushed Eric on the financial part of it." Abby paused, thinking about the possibility Eric was dealing drugs, needing the money to meet their financial obligations.

"What do you mean? I thought Eric wanted this baby as much as you did."

She nodded vigorously. "Oh yeah, he wanted a baby as much as I did." Abby paused again. "At first."

The look on Jennifer's face showed her obvious surprise.

"Don't get me wrong. He was thrilled when I became pregnant. It was the financial strain that was getting to him."

"That's understandable. But what happened? What did you mean when you said he wanted a baby 'at first'?"

"After the first year he wanted to give up. Just forget the doctors and all of their procedures. I guess he was feeling overwhelmed by the monetary burden. He tried to convince me to move on with life—that our two wonderful girls were all we needed. But I wouldn't listen. I insisted we keep going. I've always felt like another spirit was up there waiting to join our family."

"Didn't Eric feel the same way?"

"I don't know."

"Maybe he couldn't understand that maternal instinct you were feeling," Jennifer pointed out, trying to ease Abby's apparent guilt.

Abby nodded slowly. "After a while he couldn't see anything past the bills flowing in every month. Looking back, I can see I might have been a bit obsessed. I'm sure I must have driven him crazy with my fixation on becoming pregnant." Abby slowly stirred the soup. She scooped up some of the now-cooled liquid and brought it to her lips.

"So? How did Eric handle it?" Jennifer asked.

Abby set her spoon down and pushed the bowl away, suddenly losing her appetite. "Not too well. He became somewhat of a workaholic, taking in a bit of contract work in addition to his regular job. I can't blame him. I'm sure he felt a strong need to get the bills settled."

"So why would he leave?"

"I'm not sure. Like I said, he was excited about the baby." Abby pushed back from the table and carried her dishes to the sink, rinsing them out before stacking them in the drainer. She turned and leaned against the counter, carefully watching her sister's expression. "There is one other thing."

* * *

Eric shook his head, trying to figure out how and when he had gotten himself involved in this mess. *I can't think about that right now. The important thing is to get this worked out so that I'm not the one who goes to prison.*

He began pacing around the small motel room, trying to decide what to do next. He had already gathered some information that could potentially help him out of this. His plan would be risky, especially with the drug arrest on his record. He wasn't sure if anyone would believe his story—even to him it sounded far-fetched.

CHAPTER TEN

"Our accountant friend is starting to be a problem." The smoothly dressed businessman tapped his fingers as he sat at the table.

"Why do you say that?" his companion asked.

"He'd paid us what he owes, but now he's borrowed more and he seems to be having trouble coming up with the cash."

"Do you think he's trying to jerk us around?"

"I don't know. What do you think?"

His companion stroked his goatee, as was his usual habit when making decisions. "Let's give him another week, and then if he still gives us the runaround we'll send him a stronger message."

* * *

Jennifer stared at Abby, waiting for her to reveal the one thing she had been holding back.

Abby walked slowly over to the table and eased herself into the seat across from her sister. She leaned back for a moment and took a deep breath. "About six years ago, when Eric was working for a different company, he was asked to work a lot more than he ever had before. At first he didn't mind, but after a few months he got tired of it. All those hours were really stressing him out. One day a friend from work invited him to go fishing for the weekend at a cabin the guy owned. Of course I gave him my blessing. He had been working so hard, he rarely got a chance to relax."

Abby sipped her water before going on. "As soon as he left I got this feeling that I shouldn't have let him go. He didn't come home when he was supposed to, and I knew something was wrong. Sure enough, when he came home he was stoned."

"Oh, no," Jennifer said. "What happened?"

"This 'friend' of his had some pot, and even though Eric tried to resist at first, he gave in. He even told me that if the guy had had harder stuff, he would have used that, too." Abby looked down at the table, then back at Jennifer. "He had to meet with the bishop and go through the repentance process all over again. He promised me it wouldn't happen again, but I'm afraid this is something he's going to struggle with for the rest of his life."

"Oh, Abby. I'm so sorry. I had no idea you'd gone through all that," Jennifer said.

"Well, how could you know? I guess we did a good job of keeping it to ourselves, although Eric did tell his father. I think that's part of why they haven't been speaking, not that their relationship was great to start with."

Jennifer shook her head. "I wish I had known about it when it happened. What an awful thing to go through alone."

"It was a trying time. But we've been closer ever since." She looked away. "At least I thought we were."

"Now I understand why you're not telling everyone." Jennifer paused. "You're afraid he's had another relapse."

Abby's head thudded dully. She turned away from Jennifer as tears moistened her eyes. "That possibility's been on my mind." Then, steeling herself, she turned back to her sister. "I read an email today that worries me. It was for Eric. It said, 'I want the package returned immediately.'" Abby swallowed hard and tried to control the shaking in her voice. "Do you think that could mean a drug delivery? Do you think he could be dealing drugs again?"

"I don't know. I mean, having a brief relapse doesn't mean he'd turn to dealing again."

"I hope I'm just jumping to conclusions and that the email is talking about something else. I'm just trying to figure this out." Abby paused. "Maybe Eric was trying to find a way to pay off our debt. Maybe the stress of the debt pushed him back to his drug contacts." Abby paused again. "The other day I got a call from a man asking for Eric. He wouldn't give me his name and hung up." Abby couldn't hold back her fear and sorrow and bit her lip to try to keep from crying. "I don't know what to think anymore," she choked out. "What if he is dealing drugs again, and he was involved in a deal that went bad? You know how often you see news reports where someone is murdered over a drug deal. What if he's . . . got a whole life I don't know about . . . if he's . . . ?" Her crying prevented her from completing her thought.

Jennifer went over and sat next to Abby. "You should have faith in your husband until you know something. He didn't take your family's money—that's something. His stuff is still here . . . Don't assume the worst. It will only drive you crazy."

Abby wiped her eyes and stared at the tabletop for several moments before she was able to speak. "You're right," she said, looking at Jennifer. "I have to believe in him. I have to believe he wouldn't go back to using drugs. He promised, and I have to believe in our marriage. I can't even imagine how he'd have time to be with a . . . another woman . . ."

They sat in silence for a while before Jennifer spoke. "If it makes you feel any better, you're not the only one with problems."

Abby looked at her sister. "What do you mean? Your life seems perfect to me."

Trying to smile despite her mood, Jennifer said, "Yeah, well, things aren't always what they appear."

Abby momentarily forgot her own problems as she concentrated on her sister.

"Rick and I are in counseling." At the look of shock on Abby's face, Jennifer explained. "Yeah, I know. Not what you expected from the perfect Jennifer, huh? Don't worry, though. It's just your typical personality-conflict thing."

Abby stared at her sister, speechless.

"Don't worry. We'll be okay."

"Yet you came here? I'm sorry I took you away from your family." She was astonished over Jennifer's confession.

"We'll be fine. I only told you so you would realize everyone has struggles. I know yours are extreme right now, but I hope you realize that nobody has a perfect life, no matter how things may appear from the outside."

The phone rang, interrupting their conversation.

"Do you want me to get it?" Jennifer asked.

"No, that's okay." Abby stood and walked over to the phone. "Hello?"

"Abby, this is Tim. How are you?"

"I'm okay." She was a bit surprised to hear from Eric's coworker. "Do you have any news for me?"

"No. Actually, I was hoping you'd have some for me. I'm really worried about Eric. Have you heard from him at all?"

"I'm afraid not." Abby looked at Jennifer, covered the mouthpiece, and whispered, "It's Tim."

Jennifer nodded, went to the sink, and began loading the dishes Abby had used.

"I haven't found a file for you, either," Abby said.

"Okay, thanks for looking." He paused. "I think Brock will need more information soon," Tim continued. "I told him a few things, and he'll be patient until we know what's going on, but I don't think he can stay in limbo much longer. He's going to have to hire a temp worker soon."

"Oh." Abby bit the inside of her lip, fresh worry coursing through her. "I understand. I appreciate your help."

"Look. If you hear from Eric, let him know he needs to get in touch with us as soon as possible. I, uh, I think we can work out whatever's going on."

Does Tim know about Eric's past drug use? "Do you have any idea what's going on?" she asked.

He seemed to hesitate. "No, I don't."

"Do you think I should call Brock?" Abby asked, wondering if Tim knew something he wasn't telling her.

"No, I'll take care of that. You just let me know if you hear from Eric."

Relieved she wouldn't have to talk to Eric's manager, Abby said, "Thank you, Tim, for all you're doing."

"Call me if you need anything," he said before they hung up.

"It's nice to know someone's on your side," Jennifer said after Abby told her about Tim's concern for Eric.

* * *

Abby stretched as she looked at her bedside clock, then jumped out of bed in a panic that the girls were late for school. She threw on her robe and ran down the stairs where she found Jennifer sitting at the kitchen table, reading the newspaper.

"Where are the girls?" Abby asked.

Jennifer smiled. "I took them to school a long time ago. I thought I'd let you sleep in. You looked exhausted last night."

Abby let out a breath of relief. "That was really thoughtful. It did feel good to sleep in." She walked into the kitchen and poured herself a glass of orange juice. "How did you sleep?"

"Pretty good, considering our conversation," Jennifer answered.

Abby nodded. "I know what you mean." She motioned to the paper in front of Jennifer. "Anything interesting in there?"

Jennifer shook her head with regret. "Not so far, and I'm almost done."

Closing her eyes in defeat, Abby nodded. "I have to admit, I'm losing hope."

"Don't ever give up hope."

Abby smiled halfheartedly.

Suddenly closing the paper, Jennifer said, "What time do you have to go to work today?"

"Believe it or not, I actually have today off."

"Great. I have an idea. Why don't we go somewhere and wander?"

"What did you have in mind?"

"Do you have a mall nearby?"

"Yeah," Abby said, hesitating.

"What's wrong?" Jennifer asked.

"I just feel guilty doing something fun when Eric's missing."

"Look, Abby, you need a break. It's not wrong for you to take some time for yourself once in a while."

"I guess you're right. Let me change."

As they were about to walk out the door, the phone rang. Abby rushed to answer it.

"Abby? This is Nadine."

Abby closed her eyes and shook her head. "Hi, Nadine."

"Mary is sick, so I need you to work today."

Abby glanced at Jennifer, who had a questioning look on her face. "I . . . uh, I have plans today. What about Linda? The new girl? Can she cover for Mary?"

Nadine sighed. "She's already scheduled for today. You're the only one who can take Mary's place."

"What time?" Abby asked, resigned to her responsibility and wondering what was wrong with Mary.

"Not until three o'clock this afternoon. But I'll need you to stay until after we close."

"Oh," Abby said, having forgotten Mary frequently worked the evening shift. She was once again grateful to have Jennifer there to help out. "Okay. I'll see you then."

Abby hung up the phone and grimaced at Jennifer. "Looks like my day off isn't going to happen, but I don't have to go in until three o'clock."

"I'm sorry, Abby. That's too bad. But at least I'll be here to take care of the girls."

"Yeah. Thank goodness for that," she agreed as they walked to the car. "I don't know what I would've done if you weren't here." *Or what I'll do once you're gone,* she thought, wondering how long her life would be in upheaval.

They pulled into the mall parking lot a short time later.

"Your mall sure feels deserted compared to the one I go to in L.A.," Jennifer observed as they walked along the lower level.

"Yeah, this is the best time. I don't like to come when it's crowded."

After an hour of shopping, the few things Abby needed had been purchased, so the sisters stopped for some frozen yogurt before window-shopping on the upper level.

"Rick's birthday is next week and I need to get him a gift," Jennifer said.

Abby didn't think she could stand shopping for a gift for someone else's husband, not when her own husband was missing. "I'm going to wander around on my own if you don't mind."

"Are you sure? I could get something for Rick later."

"No. You go ahead," Abby said. "I'll meet you back here in half an hour."

As Abby walked away, she noticed things were picking up. It was approaching lunchtime and more people were arriving. She stopped at the railing and looked down at the people beneath her. When she saw a couple cuddling on a bench, her chest tightened with envy.

She looked away from the couple, and her gaze fell on a man who was walking away. Her back went rigid as she looked at him. He had blond hair cut in a style like Eric's and his walk seemed familiar.

She dashed toward the stairs, almost tripping in her haste. The man was beginning to disappear from sight.

No, wait! Abby silently screamed.

By the time she reached the bottom of the stairs, she couldn't see where the man had gone. She was out of breath, her heart pounded, and the baby moved restlessly in her womb.

Hurrying down the mall in the direction the man had gone, she scanned store windows as she passed. She slowed as she reached a music store, stopping in the doorway when she spotted a blond man in the back. It was the same man she'd been following. She hurried in and approached the man, whose back was to her.

"Eric?" she whispered.

The man began turning in her direction, and she gasped when she saw his profile. As he faced her she felt as if she'd been kicked in the stomach—she'd been so sure it was him.

He stared at her, alarm registering on his face. "Are you okay, ma'am?"

She felt the world spinning as dizziness began to overcome her. Desperate to keep from falling, she grabbed at the man's arm. He held on to her.

"Are you okay?" he asked again. Then he called out, "Could we get some help over here?"

As the dizziness receded, Abby let go of the man's arm and stood back from him. "No. It's okay. I'm fine," she mumbled, mortified.

The store manager rushed over. "Is there a problem here, sir?"

"Can you get some water for this woman?" the man asked.

Several people were looking their way, and Abby wanted to escape their stares. A moment later the manager handed Abby a glass of water and she gulped it down.

"I'm fine now. Really." She tried to smile at them. "Thank you for your help."

The blond man frowned at her. "I think you should see a doctor. I mean, in your condition . . ." He pointed to her pregnant shape.

"I have an appointment later today," Abby lied. "Thank you for your concern."

She left the store as quickly as she could and walked down the mall until she was out of their sight. She found an empty bench and sat down to regain her composure. Recalling the feeling of exhilaration when she'd thought Eric was within reach, she felt she would welcome him back no matter what had caused him to leave. But what might she have to face if she did? The sensation of the world crashing down on her when she'd realized the blond wasn't Eric was the worst feeling she had ever experienced. Worse than when she had first discovered Eric was missing.

When she'd recovered physically, she headed back to where Jennifer was shopping. As she reached the store where she was supposed to meet her sister, she decided to keep quiet about the incident downstairs. It was too embarrassing. Besides, Jennifer would make her go to the doctor when all she needed was for her husband to come home.

She found Jennifer next to a rack of shirts. Putting on a bright smile, Abby walked over to her and asked how it was going.

"I think I'm going to get this one," Jennifer said, holding up a blue shirt. "How about you? See anything interesting?"

"No. Are you about ready?"

Jennifer scrutinized Abby's face. "Are you okay? You look pale."

"I'm just tired like usual."

They left the store a short time later, walking down to the lower level to head to their car. To Abby's chagrin, the blond man was walking toward them. She tried to ignore him, hoping he wouldn't notice her, but he walked right up to them.

"How are you feeling?" he asked.

Jennifer looked at him with curiosity. "Can I help you?"

He looked at Jennifer. "Your friend here nearly passed out a few minutes ago. I was wondering if she's feeling better."

Jennifer looked at Abby. "What is he talking about?"

Abby looked at the man. "I told you before, I'm fine."

He glanced at the two women uncomfortably, then nodded and strode away.

Jennifer turned back to Abby. "Do you care to explain what happened?"

Abby became defensive as her embarrassment surfaced again. "Who are you, my mother?"

Jennifer's voice softened. "No. I'm your sister and I love you. Please tell me what happened."

Abby immediately felt contrite. "It was nothing, really. I felt dizzy for a minute." She looked at Jennifer, hopeful she would drop the subject. "I'm fine. Really."

Jennifer hesitated. "Well, I guess you're old enough to know how you're feeling."

"Thank you," Abby said.

After eating lunch back at Abby's house, the sisters settled down to talk about what strategy they should use next.

"I don't think the police are actively pursuing this," Abby said. "I think it's going to be up to us."

"You may be right. But don't forget I have to leave in a few days."

"I know. And I think you should go back to your family. They need you." Abby smiled gratefully at her sister. "It's been wonderful having you here. I'm glad you were able to come."

"Me too. But I'm not leaving yet. Anyway, it's good for my family to have me away for a while. It helps them appreciate all I do for them."

Abby laughed in agreement.

"What about Eric's files?" Jennifer said suddenly.

"What files?"

"On the computer." Jennifer became animated as she spoke. "Maybe he left something in his computer files that could give us a clue."

Jennifer's excitement was contagious.

"Great idea," Abby agreed.

They went straight into the office and over to the computer. Abby sat at the desk and turned on the computer.

As the screen came to life, Abby turned toward Jennifer. "How much do you know about computers?"

Jennifer grinned. "I actually know a thing or two."

"Great. I know how to use a few of the computer programs and how to go online, but that's about the extent of my knowledge." Abby stood. "You sit here. I'll watch."

Jennifer took Abby's place and began clicking on icons. Abby tried to follow what she was doing but wasn't having much success putting the steps to memory.

"Can you teach me what to do?"

"Sure," Jennifer said. "You see this icon here? You can go in here and see an overview of what's on the hard drive."

"Okay," Abby said, relieved to now understand what Jennifer was doing.

They looked things over for a few minutes.

"I think I'd like to try it," Abby said.

Jennifer relinquished the desk chair to Abby, who started clicking on different folders as soon as she was seated.

They looked for more than an hour, at which point Abby turned toward Jennifer. "I don't know if there's anything here."

Jennifer stood and stretched. "Let's take a break. We can come back to it later."

CHAPTER ELEVEN

As the afternoon wore on, Abby and Jennifer began debating whether to contact the media to broadcast information about Eric. Abby was against it, Jennifer for it.

"Your paper's a daily local. I think we'd get a lot of leads if there was a story about Eric. If someone sees him, they'll call the number we set up," Jennifer said.

Abby shook her head, not convinced. "But what if he's gone back to using drugs? I mean, how humiliating would it be if it comes out that he's a drug addict and we have the whole city out searching for him? Or what if he's gone off to set up a totally new life and he doesn't want to be found?"

Jennifer nodded in agreement. "Yeah, I guess you're right." She sat up straighter. "But Abby, what if it has nothing to do with either of those things and something's happened and he's not able to get back to you? What then?"

Abby closed her eyes for a moment before speaking in a whisper. "I don't know." She shook her head slowly from side to side. "I just don't know."

They sat in silence for several minutes before Abby finally spoke. "Okay. What about this? We call the local paper and have them run a *small* story about Eric.

Nothing major. Just a small photo and description, mentioning that I haven't heard from him in several days."

A broad grin curved Jennifer's mouth. "Great. I think that's the best course of action. I mean, what have you got to lose?"

Abby grinned back tentatively. "I have no idea." But she was relieved to have made a decision.

The newspaper reporter on the phone wasn't enthusiastic about Abby's story, but he agreed to run it.

"Thank you," she said, grateful he was showing even a small amount of interest. "I'll bring a picture by later this afternoon."

"Sure. See you then."

Abby hung up the phone and told Jennifer the situation.

"Sounds like it will be a small mention. That's what you wanted, wasn't it?"

"Well, yes. I guess so. Although I was surprised it was such a non-story," Abby said.

"They probably have people asking them to run similar stories more often than you think. Anyway, you better get ready for work."

Abby agreed and headed upstairs.

* * *

As Abby approached the newspaper office, she felt intimidated by all the commotion. She wished Jennifer had been able to come with her but was glad she was staying with the girls. Abby forced herself to walk with confidence. There didn't seem to be a receptionist, so she approached the first person she saw.

"Excuse me," Abby said in a near whisper.

The woman looked up, annoyed at being interrupted. "Yes?"

"Would you point out Steve Adams for me?"

The woman looked Abby over for a moment before responding. Then she jerked her thumb over her shoulder. "Over there. The one on the phone."

Abby looked in the direction the woman indicated and saw several men talking on phones. "I'm sorry to bother you," she said to the woman, who was again typing, "But could you be more specific?"

The woman rolled her eyes, then stood. "Hey, Steve. This lady's looking for you."

A tall man who looked like a recent college graduate approached Abby.

"I'm Steve," he said, smiling good-naturedly in her direction.

Abby stepped forward, feeling better now that she'd seen his friendly demeanor. "I'm Abby Breuner. I spoke to you earlier about my missing husband."

"Oh, yeah." He nodded. "Come on over here and have a seat." He pointed to a desk covered with memos, Post-it Notes, and yellow legal pads. In the center was a laptop computer.

Abby sat in an empty chair and tried to shut out all the noise. "How can you concentrate with all this racket?"

He grinned. "You get used to it." He shuffled some papers and asked, "Now. What can I do for you?"

Abby reached into her purse and pulled out a wallet-size photo of Eric and handed it across the desk. "Here's the picture I promised you. When do you think the story will be in the paper?"

Steve looked at the photo for a moment before answering. "Not for a few days. I'd guess Monday's edition."

"Oh." She was disappointed, but tried to smile gratefully.

Steve looked at her with sympathy. "It's the best I can do."

Abby nodded. "I understand." She bent to pick up her purse and stood. "Thank you for your time."

"Wait a minute. I have a few questions to ask."

She sat back down. "Sure."

Steve pulled a notepad in front of him and turned to a blank page. "I want to get my facts straight. You said on the phone he was supposed to come home for lunch and didn't show up." He looked at Abby for a confirmation.

"Yes. That's right."

"Okay. What's the name of his employer?"

"Central Valley Construction."

Steve paused for a moment before writing the information down. He didn't look up from his pad. "And his supervisor's name?"

"Brock Mendez."

"And what does your husband do there?"

"He's an accountant."

Steve looked up at her sharply. "An accountant?"

"Yes. Why? Is something wrong?"

He hesitated before answering. "It's just that I've heard rumors."

"What kind of rumors?" Abby asked.

Steve set his notepad down and held up his hands. "I can't really say." He chuckled. "Don't want to give you possibly false information."

Abby leaned forward in her chair. "Look, Mr. Adams. My husband has been missing for four days now. I have no idea where he is or what could have happened. If you know something that could help me find him and you don't tell me, I . . . I . . ." She let her words trail off, not sure what she could threaten him with. Abby glanced at the man's left ring finger and saw a gold band. "You're married?" she asked, pointing to his left hand.

"Yeah. What's that got to do with it?"

"If your wife was missing, wouldn't you be desperate to know where she was? To know if she was even still alive?"

He sighed audibly and looked around the room before looking back at Abby. He leaned across the desk. "Okay. You didn't hear this from me, but I've heard Central Valley Construction has been having financial issues. Apparently there have been discrepancies in their records."

"What do you mean by 'discrepancies'?"

"You know. Things don't quite add up at the end of the month."

"And how would you know this, Mr. Adams?"

"I told you, they're only rumors. But I have a source that's reliable. Someone close to someone on the inside."

"Let me see if I have this straight. You're saying someone in the accounting department may be doing something illegal?"

Steve didn't answer; he just looked her in the eye. Finally he said, "I'm not saying anything, Mrs. Breuner. Nothing at all."

Abby stood slowly from her chair. "Thank you for your help, Mr. Adams."

She wove her way out of the room and headed to her vehicle. On the drive to work she thought about the implications of Mr. Adams's "rumors."

Could Eric be involved in something else illegal? Is that why he disappeared? Should I be happy it isn't drugs or feel even worse?

Once at work, Abby got busy shelving books. She was surprised when Mary appeared half an hour into her shift. "Mary," Abby said, straightening from her task. "How are you feeling? Nadine said you were sick."

"Hi, Abby. I must have just eaten something that disagreed with me. I'm fine now." Mary smiled. "What about you? Are you ready to tell me what's going on?"

Now that Abby had asked the newspaper to print a story about Eric's disappearance, there was no point in keeping the information from Mary. "I guess I am."

Mary's eyebrows lifted in surprise. "That was easy."

Abby tried to laugh, but thinking about the information she was about to share kept her from enjoying Mary's comment. "Eric's missing."

The smile vanished from Mary's face. "What?"

"That's what's been going on. Eric was supposed to meet me for lunch the other day and he never came. I haven't heard from him since, and I have no idea where he is." She noted with surprise that it was actually a relief to tell her friend.

"You're joking," Mary said, obviously having a hard time taking in the information.

"I wish I were." Abby felt the familiar pang of worry in her chest. "I don't know what to think. I just came from the newspaper. They're going to run a story on Monday. I don't know if it will help, but I felt like I needed to do something."

"You've talked to the police, haven't you?" Mary asked, her hand going toward her mouth.

"Yes, but they won't do anything since there's no appearance of foul play."

"Foul play?" Mary asked, the idea obviously shocking her. "Why would there be foul play? Your husband's an accountant, right?"

"Yes, he is. That's why it doesn't make any sense."

"Do you have any theories?" Mary asked, her mind evidently in detective mode.

Abby knew Mary loved a good mystery and hoped all the years she had spent reading them might come in handy now. It felt good to talk to her friend about this, to get another viewpoint. Abby took a deep breath. Then she told Mary about all the horrible things that had happened since Eric's disappearance. She even showed Mary the awful picture of Eric with the other family.

Mary seemed in shock when Abby finished. After hugging her friend, she asked, "Is there anything I can do to help? Hey, what are you doing here so late? Who's watching your children?"

"I'm here because Nadine said you were sick, but don't worry, my sister's in town helping me out. The girls are with her." Abby was touched Mary had thought of her daughters, but before she could express as much they both turned at the sound of someone clearing her throat. Nadine was standing there.

"Is there a problem here, ladies?"

With Mary as an ally, Abby didn't feel so intimidated by her supervisor. "No, everything's fine, Nadine," Abby said. "I was asking how Mary was feeling. You didn't tell me she was going to be coming in after all."

Nadine looked taken aback to be caught making a mistake. "Yes, well, she didn't give me much notice." Nadine shot Mary a look that said she didn't appreciate the changed plans.

"Sorry. I'm feeling better, though. Thank you for caring," Mary said, trying to keep the sarcasm out of her voice.

"Good. Then I suggest you get to work." Nadine turned and stalked off.

Abby had to cover her mouth to keep from laughing out loud. "You're priceless, Mary."

"Thank you. I try to be." She grinned back. "Since I'm here, I guess you can go home."

"Actually, I think I'll stay. I might need the money soon. And it's nice to have something to keep me busy."

"Okay. Will you keep me up-to-date on what's happening and let me know if I can help?"

"Yes," Abby said, happy to have another person to talk to about her problems.

"And can I look at that horrible picture once more? I hate to ask, but this way I can keep my eyes peeled. That woman looks strangely familiar . . ."

Abby's eyes lit up with hope. "She does?" she asked as she quickly pulled out the photo. "From where?"

Mary looked at it closely. "Yes. She does, but I don't know why. I'm so sorry, Abby. But I'll try to remember, and I'll call you if I do. Promise to call me if any clues develop—it might help me think."

Abby nodded that she would, but disappointment and frustration filled her. Where were the answers?

CHAPTER TWELVE

The weekend passed uneventfully. Abby and Jennifer tried to keep the girls occupied so they wouldn't notice their father's absence so much, taking them to movies and roller skating. On Sunday they went to church, but since the newspaper article had yet to run, no one knew why Eric wasn't there. She politely evaded questions about his health and steered conversations in another direction. During sacrament meeting, Abby thought back to the previous Sunday when Eric had been sitting next to her. *How things can change in only a week,* she thought, looking at the families around her and wondering what trials they faced.

The rest of the day passed uneventfully, and on Monday morning Abby scoured the paper for mention of Eric. She found it on page three of the local section. She stared at the photo and thought about the conversation she'd had with Steve Adams at the newspaper. In the accompanying article no mention was made of the "rumors" at Central Valley Construction, which was a relief.

What of those rumors? she wondered. *A kernel of truth can be found in some rumors.*

She set the paper on the counter and headed up the stairs to see if Jennifer needed any help packing. She would be leaving later that morning, and Abby needed to drive her to the airport.

Jennifer was piling her things into her suitcase. She smiled when she noticed Abby standing there.

Abby smiled back sadly. "I'm going to miss you."

Jennifer stopped packing. "Me too." She walked over to Abby and put her arms around her sister. Abby returned the hug. "Are you sure you don't want me to stay longer?" Jennifer asked.

"I don't know how long Eric will be gone. Besides, your family needs you. We'll be okay."

"You'll have to keep me up-to-date on everything that's happening."

"Believe me, I will."

"Good. Now help me shut this thing. I think I'm going home with more than I brought."

* * *

Once home from the airport, Abby noticed how empty the house seemed with Jennifer gone. She wandered around the family room and ended up in front of the bookcase. The origami bird stared at her from its perch. Abby reached up and touched one paper wing. She plucked the bird from the shelf and set it in her empty hand.

Slowly she began unfolding the little bird. She bit her lip and paused. She'd promised herself she wouldn't open it without Eric. With a sigh she repaired the damaged wing and set it back up on the shelf.

The baby moved inside her, jarring her out of her thoughts. Abby wandered over to the couch and sat down, tucking her feet underneath her. She laid her head back and closed her eyes, fighting with herself over whether to feel self-pity or to do something more about her situation.

Resolve won the battle as she lifted her head and stared at the wall across the room. In her mind's eye she pictured Tim Meher. It had been several days since she'd spoken to him. Maybe he would have some new information for her and perhaps she could get up her nerve to ask him what the reporter was talking about when he said there were discrepancies in the accounting department at Central Valley Construction.

"This is Tim," he said when the secretary put Abby through.

"This is Abby Breuner."

He was silent for a moment. Then his voice suddenly became warm. "Yes. How can I help you, Abby?"

She was encouraged by his friendly tone and hoped he would be able to answer her questions. "I was wondering if you have free time for me to stop by and talk to you."

"I won't have time until tomorrow morning. How does nine o'clock sound?"

"That would be fine," Abby said.

"I'll see you then."

It wasn't until Abby had hung up that she realized Tim hadn't asked about Eric. It was almost as if he knew there had been no contact.

Of course he knows Eric's still gone. If he were back, he would've gone to work.

As Abby thought about Eric, it occurred to her that she should let Eric's father know his son was missing. After the pleasantries were over she got right to the point.

"Harry, I wanted to let you know something. Please don't get too upset when I tell you this."

"What's going on, Abby?"

"Eric's missing." Abby shut her eyes, waiting for his response.

"What? What do you mean? He's not using drugs again, is he?"

"Truthfully, I don't know. I'm praying that's not it. I have no idea where he could be or what he's doing." Abby stared at the photo of her family on the desk and felt a lump forming in her throat.

"Have you contacted the police?"

Abby explained the situation and added, "But I did arrange for the local paper to run a small story. It came out in today's paper."

"Perhaps that will lead somewhere." He paused. "I wish I could tell you something more to help you. Is there anything you'd like me to do? Do you want me to come out there?"

"That's thoughtful of you. But actually, my sister just left. And I don't think it would be best if you came out here only to find he's had another relapse."

"I agree. The last thing that would help him is to have his old man show up," Harry laughed. "I don't think he would respond well to my counsel."

"I think we'll be all right for now. But if you could pray for his safety, I think that would help. I'll let you know when I find out anything concrete."

"Sounds good, Abby. You take care of those girls. And that baby. Okay?"

"I will."

* * *

That afternoon, when the phone rang, Abby was surprised to hear Bishop Dunlap on the line.

"Sister Breuner, how are you?"

"Okay. And you?"

"I'm good. But I hear, or rather, read, that things might not be okay at your house. Would it be possible for me to come by your home this evening to visit with you?"

"Sure. I guess so." Even as she said it, Abby felt some measure of relief, and that lasted all afternoon.

That evening, after the girls were settled in the family room watching a movie with the bishop's wife, Abby and the bishop sat in the living room to talk.

"What's happening in your life, Sister Breuner?"

The frank concern and caring in his eyes left Abby on the verge of tears, and she had to swallow several times before she could speak.

"I'm sorry I didn't call you," she began.

"That's perfectly fine. But now that I know, do you mind telling me more about it? I'd like to help if I can."

Abby wasn't sure what the bishop could do to help, but having him offer was a tremendous relief. She had been hesitant to let people know too much for Eric's sake. In fact, Abby didn't think Bishop Dunlap knew anything about Eric's struggle. She wasn't sure how much to reveal.

"Well, I'm feeling pretty devastated by the whole thing. I mean, I have no idea where my husband is." Saying those words in such a factual way brought the situation into sharper focus, and Abby began to weep.

"Take your time now."

When she'd calmed a little, she said, "There's something you should know about Eric that might shed a whole different light on this."

Leaning forward in the chair, Bishop Dunlap nodded. "If it's about Eric's problem with using drugs, you don't need to say anything."

Shocked by his knowledge of Eric's history, Abby didn't know what to say.

Seeing her surprise, the bishop went on. "Eric came to me a while ago and told me he felt he needed to share some things. He said he hadn't used anything in a long time, so I'm not sure why he believed he needed to tell me about his past. I know he'd fully repented of his mistakes in your last ward."

"That's a relief," Abby said. "I had no idea he'd told you about that. You can see why I'm trying not to draw too much attention—I wouldn't want that to get out."

"You suspect he's gone back to using drugs again?"

Closing her eyes in misery, Abby shook her head. "I hope he hasn't. But there are other . . . things." Then she told the bishop about the rumors concerning Eric's employer and the strange book and photo. "I thought things were okay," Abby said in confusion. "Why would he have left?"

The bishop was silent for a few moments, looking thoughtful. Finally he spoke. "I don't know the answer to that, but I'd like to counsel you to have faith that Heavenly Father will watch over Eric and protect him. Things may not be as they seem. Do you think you can do that?"

"Yes. In fact, I do feel He's watching over Eric." Fresh tears filled her eyes. "But it's difficult not knowing where he is . . . and my poor daughters. They don't understand why their daddy hasn't come home or called."

"What have you told them?"

Abby repeated what she'd told Tiffany and Susannah.

"I think that's the only thing you could have said. Now, is there anything we can do for your family?"

"I think we're doing okay. But if you could pray for us and for Eric."

"I'd be happy to. In fact, I'd like to say a word of prayer with you before I go."

Abby agreed, and after the prayer, the bishop and his wife left with the promise to stay in contact. Closing the door behind them, Abby replayed the meeting in her mind. Tremendous gratitude filled her heart as she thought about the love and support she was receiving. She was thankful for the gospel and the peace it brought into her life—she'd never needed it as much as she did now.

CHAPTER THIRTEEN

Tiffany finished writing her spelling sentences as the morning-recess bell rang. She put her paper and pencil in her desk and pushed her chair in.

"Tiffany," Mr. Phillips called. "Would you come here a minute?"

Tiffany walked toward her teacher as the rest of the students raced out the door. She stood in front of his desk, waiting for him to speak.

Mr. Phillips smiled. "I saw in the newspaper that your father is missing. Is he back yet, Tiffany?"

Tiffany was ashamed to admit her dad had abandoned her family. She glanced at her teacher before looking down at the floor. "No, he's not back. But I talked to him on the phone last night."

"That's great, Tiffany." He paused. "Where is he?"

Tiffany realized she had made a mistake in lying to her teacher, but she was too embarrassed to admit it now. Her heart beat faster as she tried to think of what to say. Finally she answered, "I don't know. He talked to my mom for a long time, but he only talked to me for a minute." Tiffany shifted from one foot to the othcr, suddenly anxious to leave the classroom and be with her friends on the playground.

Mr. Phillips stared past Tiffany's shoulder.

"Can I go now?" she asked, feeling uncomfortable.

"What?" he asked, seeming to having forgotten Tiffany was standing there.

"Can I go to recess now?" she repeated.

"Yes." He smiled. "I'll see you after recess."

Tiffany walked to the door and then ran out to the playground. As she began playing with her friends, she forgot about her encounter with Mr. Phillips.

* * *

The sun was shining as Abby pulled into the parking lot at Central Valley Construction. She glanced around at the other vehicles, but, as expected, Eric's wasn't among them.

"How are you, Abby?" Tim asked when she was seated in his office. He took the chair next to hers.

"I'm okay."

"Good." He leaned toward her. "Have you heard from Eric?"

"No, I haven't heard anything. That's one of the reasons I'm here. So you haven't heard from him either?" Abby asked, worried about Eric's job.

"No, and I wouldn't really expect him to contact me before talking to you."

"Of course. I'm sure your right." Abby paused before saying, "Tim, I need to know if anything unusual has been happening around here. Specifically in the accounting department."

Tim looked at Abby more closely. "Did you have something in mind?"

Abby looked back at him, not sure what to say.

"We're not exactly in the habit of giving out company-related information to employee spouses," he tried to explain.

"Of course not. But I've heard rumors there might be problems in your department."

He squinted in Abby's direction, his friendliness fading. "Where did you hear these rumors? From Eric?"

Abby should have guessed he would jump to that conclusion. "No. Eric never told me anything about the business."

"Then who did?"

Obviously he wasn't going to give out information willingly. She closed her eyes briefly, already feeling exhausted by the effort this conversation was taking. She opened her eyes to a suddenly concerned Tim.

"Can I get you something? Water perhaps?"

Abby shook her head, feeling drained. "No. Please just answer my questions."

"I'd be happy to. What was it you wanted to know?"

Abby clenched her teeth, suddenly irritated by what seemed to be a game they were playing. "I asked if there were any problems in your department. For example," she said, forcing herself to calm down, "have significant discrepancies been found in any accounts?"

Tim sat quietly for several moments, staring at one of his paintings. Abby thought he wasn't going to answer. When she was about to ask the question again, he shifted his gaze to her.

"Abby, can I be honest with you?"

"I'd like nothing better," Abby said, relieved he was finally going to answer her questions.

He stood and walked around to the other side of the desk and pulled out his large leather chair. He settled himself in, and when he was comfortable, spoke again, this time in a serious tone of voice.

"Abby. We think Eric has embezzled company funds."

"What?"

"Your husband has taken money that does not belong to him."

Abby's heart pounded. She couldn't believe what she was hearing. "Can I have that glass of water now, please?" Her voice was shaky.

Tim smiled sympathetically as he stood. "Certainly."

She stared at the wall as Tim filled a glass with water. Her hand trembled as she took the full glass from his outstretched hand.

"Thank you," she whispered.

He went back around to his side of the desk and sat down. She noticed him watching her as she swallowed the last of the water. When she set her glass down on his desk, he picked it up and set a coaster beneath it.

"Do you feel better?" he asked.

"No," she said, trying to control her complete astonishment.

"Now, what I would like you to do is this. When you hear from Eric, tell him if he turns himself in and gives the money back we won't press charges."

"Charges?" Abby choked, the realization hitting her that Eric would have to go to prison if what Tim said was true.

He spoke to her as if to a child. "There won't be any charges if he gives the money back." He stood and helped Abby to her feet. "You'll tell him, won't you?"

Abby nodded, unable to respond in her shock.

Tim led her out of his office, and Abby was grateful the secretary wasn't there to witness her shame and embarrassment.

As she walked down the hall, she felt like everyone was looking at her, knew who her husband was and what he had done. It was humiliating. She shoved through the door of a nearby ladies' room and gazed into the mirror, deciding she looked awful. Her face was pale, and her hair looked like it was having a worse day than she was. She went to reach for her lipstick or blush, hoping to hide her reaction to Tim's revelation.

She looked around the small restroom and wondered where she'd left her purse. Nausea rose up when she realized she'd left it in Tim Meher's office. Swallowing several times to keep the bile in her stomach, she braced herself for a second round of humiliation.

Peeking out the bathroom door, she didn't see anyone around, so she moved slowly back down the hall toward Tim's office. She was disappointed to see the secretary still missing from her post. She had hoped the woman would be able to retrieve her purse for her.

Abby walked toward Tim's office door and noticed it was ajar. When she lifted her fist to knock, she heard his voice, apparently talking to someone on the phone. She paused, not wanting to interrupt him again.

The words on his end of the conversation floated out to her.

"Yeah. I told you I'm working on it . . . Look, I know you're serious, and I'm doing all I can to take care of it. We just need a little more time . . . Fine. I'll see you on Friday."

Abby stood silently, trying to comprehend what she was hearing.

What is he talking about? Could it have something to do with the conversation we just had? Who else knows about Eric stealing?

Slowly backing away from the office door, not sure what to do, she met the secretary as she rounded the corner.

"Mrs. Breuner? Is everything all right?"

Abby was caught off guard, but recovered quickly. "Oh. Yes. I've misplaced my purse. I think I may have left it in Tim's office. Would you check for me?"

"Absolutely. Right this way."

Abby was headed toward Tim's office once more. She followed the secretary as the woman knocked on the door and walked right in.

Tim seemed concerned to see Abby there.

"Is something wrong, Carly?" he asked.

She smiled brightly. "No, no. Mrs. Breuner thinks she may have left her purse in here. Ah, yes. Here it is." She bent to retrieve it from the floor near the chair Abby had occupied, then handed it to Abby with a cheerful smile.

"Thank you," Abby said, a tentative smile on her face. Then she turned and left the office without saying another word, but wondering about the phone call she'd overheard.

CHAPTER FOURTEEN

As she sat in her minivan outside Eric's workplace, Abby tried to calm down before attempting to drive home. She looked at her hand and saw it was trembling.

Tim Meher's accusations rang in her ears. *Is Eric really suspected of embezzlement? Maybe I would prefer a drug relapse, or whatever that picture means. At least that wouldn't send him to prison.* She shook her head and tried to push the thought away.

As Abby backed the van out of the parking spot, she glanced up at the window where she thought Tim's office was. She wasn't certain—it was four floors up—but it looked like someone was standing near the window, looking in her direction. She tried to ignore the feeling of helplessness and embarrassment that clenched her insides, and looked away to concentrate on getting home.

The phone was ringing as Abby walked into the house. She jogged into the kitchen, dropping her purse on the counter, and grabbed the receiver midring.

"Hello?" she asked breathlessly.

There was no answer, but she thought she heard a sound in the background.

"Hello," she nearly yelled into the phone.

She tried to remember the bishop's counsel to have faith that Heavenly Father was watching over Eric. She slammed the receiver down and decided that Eric being a criminal was better than his being hurt or killed by drug dealers. She focused on Tim's accusation—almost a comfort at this moment of uncertainty. Did he really believe she could pass on a message, that she was in contact with Eric? A cynical laugh came from her throat at the thought.

The oddity of his request suddenly took on new meaning. Abby walked over to the counter and picked up a pen and pad of paper. She wanted to record and examine the questions that raced through her brain. It seemed like when she was pregnant she lost some of her usual mental acuity, and she wanted to make sure she wasn't missing something. She tried pulling the questions out one by one as they flashed by, listing them on paper as quickly as she could. *Why does Tim think I'm in contact with Eric? Why does he suspect Eric of embezzlement? Who was he talking to on the phone? If Eric hasn't abandoned us, what does the picture mean? What package does Eric have . . . is it here?*

She took the paper to the couch and sat down, laying her head back in exhaustion, frustrated by all the unanswered questions. Memories of Eric floated through her mind. An image of him with red-rimmed eyes and clothing that smelled of marijuana passed in front of her. Then she remembered the email message she'd read recently.

Is Eric that desperate for money? I know our bills have been a burden lately, but I can't believe he would go to that extreme.

She recalled the conversation she'd had with Jennifer a few nights before when she'd told her sister that Eric had somehow always managed to come up with the money they needed for the infertility treatments. The thought sickened her. *It's all my fault. I pushed him into this.* At the realization, despair began to engulf her.

The ringing of the phone yanked Abby back to her present surroundings, her despair giving way to fear.

She reached for the ringing phone. Would it be another silent answer? She cautiously picked it up and brought it to her ear.

"Hello?" It came out almost a whisper.

"Abby? Is that you?"

"Yes. Who is this?"

"It's Tess."

Relieved that it was someone familiar but annoyed at who it was, Abby responded, "What do you want?"

Tess paused at Abby's abruptness. "Well, I . . . I was wondering if you wanted to go to lunch with me. I know we haven't really gotten to know each other, and, well, I've had something to celebrate for several days now—but haven't had anyone to share it with."

Abby closed her eyes briefly, shame at her own behavior and surprise at Tess's honesty filling her. Remembering her desire to be friendlier to her neighbor, she apologized. "I'm sorry Tess. It's been a stressful day. I'd love to hear your news. When did you want to go?"

"Could you do it today?"

Abby was scheduled to work at one o'clock that afternoon. She wondered what would happen if she asked for time off. She decided she might have a nervous breakdown if her stress went any higher. She resolved to

talk to Nadine that afternoon and then turned her attention back to the phone. "Yeah, I guess so."

"Great. I'll meet you at that new Mexican place
downtown at, say, eleven thirty?"

"Okay, see you then."

Abby hung up the phone, feeling grateful that she
had something positive to look forward to.

* * *

An hour later Abby was sitting at a table waiting for
her neighbor to show up. Shortly after, Tess waltzed in,
all eyes following her in her miniskirted glory. She
walked up to Abby's table and swished into the seat
across from her. Abby noticed Tess looked extra radiant
today.

Despite her showy nature, Tess's cheerfulness was
contagious, and Abby began to feel better as she got to
know her neighbor. They chatted about everyday
things and ordered their food. While they were waiting
for their entrées Tess smiled happily at Abby.

"Well, you're probably wondering why I asked you
to lunch today," she began.

Abby smiled back. "I am curious. I mean, this is the
first time we've done this."

"Well . . ." Tess paused dramatically. "I got a
promotion at work!"

"Really?" Abby tried to control her astonishment.
"Doing what?"

"Don't be so surprised. I have lots of skills, you
know," she pouted.

"I didn't mean it that way. It's just that I had no idea
you were looking to move up that career ladder. I

thought you were working on a dance career or something."

"Yeah, it was kind of strange, actually," she said, perking up. "But I can see an opportunity when it's in front of me. I'm Mr. Meher's personal secretary. In fact, he asks about your family a lot. He must think highly of Eric."

The waitress set their food down in front of them, and Tess scooped a forkful of salad into her mouth.

"Uh, how kind of him," Abby said, finding Tess's revelation an odd coincidence. "I didn't know they were looking to expand their secretarial pool."

"They *are* the largest construction firm in the San Joaquin Valley, you know."

"Oh yes. I guess they're probably expanding often. What will you be doing in your new job?" Abby asked, trying to show more pleasure at Tess's news.

"Oh, some of the same stuff and a little accounting. I actually started a little while ago. But now that I'm in the accounting department, I thought I'd see more of Eric. That's why I was wondering where he's been."

"Were you working this morning?" Abby asked, wondering why she hadn't seen her there.

"No. He only needs me part-time."

"I see." Abby also wondered if Tess had heard the accusations against Eric. Judging by her comments, she guessed she hadn't.

"So what's the deal?" Tess asked, missing the inflection in Abby's voice. "Is he still out of town?" She sipped her drink innocently.

Abby found her voice quivering as she spoke. "Eric seems to be missing, Tess. I put a story in yesterday's paper."

Tess's mouth fell open. "I had no idea. I thought he was on a business trip."

"That's what I told you because I wasn't ready to tell anyone the truth yet." Abby looked beyond Tess's shoulder. "But now I'm feeling more desperate." She brought her gaze back to Tess's shocked face. "I'm surprised Tim didn't mention it."

"Me too," she said, her brows furrowed. "What do you think happened to Eric?"

Abby wasn't about to share Tim Meher's accusations. "I don't know." She shook her head helplessly.

"Is there anything I can do to help?"

"No. But thank you for asking." Abby pulled herself together. "But we're here to celebrate your good news, so tell me why you like this job."

Tess explained how it opened up opportunities for her and why she was interested in accounting.

"Wow. That's great," Abby said, trying to be enthusiastic despite the panic pushing to the surface as each minute passed. She was fully aware that if Tess was in contact with Tim, there was a good chance she would hear rumors about Eric embezzling. The thought nauseated her.

"Abby? Are you okay?" Tess asked, reaching a hand across the table. "Maybe we'd better get you home."

Abby held up a hand. "I'm just a little dizzy. I'll be fine. So let's get to know each other. Tell me about where you grew up . . ."

* * *

On the drive to work, Abby thought about Tess and her new job. *What a strange coincidence. Well, I won't have to worry about her flirting with Eric. I'm sure he's fired.*

Misery coursed through her. She had to find out where Eric was and what he was up to. Not knowing was driving her crazy. She missed him terribly, but she was also angry with him for putting her through this nightmare.

As soon as Abby entered the library she looked for Nadine. When she found her, Abby asked to speak with her privately.

"What is it, Abby?"

Abby hesitated, not sure now if this was a good idea. "Perhaps you've heard that my husband is missing."

"Yes. I was sorry to see that."

Abby was surprised to hear any sympathy from Nadine and decided to press her luck. "I was wondering if it would be possible for me to take a few days off while I get a handle on my situation."

"I suppose, under the circumstances, that would be okay." Nadine paused. "It would be without pay, of course."

"Of course," Abby said, relieved she would still have a job. "Thank you, Nadine. I appreciate it."

A brief smile graced Nadine's lips. "I do hope you find your husband, Abby."

As Nadine walked away, Abby looked for Mary, hoping to let her know she wouldn't be there for a while. She found her in the children's section of the library.

"Mary," she whispered.

Mary looked up from the shelf, then pulled Abby by the arm to an empty aisle. "Abby, what's going on?"

"Nothing much," Abby said, thinking about the accusations Tim had made only hours before. She wasn't going to say anything about the embezzlement claim until she had more information. "There was one interesting development, though."

"Oh? What's that?"

"You remember my neighbor, Tess? I pointed her out to you that time she came in to get a book."

"Oh, yes. I remember. Miss Hips."

Abby chuckled at the nickname. "Yes, her. Well, I had lunch with her today—which was unusual enough—but then she told me she's been promoted and now works in Eric's department."

"Hmm. That is a coincidence, isn't it?"

Abby could see the wheels spinning in Mary's mystery-chasing mind. "What do you make of it?"

Mary shook her head. "It's probably nothing."

"Yeah, you're probably right," Abby said, disappointed Mary couldn't come up with something sinister. "By the way, Nadine let me take some time off, so I won't be around for a while."

"Now there's a shock."

"She was actually pretty nice about it." Abby smiled. "I'd better let you get back to work, Mary. I'll talk to you later."

Abby drove directly home, relieved not to have to think about work for a few days. She went up to her bedroom, wanting to take something for the headache she felt coming on. She dropped her purse on the bed on her way into the bathroom. After taking some medicine, Abby walked over to her little alcove and settled into the soft cushions. Guilt flowed through her as she remembered the pressure she had put on Eric to continue with the fertility treatments. He had wanted to stop, but she had insisted. She knew the financial pressure on Eric had been enormous.

Was it bad enough that Eric would resort to embezzlement? she wondered. *And what of that email message demanding a package?*

She couldn't believe Eric would steal. He had always been very honest with her. He could have chosen never to tell her about his past, but he wanted to be fair—to let her make a decision with open eyes. And she remembered the time he'd taken the bus home from work when their car was in the shop. He had found a wallet containing a large amount of cash and had turned it in without a second thought.

Of course, that was before their finances had been tapped out, and she didn't know everything about his drug-dealing days. That wasn't exactly an honest profession.

She sighed, reined in her emotions, and went outside to get the mail. Sitting down at the office desk, she used the letter opener to rip open the envelopes. The first one was a credit card bill with a charge from the local bookstore. The date was three weeks previous and was for a hundred dollars. It couldn't be for the book she'd found in his drawer—that was a library book, but as she thought about it, it occurred to her that he could have bought other books relating to his escape. *Maybe he bought books on the place he was planning to go,* Abby thought, hope pushing her from her chair and up the stairs into her room.

She slowly looked around the room, trying to get an idea of where Eric would have hidden something. She had searched the dresser drawers already after finding that horrible book and photo. Her gaze rested on the open closet door. Abby rushed over to the walk-in closet and turned on the light. The tiny space revealed nothing. She studied the clothes hanging above and the neat pile she'd stacked in the corner. Her gaze lifted to the shelves, but she couldn't see much of what was up there.

She left the bedroom and came back a few moments later, dragging Tiffany's desk chair behind her. She placed it in the closet and stood on it to survey the shelves. There were several shoe boxes, games, the camera equipment, and other assorted items. She lifted the camera off the shelf and carried it over to the bed, then trudged back to the closet and climbed onto the chair again. She took several shoe boxes down at once and dumped them onto the bed.

Junk. All junk, she thought as her hopes faded.

Ten minutes later she was standing on the chair looking at nearly empty shelves. The only things remaining were half a dozen board games.

She shook her head. *Well, I took everything else out; I might as well make a bigger mess.*

The games came down and were piled onto the bed. She flipped the lids off one by one, not finding anything but what should be there. She got to the last box, a game of Monopoly, and lifted the lid. What she saw stopped her cold. The game pieces were gone. In their place were stacks and stacks of cash, mostly twenties. She turned the box over, and the bills tumbled onto the bed. Carefully she counted them.

Fifteen thousand dollars!

Tears sprang to her eyes as she realized this could be the embezzled money Tim Meher had talked about. Her head shook from side to side in denial.

What else could explain the money? a voice seemed to whisper. *But what if it's not the stolen money?* she argued. *What if it's money Eric put aside for . . . a lot of rainy days? It would help us get by.* She knew that wasn't realistic—if these were legitimate earnings, she was sure he'd have deposited them at the bank. But she had no concrete evidence of where the money had come from.

Abby carefully stacked the money in the box and placed it in the closet while she decided what to do.

The doorbell rang and Abby rushed downstairs to see who it was. She was relieved to see her daughters home from school. She tried to be attentive to their conversation as she fixed them a snack, but a vision of the money she'd found kept pulling at her, and she wondered if Eric had stashed more in other places in the house. Though she knew she shouldn't spend the money, knowing it was available made Abby feel a little better, though it was as if one weight had been lifted from her shoulders to be replaced by a new one.

What is Eric doing with that much cash, and why has he hidden it in our house? The thought occupied the rest of her night.

CHAPTER FIFTEEN

The next morning passed quietly except for the many times Abby went to her closet to make sure the money was still in the Monopoly box. *I have to get this out of here. It's driving me crazy. What on earth was Eric doing with this much money?* The only answer her mind supplied was numbing. *Doesn't the presence of the money confirm Tim's allegations?*

Abby thought of Jennifer's counsel to trust her husband until proven guilty. Abby agreed she wasn't ready to completely believe Tim until she had spoken to Eric and given him a chance to explain himself. Then she remembered glancing at his Internet bookmarks when she was looking for the banking website. She hadn't paid much attention to them then.

A few minutes later she was dismayed to see that Eric had bookmarked the FBI's website and two sites relating to embezzlement. Quickly shutting down the computer, Abby breathed deeply, trying to slow the racing of her heart as her faith in her husband slipped just enough to warrant deep questions about the man she was married to.

Even though Tim had accused Eric of a crime, Abby decided to check with the police to see if the article she'd put in the paper had provided anything new. But as she was shown into the office of Detective Carlson, she nearly regretted calling attention to the fact that Eric was missing. What if he had stolen money? Would his disappearance further prove his guilt?

She tried not to think of that as she sat across from the detective.

"Mrs. Breuner, next time you place a missing-person's story in the paper, I would appreciate it if you'd check with me before telling the public to call here."

"I'm sorry. I didn't think you'd mind," Abby said, wondering if she was making an enemy of the police by irritating them.

Carlson let out a heavy sigh. "Do you realize how many false leads come in? It ties up my men when they could be out chasing the real criminals."

"Are you saying you haven't been looking for my husband?"

The expression on Carlson's face said it all.

"He's been missing for over a week. Doesn't that count for anything?" Abby asked.

"Look, Mrs. Breuner, unless we have something to indicate there's been foul play, we don't have the manpower to look for every husband that decides to cut loose from his marriage."

His words stung, but Abby steeled herself against his comment. "Isn't there something you can do?"

"I'm afraid not. But if anything new happens, let us know and we'll see if there's more we can do."

Abby stood up. "Thank you for your help, Detective Carlson."

* * *

Eric held the note in his hand, contemplating whether to destroy it. He considered the implications of the message as he read it over:

Here's the money you asked for. I followed your instructions, and there's $20,000 more stashed in the prearranged areas. The Feds may be on to you—watch out.

He'd found the note under the driver's seat of his Jeep on the day he'd left. There had been several thousand dollars bundled with it, and that was in addition to the five thousand dollars he'd found in his home office. He hadn't found the remaining money the note mentioned, and he wondered if it was truly there. He set the note down and picked up a set of documents. They were identical—except for the name of one supplier. These lists would lead someone to suspect embezzlement. He wondered if anyone had noticed the discrepancy.

* * *

Abby decided that putting the money in a safe place was now a top priority. She couldn't take a chance on Tim Meher or anyone else discovering it. That would only prove whatever case they were making, not to mention the fact that she might need it to survive.

Once home from the police station, she placed all of the money in her roomiest purse and zipped it closed. She drove to her bank and secured a safe-deposit box. She hoped her nervousness had not been apparent when the woman had handed her the key.

Secreting herself in the small room, Abby began transferring the cash to the safe-deposit box. Once done, she stared at the piles of cash and hoped she was doing the right thing.

It was nearly time for the girls to get out of school when Abby pulled into her garage. She decided to surprise them by walking them home from school. After putting her purse in the house and changing into comfortable shoes, she headed off to the school.

Betterman Elementary was only a few blocks away, but it felt good to Abby to stretch her legs. It also gave her time to think. She'd been thinking and rethinking her notes on her situation. She couldn't understand what made Tim Meher think she had been in contact with Eric.

Before she could let her thoughts run any further, she found herself standing next to the door of Tiffany's classroom. The bell rang and the students poured out. Tiffany's face lit up when she saw her mother waiting for her. She put her arms around her mother's waist, and Abby smiled down at her.

"Where do you usually meet Susannah?" Abby asked.

"I'll show you."

Mr. Phillips stepped out the door after all the students had exited. He extended a hand to Abby. "Good afternoon, Mrs. Breuner."

Setting her hand in his, Abby smiled, but noticed something odd in his expression. "Is everything all right, Mr. Phillips?"

He seemed preoccupied. "Yes, everything's fine." Focusing on her more closely, he said, "I should be asking you that question. I understand your husband is still . . ." He glanced in Tiffany's direction.

Letting out a sigh, Abby tried to control the sudden tightening in her chest. "Thank you for your concern. I'm sure everything will be okay." Abby wished she felt the confidence she pretended.

"Let me know if there's anything I can do to help." He paused for a moment. "Well, I've got things to do. It was nice talking to you."

Abby nodded and took Tiffany's hand. "Okay, Tiff. Show me where you meet Susannah."

* * *

"It's been a week and he's still trying to postpone payment," the man said, sitting at his usual table eating dinner.

"What do you want to do?"

"He can't pay us back if he's dead."

"No. But we can go after people close to him. You know, family."

His boss smiled. "See that it's taken care of."

* * *

Eric sipped his soda and peered over the dashboard. It was Wednesday night and he'd been staking out this house for two hours. He hoped he could bring the situation closer to a resolution soon. He'd had about all he could take of this hiding game and was determined to do all he could to end it.

He looked at the purchase orders on the passenger seat. They were for a phony supplier, and his signature was scrawled across the bottom of each one. This wasn't going to be pinned on him if he could help it.

CHAPTER SIXTEEN

It had only been a couple of days since Abby had asked Nadine for time off, but she could see now that going back to work would nearly kill her. The stress from worrying about Eric was starting to take its toll. She had been feeling dizzy more often and was concerned about her blood pressure. She didn't think her job was worth the risk of her health deteriorating; she had to think of her unborn child. Maybe she could use the money she had found hidden to live on for a while. At least until Eric got back.

But that was the problem: she didn't know if Eric ever would come back, and because of that, she might never know where the money had come from. It wasn't hers to spend. It was ridiculous to consider keeping the money. Of course, since she wasn't certain whom it belonged to, she couldn't exactly give it back. She would keep it secure in the safe-deposit box until she knew whose it was.

That still didn't solve her job problem. Abby decided to call Nadine and see if she could extend her leave.

She bit her lip as she waited for Nadine to come on the line.

"This is Nadine."

"Hi, Nadine. This is Abby Breuner."

"Yes, Abby. Have you found your husband yet?"

"No," Abby said, feeling a rush of anger for the blunt way Nadine asked the question. "That's why I'm calling. I was wondering if I could extend my leave for a while. Perhaps until he's found." Abby cringed, waiting for her reply.

"That would put me in a bind, you realize. I need a more definite time frame. I mean, if we're talking weeks, I need to hire someone to take your place."

Suddenly Abby was exhausted. The job simply wasn't worth it. "Nadine, let me put it this way. I won't be coming in for a while. I don't know how long it will be, but I'd like to have a job there when I return."

"As much as I'd like to hold your job for you, I just won't be able to. I'm sorry, Abby. I think it would be best if you consider other employment."

"Maybe you're right," Abby said after a pause, surprised at the relief she felt now that a decision had been made. "I enjoyed working there, but I guess now isn't the best time for me to be working."

"Perhaps in the future you can apply to work here again. Good luck with everything."

Abby hung up the phone and decided to call Jennifer. She'd called her sister many times since she'd left, and Jennifer had been a great support—especially concerning Tim's accusations. Although she hadn't yet told her sister about the money, Abby knew she could talk to her about most things.

"It's probably for the best, Abby," Jennifer said when Abby called. "I mean, you're going to have a baby in a few months. What were you planning on doing then?"

"You're right. In the long run I'm probably better off."

They talked a while longer, brainstorming a few ways Abby could work from home, both of them promising to call again soon.

* * *

Wandering up and down the grocery store aisles, Abby took in the food choices, her mind on Eric. *Is he eating all right?* His favorite brand of tuna beckoned her. She put half a dozen cans in her shopping cart, stocking up for his return. Her grocery list forgotten, she piled all of Eric's favorites in her cart and made her way to the front of the store.

The clerk, familiar with Abby's shopping habits, gave her a funny look when Abby stacked her purchases on the conveyor belt. Nothing she'd bought was on sale. Abby just smiled benignly and concentrated on filling out her check. She handed it to the clerk and accepted her receipt. Then Abby pushed the shopping cart into the parking lot, transferring the bags to the back of the van. She was oblivious to the other people in the lot or she would have noticed the man parked several slots away who eyed her with interest.

She drove home on automatic pilot, and once the last bag of food was put away, Abby went to the office to balance her checkbook and pay some bills. She tried to get comfortable in the chair, then opened the envelopes one by one. As she wrote the checks and entered the information into the check register, she was comforted by the thought of the cash available to her in the safe-deposit box. Even though she was expecting a direct-deposit paycheck from Eric's work, it would only be enough to cover the mortgage and a few other bills. It wouldn't go far.

Using the money Eric had hidden wasn't something Abby wanted to do, though. If it belonged to his firm, it would need to be given back. The temptation loomed large as she thought of upcoming bills, but then an image of her visit with the bishop filled her mind. She realized it might be possible to ask the Church for assistance. She felt embarrassed to even consider it. After all, she could beg Nadine to take her back. Then she felt the baby kick and knew it simply wasn't possible for her to work and stay healthy under this level of stress.

If this isn't all sorted out in the next two weeks, I'll call the bishop, Abby decided as she wrote out the check for the utility bill.

Once the stack of unpaid bills had been exchanged for a pile of stamped envelopes, Abby leaned back in her chair, relieved the task had been completed. Energized and in the mood for order, she picked up her purse and began cleaning it out.

One by one, unnecessary receipts and old to-do lists were dropped into the trash. She could see the bottom of her purse now and chastised herself for not doing this sooner. Sorting through the remaining items, she dumped them on the desktop. The pile contained a couple more receipts and a note she had jotted to herself, along with a folded piece of paper unlike the others.

She picked up the folded piece of paper and looked at it curiously. Unfolding it, she realized she hadn't seen it before. Her heart nearly stopped as she read the message:

Trust me. Trust in our love. Eric

The slip of paper fluttered to the ground, shock making Abby's hands stiff and cold. Then she began shaking uncontrollably. Her breath came in short, uneven bursts and her heart seemed to skip beats. Slowly bending over to snatch the piece of paper from the floor, she had to put it on the desk to read it because her hands were shaking so badly. Her mind devoured the words as she read the brief message over and over.

Then the questions flooded her mind. *When was this put in my purse? Was it the morning of the ultrasound? What does this mean? Is he coming home to me?*

Abby thought hard, trying to recall when she had last cleaned out her purse. It was before Eric had vanished—she was sure of it. Her elation was reduced as she considered when he might have put it there.

Was it possible he had been close enough to touch and she had been unaware of it?

The thought brought agony to her heart. But the message of the note, to trust him and to trust in their love for each other, buoyed her up. She thought about Tim's accusations and contrasted that with the message Eric had given her.

Maybe he knew Tim would make false allegations and he doesn't want me to believe them. "Trust in our love . . ." Maybe that picture really is a lie—but who, and why . . . ?

Then she thought about the money she had found, and doubt again pushed its way into her mind.

CHAPTER SEVENTEEN

Thursday night Abby had a lovely dream about Eric. He was lying next to her, stroking her face. He gently kissed her lips as tears filled his eyes. It felt so good Abby didn't want to wake up, even as she heard Susannah calling for her. Abby forced herself awake and was startled when she detected the lingering scent of Eric's cologne.

It must be my imagination, she reasoned as she rolled to a sitting position on the side of her bed. She went down the hall to Susannah's room to see what was the matter.

Susannah was sitting up in bed, her eyes wide, staring off into the distance.

"Susannah? Are you okay?" Abby asked.

Susannah's head whipped around to look at her mother. "Mommy?" Her arms reached out toward Abby, and Abby went to her, pulling her into a warm embrace.

She ran her hand over Susannah's damp brow. "No fever. How do you feel?"

Susannah pulled back from her mother's encompassing arms and stared into her eyes. "Daddy was here, Mommy."

Startled to hear her daughter say what she had been thinking only moments before, Abby didn't speak for a moment.

"Mommy? Didn't you hear me?" Susannah prodded. "He was here. Did you see him?"

"Susannah, I wish Daddy were here too. But wishing won't make it true."

Disappointment filled Susannah's face. "Don't you believe me?"

Abby looked into her daughter's eyes. "Tell me what happened."

Susannah took a deep breath. "Well, I was sleeping and I had a dream about Daddy. Then I woke up and saw him." She looked at her mother with imploring eyes. "But I don't think he saw me wake up."

"Why do you say that?"

Tears trickled down her cheeks. "Because he didn't talk to me."

"You miss your daddy, don't you?"

Susannah nodded.

"I miss him too." Abby pulled her daughter into a hug and held her while she cried, forcing herself to control her own tears.

At last Susannah's tears subsided, and Abby was able to go back to her own bed. She stared up at the ceiling, thinking about what might have happened.

Is it possible Eric's been here? And if he was, why didn't he wake me?

Abby finally allowed the tears to come as she turned into her pillow to muffle the sobs.

CHAPTER EIGHTEEN

Touching Abby but not being able to speak to her had been one of the hardest things Eric had ever done. Even though he knew he should stay away until his situation had been resolved, he couldn't. Not only that, he needed to search for the rest of the money. His nocturnal visit had been unsuccessful, except for the message he'd left and prayed Abby would find.

Now, trying to be as inconspicuous as possible, Eric walked into the bank. He signed the signature card, got his box, then entered the small room. He opened the metal box and carefully picked up the note that implied he had asked someone to put the money in his house. Setting it aside, he pulled out the few papers that were there and placed them on the counter. Gazing at the remaining contents of the box, he gently patted the money that lay inside. It looked like it was all there. He put the note back inside, closed the lid, then returned the safe-deposit box to its slot.

Back in his rental car, Eric drove to a copy shop and made copies of all the documents he had taken from the safe-deposit box. After taking the originals back to the bank, he returned to his motel room and examined the documents.

There were only a few, not nearly enough to protect himself from the authorities. He needed more, but the only way to get what he needed was to go to Central Valley Construction and get into the computer in his office.

Eric had been hoping he could avoid that; it would be a difficult endeavor, but now it looked like the only way. He knew Tim often left early on Fridays, so he was fairly certain he could count on him being out of the office by late Friday afternoon, and others in the office went home early on Fridays too. That was when he would make his move.

* * *

The next morning, after she took the girls to school, Abby logged onto the computer and checked Eric's email. She sighed when she saw there was nothing new. Then the phone rang, pulling her attention away from the computer.

"Abby, this is Brock Mendez."

"Yes?" Abby answered, biting her lip.

"What's going on with Eric? He hasn't been at work and Tim tells me he hasn't heard from him, that apparently Eric's missing. Is this true?"

"Yes, I'm afraid so." Abby's heart pounded as she spoke to Eric's boss. She tried to think of what to say and wondered what he believed about the embezzlement.

"As you can imagine, I'm very concerned," he said. "Have you spoken to the police?"

"I have, but they don't seem to be worried at all."

"And you have no idea where he could be? He hasn't contacted you?"

Not this again. "No. Like I told Tim earlier, I haven't heard from Eric and I don't know what's going on." Abby chewed her lip again, waiting to hear the same accusations that Tim had thrown at her.

"Well, I hope he's okay. How's your family doing? Are you all right?"

Surprised by his response, she said, "Uh . . . we're getting by, I guess. Thank you for asking."

"Okay, good. Will you let me know if you hear from Eric?"

Confused that he hadn't brought up the embezzlement, Abby almost mentioned it herself, but decided she would follow his lead. "If I hear anything, I'll be sure to let you know."

"Good. I'll be in touch."

Abby hung up the phone and considered the conversation she'd just had. *Does Eric still have a job? Why didn't Brock mention the embezzlement? Maybe he's just being gracious because Tim told him I'm as clueless as they are.*

Trying to turn her focus away from her problems, Abby got up from the desk and wandered into the living room, opening the windows to let the cool morning air into the house. As she looked around the room, she couldn't ignore the shape the house was in. Things were piling up, and the carpets needed vacuuming. She started with the bathrooms, and when they were finished, she moved on to the master bedroom. Abby dragged the vacuum and dust rags into her room and remembered how dusty Eric's dresser had been the day Jennifer had shown her the book.

Now, as she stood in front of Eric's dresser, she stared at finger marks that were out of place on the dust-covered top. That wasn't where she touched the dresser, and the girls weren't tall enough to reach the top.

Abby's heart hammered against her ribs as she recalled the odd feeling of Eric's presence the night before. Her hands hovered over the dresser, poised to open the drawer, as her mind questioned what she saw. *Why would Eric come home and open his drawer but not wake me? Was he looking for the money or the book on disappearing . . . ?*

She slowly reached for the drawer handles, but once the decision was made, she yanked the drawer open. She gasped when she saw it—a note addressed to her in Eric's writing.

With shaking hands she pulled it out, then walked unsteadily over to the love seat and sagged into the cushions. The terror of what the message might say was outweighed by the sheer need to know for sure that he'd been there and tried to communicate with her.

One corner ripped as she tried to unfold the note with trembling hands. She carefully opened it the rest of the way and spread it out on her lap.

Abby,

I hope you found this without too much trouble. Know that I love you and I'm trying to come home to stay. I can't tell you any more than this because I don't want to put you in a position to say something you shouldn't. Just sit tight, but for my safety don't tell anyone I contacted you. Destroy this note.

Love always,
Eric

Elation filled Abby's soul. He still loved her. Then her spirits came crashing down. He was in danger and she couldn't help him. What was it all about?

Abby stood abruptly and began pacing the room, trying to decide what to do. She couldn't tell anyone about the note—that much was clear. Not even Jennifer. But how was she supposed to act? Did he expect her to go on as normal? And how much danger, exactly, was he in?

The fear of the unknown took over. Abby read the note again, memorizing every word, then walked into the bathroom. She lifted the lid on the toilet and tore the note into tiny pieces, then let them slip from her hands and watched them float in the water for a moment before she pressed the lever. They didn't go down with the first flush, and she had to try several times before all the pieces of paper were gone for good.

She left the bathroom and walked over to the closet she shared with Eric, staring at the pile of clothes stacked neatly on the floor. Calmly, she picked up each piece and attached it to a hanger. With that done, she made sure his shoes were lined up on the floor. Then she turned to her side of the closet and made sure everything looked presentable. The order helped her think more clearly, and she desperately wanted to know what kind of trouble Eric was in so she could help him. Could it be as simple as embezzlement? She decided to leave a note of her own, just in case he came back.

Pulling out a sheet of her personal stationery, Abby jotted down a few of her thoughts, then tore the paper up and tossed it in the trash. She knew she had to do this right; it might be the only opportunity she would have to communicate with her husband.

After several stops and starts, she had a message she hoped would be acceptable.

Eric,

I love you so much. I trust you're doing all you can
to come home. Please let me know if I can help you.

Yours forever,
Abby

She folded the note neatly into thirds and stared at it, wondering where to put it so that Eric would find it.

She thought of the dresser. After all, that was where he had left his note for her. She pulled the drawer open and stared at his socks and underwear. Shutting the drawer, she walked over to the closet, stood on tiptoe, and pulled down the Monopoly game. She set the note inside, then carefully slid the box back on the shelf.

Maybe he'll come looking for the money and he'll find the note.

Her spirits higher than they had been for days, Abby finished cleaning the house and then stopped for lunch. The ringing of the phone interrupted her meal. She picked up the phone, half expecting to hear Eric's voice. Instead it was Mr. Phillips.

"Mrs. Breuner?" he asked.

"Yes?" She hoped Tiffany wasn't sick again.

"I've been getting more and more concerned with Tiffany this week. She seems distracted in class, and her scores have dropped noticeably. I think we should discuss this."

"Well, you know about my husband. I wouldn't be surprised if that was affecting her."

Mr. Phillips was silent for a moment. "Have you heard from him at all?"

Abby thought about the note she had found earlier. Her heart pounded as she knew she would have to fudge the truth. And she realized that if doing so only to her child's teacher could send her into such a nervous state, she would have a real problem if Tim Meher confronted her. She swallowed quickly before replying, "No I haven't, I'm afraid."

"I can see why Tiffany would be upset." He paused for a moment. "I wonder if it would help if I gave her extra tutoring—maybe help her catch up while she's off-track these next couple of weeks."

The suggestion made Abby uncomfortable. She wasn't sure why. "I'll have to think about it."

"I know it's unprecedented . . ." He paused. "But I can come to your house if that would ease your mind. I really feel for your family and want to help if I can."

"I don't know. Can I get back to you?"

"Sure. Let me give you my home number."

Abby grabbed a pen and paper and wrote the number down. "Thank you. I'll let you know."

After she hung up the phone, Abby stared at the piece of paper and tried to examine her feelings of discomfort. Though a very unusual offer, maybe he did just want to help. Having him at her home seemed unsettling for many reasons under the present circumstances. And he had seemed a little eager to have Abby agree to it.

She wasn't sure if it was that he was a single man, or that the offer seemed to cross professional boundaries, or if it was the Holy Ghost. All she knew was that Mr. Phillips' suggestion made her anxious.

Abby set the piece of paper on the counter, then finished eating her lunch. A short time later she left to run a few errands. When she was miles away, she realized she'd neglected to set the alarm. Cursing her stupidity, she weighed her options. She only had a little time to finish her errands; she'd just have to hurry and pray nothing happened.

* * *

The moment Abby drove away, he made his way into the house, amazed to find the alarm unarmed yet again. If only he could be this lucky at poker. He needed to find the money, and he would do what was necessary to accomplish that. He entered the house without incident and searched fruitlessly, except for finding a note he hadn't been expecting. Things had gone wrong and he needed the money back. His survival depended on it.

* * *

The first thing Abby noticed when she returned from running her errands was that the couch cushions were askew. She only noticed because she had straightened them that morning in her quest to bring order to her home.

Dropping the packages she was carrying, Abby walked swiftly into the other main-level rooms of the house, noticing items out of place here and there. Nothing obvious, but enough that she could tell someone had been there.

Once the realization hit that someone could *still* be there, Abby quickly ran out of the house and climbed into the minivan. She backed out of the driveway, not sure where to go. Then, knowing the girls would be walking home from school soon, Abby headed toward the school to intercept them.

As she waited by the school fence, Abby's mind darted from one thought to another. She needed to figure out what to do. *What were they looking for? Did they know Eric had been there? Were they looking for the cash? Had it been Eric again?*

Abby didn't know whether or not to call the police. She still didn't know if Eric was involved in embezzlement and didn't want to hurt him by getting the police involved.

Then she thought about the note, thankful she had destroyed it according to Eric's directions, and wondered how much danger he was in and if the danger would affect her and her daughters. She knew she should have set the burglar alarm, although she wondered if that would have stopped them.

But what about the note I wrote? Alarm twisted her stomach. She could only pray that whoever had been there hadn't looked in the Monopoly box. With reluctance, Abby decided to call the police.

Once home, Abby sent the girls to friends' houses so she wouldn't have to explain to them why the police were coming. An hour later a uniformed officer arrived and accompanied Abby into the house. He looked around the spotless room. "You say you think someone broke into your house, ma'am?"

"I'm pretty sure. You see, I had just cleaned up the house this morning. And when I came home from running errands I noticed a few things out of place," Abby said, hoping the officer wouldn't scoff at her worries.

"Is anything missing?" he asked, pulling out a small notepad.

"Not that I can tell."

He walked around the house, checking the rooms, doors, and windows. "It doesn't look like anyone forced an entry," he said.

Abby bit her lip. "I . . . I didn't know what to do. That's why I called."

"Since nothing's missing and there's no sign of forced entry, all I can do is file a report," he said. "If there's nothing else I can do for you, I'll be on my way."

His casual response made her feel foolish. "Thank you, Officer. I appreciate you coming here." But as Abby watched the officer drive away, she knew she shouldn't feel foolish. Someone had been there. She could feel it.

* * *

An hour or so later, Abby stole upstairs to peek in the Monopoly box. What she found caused her knees to buckle, and she stumbled to the bed as her stomach churned violently. It was a note, but not the one she'd left.

Mrs. Breuner,

We know you have the money. Send an email to the address below and tell us where you will leave it for us. Do not take these instructions lightly.

CHAPTER NINETEEN

Abby had always considered herself a planner, carefully outlining the paths she would follow before setting off. That luxury was absent now. After having her home violated, she didn't feel secure staying there. And because the police couldn't do anything to help unless she told them about the cash, she knew she had no choice but to ensure the safety of her children on her own.

That was how they found themselves pulling into the parking lot of a motel in the next town. The girls decided it was a grand adventure, staying in a motel when their home was close by. Abby indulged them by promising they could eat out and stay up to watch television.

Not wanting Jennifer to worry, Abby had taken a minute to leave a message on Jennifer's answering machine to clarify that they were going away for a few days. She had also arranged for a substitute for her Primary class.

As Abby approached the motel office, she thought it might be best to sign in under an assumed name and to pay in cash. "Tiffany, you and Susannah go sit in those chairs while Mommy checks us in," she whispered as they entered the lobby, a reassuring smile on her face.

They did as instructed, and Abby walked over to the long counter. She spoke softly as she gave her name, not wanting the girls to overhear. She paid in advance for three nights and accepted her key card.

As the three of them entered the generic-looking room, Tiffany and Susannah quickly claimed the beds, tossing their suitcases on the floor before beginning to jump on the mattresses.

"Okay, okay," Abby said. "One of those beds is for me. You're going to have to share the other."

"Mom!" they complained in unison.

"I know, I know. Now, who wants to go swimming?"

After their swim in the motel's pool, Abby unlocked the door to their room and glanced around, half expecting to see the room ransacked. Nothing appeared out of place, and she allowed the girls to enter. After settling them in front of the television, Abby took a quick shower, trying to wash away her worries.

"Mom, let's go to the carnival!" Susannah yelled as soon as Abby opened the bathroom door. On television a commercial trumpeted the arrival of a carnival the next day, Saturday.

Several excuses for why they couldn't go ran through Abby's head. The looks on the girls' faces, however, made her rethink her automatic decision. They were supposed to be on an adventure, and she needed to keep them occupied.

"Okay. Sounds like fun," she said with more enthusiasm than she felt. "We'll go on Saturday afternoon."

* * *

The clock seemed to tick slowly while Eric waited for Friday evening to arrive. As he pulled into the parking lot of Central Valley Construction, he looked around, gratified to see that few vehicles were there. Most importantly, Tim's car was absent. Taking one last look in his rearview mirror, Eric adjusted his mustache and ball cap. If anyone looked closely at him, he would probably be recognized, but that was a chance he would have to take.

As Eric approached the front doors he wished he'd been able to get this evidence before taking off. He'd gotten some of the purchase orders, but unfortunately he'd had to leave in such a hurry there hadn't been time to do this right.

Eric pulled the door open and looked around. The receptionist's desk was vacant and he assumed she must have left for the day. He avoided looking at the cameras stationed around the building and went directly to the stairs.

Four flights later he opened the door and glanced around. He was surprised to see Carly at her desk, and he closed the door to decide what to do. Waiting was the only option. He pulled the door open a crack and peered in Carly's direction. She was talking on the phone and writing something down. After only a moment she left her desk and went down the hall.

Eric sprinted through the stairwell door and to his office. It was locked, and he had to fumble for his keys before getting safely inside. He looked around, not knowing what he expected to see, but surprised nonetheless by the mess he found. Obviously someone had searched his things.

His computer was gone.

He knew he shouldn't be surprised. He sat in the desk chair, staring at the empty desktop and thinking about his next move. Whatever it was, he didn't want to have to come back here again. He had to get what he needed today.

Maybe I can get into Tim's computer.

Eric pressed his ear to the door, listening for Carly's voice. Not hearing anything, he slowly turned the knob. Peeking through the crack in the door, he looked toward the secretary's desk. It was still vacant. He hoped she had gone home, but he didn't know if his luck was that good.

His heart pounded as he pulled his door open and darted to Tim's office. He turned the knob and wasn't surprised to find it locked. He knew Carly kept a spare key in her desk. Walking quickly, he approached her desk and rapidly searched the drawers. He found the keys and stepped over to Tim's door. As he pushed the key into the lock, he heard voices down the hall. His heart racing, Eric turned the key and felt the doorknob turn in his hand.

He closed the door behind him and pressed the lock. Tim's office looked the same as always, and Eric strode over to the desk and sat down in front of the computer monitor. When the password prompt appeared, Eric smiled. He knew Tim kept his password written down. The company required its employees to change their password every thirty days, and Eric knew Tim had a hard time remembering his current one.

He turned the keyboard over, but there was nothing there. Next he tried the mouse pad and was gratified to find a sticky-note with a group of letters and numbers written down. He quickly typed them in and hit the ENTER key. He was in.

After a few minutes Eric found what he was looking for. He printed out all the purchase orders and invoices for the phony company, grateful Tim had a printer in his office. He also burned the data onto a pair of CDs he had brought along.

He wasn't sure how much money needed to be involved before the FBI would investigate, but over one hundred thousand dollars was probably enough for them to take an interest. Not only that, but because the checks were mailed to an out-of-state address and used the banking system, that made it a federal issue.

Once he'd gotten everything he had come for, he was able to return the keys to Carly's desk and get down to the lobby without incident. The receptionist's desk was still empty, and Eric hurried toward the door.

* * *

The atmosphere of the carnival was as Abby remembered from her own childhood, and she smiled, glad she had decided to bring the girls.

Susannah pulled on Abby's arm. "I want to go on the rides, Mom."

Abby glanced at Tiffany and was pleased to see her looking happier than she had in a while. "Sure. Which one do you want to go on first?"

She watched as the girls went on the bumper boats, trying to get each other wet. By the time they climbed out of the boats, they were thoroughly in the mood for a good time.

"Mom, there's Mr. Phillips," Tiffany said suddenly, pointing him out.

Abby's head jerked in the direction Tiffany indicated. She took a step toward him to say hello, but was surprised to watch him rush off the opposite way.

She had been almost certain he had seen them. *Why would he ignore us?* Suspicion flooded her at the thought. Then she felt foolish for conjecture, knowing she was being paranoid. Still, she couldn't shake her feelings of uneasiness about the man.

Abby led her daughters to the mini roller coaster. Though she tried to show enthusiasm when the girls turned their attention to her, her earlier excitement had completely left her; she was distracted watching for suspicious characters in the crowd.

It wasn't until they were driving back to the motel that it occurred to Abby that Mr. Phillips seemed to have been at the carnival by himself. She found that peculiar.

CHAPTER TWENTY

By Monday morning, Abby and her girls were beginning to get on each other's nerves. She knew it was time to make a decision. It was obvious that running away was not the answer. They couldn't put their lives on hold indefinitely. She'd just have to call the authorities again and take other precautions when they got back. Reluctantly, she instructed the girls to pack their things.

Over their protests, Abby took the girls to school before going home. She didn't know what she would find at the house and didn't want to endanger her children. Abby drove home, her heart hammering in her chest in fear of what she might find. But what she saw as she approached her house was the last thing she expected.

Eric's Jeep was parked in the driveway. She managed to pull up to her house before turning off the engine and throwing open her door. Then she raced into the house.

"Eric! Eric!" she screamed, running through the first floor as fast as she could in her expectant shape.

Not finding him there, she rushed up the stairs, her breath coming in gasps. She immediately went to the master bedroom, stopping in the doorway. The room was empty and nothing looked out of place. She went down the hall to the other bedrooms.

"Eric? Eric, are you here?" she cried out, crushed by disappointment.

No one was home.

Abby went back to the master bedroom and examined the closet and bathroom. Nothing had been added to the things already there. Nothing had been removed. She sank onto the bed, disoriented at not finding Eric home when his Jeep was.

The Jeep, Abby thought as she rose from the bed and descended the staircase. Why hadn't the police found it? Where had it been hidden?

She went back outside and saw that the Jeep really was parked there. She hadn't hallucinated. She went over to the driver's door and peered in the window. A folded piece of paper lay on the seat. Abby grabbed at the door, but it was locked. A set of keys was next to the note. Abby tried the passenger door. It too was locked. *This is too weird,* she thought.

Racing back into the house, Abby grabbed her purse and returned outside. She frantically rummaged around for her keys. Her hand shook so much she was having trouble grabbing onto anything. In frustration she dumped everything onto the driveway.

Snatching her keys from the pile of things on the ground, she flipped through the keys on the ring. At first she thought her eyes were deceiving her. Then she realized the keys to the Jeep were missing from her key ring. She remembered Eric had borrowed her set when he last took his car in for a tune-up. He had never given them back.

Laying her forehead against the driver's side window, she gazed at the note resting on the seat. She had to get her hands on it. After punching in the code for the garage door opener, Abby walked over to Eric's workbench. The hammer seemed to call to her. She took it from its pegs and allowed her disappointment at Eric's absence to be replaced by anger. She used all the frustration she was feeling to power her swing. The glass didn't break right away, but after several hits, the window shattered.

Abby carefully reached in the window and picked up the note and keys that had been placed on the seat. Rapidly unfolding the note, Abby tried to focus on the words. It was addressed to her.

Abby,

The Jeep was found with the keys under the mat. Thought we'd drop it by. Return the package or your husband will be permanently in our debt. We will have to find alternate means of repayment. Have a great day.

CHAPTER TWENTY-ONE

"Agent Franklin," the voice on the phone answered.

"Yeah, I'm the one who sent you that disc. Did you get it?" Eric pressed the phone against his ear, glancing around the gas station.

"Yes, I did, Mr. . . . ?"

"Brown. You can call me Mr. Brown."

"Okay, Mr. Brown. Our people are examining the data. I have a question for you, though. What part do you play in this? You didn't give me much detail the other day. What is it you do there?"

Eric felt sweat forming under his arms and wondered if they were trying to trace the call. He still didn't feel comfortable telling any more than was absolutely necessary. "I'd rather not get into that now. Suffice it to say I know who's doing this."

"We would appreciate your cooperation, Mr. Brown. Your full cooperation."

"What do you mean? I'm the one who brought this to your attention." Eric looked around at the people in the surrounding area. Everyone suddenly seemed suspicious.

"We have some information you might be interested in," Franklin said, baiting the hook and pulling Eric back to the conversation.

Adrenaline rushed through Eric's body. "What do you know?"

"It's your turn first," Franklin said calmly.

"I have some of the stolen money, but I didn't take it. Now tell me what you know."

He paused before speaking. "People are keeping tabs on your family. Apparently someone is giving these people reward money for information about your whereabouts. We aren't sure who is doing this, but we're trying to track them down now to question them."

"Are you sure? That's crazy." Eric was so taken aback that he failed to register that the FBI knew who his family was.

"We thought so too. But there it is."

"Does this back up my story at all? That I'm innocent?"

"Well, there is the small matter of your possession of stolen funds. What are we going to do about that, Mr. *Breuner?*"

* * *

Abby stared at the anonymous note. Chills ran up her spine. *What kind of people is Eric dealing with?* She felt frightened on his behalf and wondered if she should be frightened for herself and her children. *What package are they talking about? Do they mean the money? How am I supposed to give it to them? What will happen if I don't?*

She began cleaning up the glass as she thought about the questions. Once done, she searched Eric's Jeep. She didn't find anything unusual, but just as she was finishing up, her elderly neighbor, Mrs. Johansen came quickly toward her.

"Abby," she breathed. "I've called the police and I believe they're on their way over. I was just out watering my roses when I noticed a man pull this Jeep up to your house. When he got out, I knew it wasn't Eric, and I was worried someone might have stolen your car. He looked really shifty—as if he was hoping no one would notice him. He was too tall to be Eric, and he acted quite suspicious, slinking about the vehicle and whatnot. I thought I'd let you know. What's going on over here anyway? I haven't seen Eric come home in days, and you seemed to run off pretty quickly the other day, and a few days ago I thought I saw another man go in your backyard. I went over there and rang the doorbell and tapped on a window, but no one answered, and I couldn't see if he'd gone in or not . . ."

Abby was moved by the woman's concern and tried her best to assuage her neighbor's fears about the safety of their family. She explained that things were okay, but that her husband was out of town and they'd had some problems with mysterious phone calls and that Abby suspected a break-in. Mrs. Johansen was just vowing to watch Abby's house during the day when the police pulled up.

"Good afternoon, ma'am," an officer began after he and his partner got out of the car. Then he recognized her.

"Yes," Abby responded, slightly annoyed. "You were over here the other day when I called about a break-in. Now I have more evidence that something is going on. Do you suppose I could arrange to have the police patrol the neighborhood until we figure things out?"

The officer smiled back apologetically and started to explain that he had to follow police procedure.

His partner interrupted him. "Ma'am, we don't have the resources to have a car here twenty-four hours a day, but we can have an officer patrol the neighborhood at night, and we can get your statement so someone can get going on this case." He glared unpleasantly at his partner, then nodded for Abby to go ahead with the details.

After Abby had finished explaining about the break-in and how the Jeep had shown up, the officers left and Abby began walking Mrs. Johansen home. As they stepped onto the older woman's porch, Mrs. Johansen turned and firmly said, "Abby, I certainly hope that you'll be changing your locks."

Abby nodded in agreement, but before she could say anything, Mrs. Johansen added, "And you'd better change them all to high-security ones, with keypads instead of keyholes that can be compromised. I know an installer who has wonderful options. I'll call him for you and give him your number." Before Abby could protest, she added, "Young lady, you have little girls to protect, and with your husband gone, well, I'll foot some of the bill. Now you just get home and change that alarm on your house and wait for the call. I won't hear another word of disagreement."

Abby's eyes filled with tears and she hugged her neighbor. Then she headed home in obedience and pulled out the instruction manual for the burglar alarm. She carried it with her to the keypad and carefully changed the code. She decided to use their anniversary year. It would be easy to remember. And maybe if Eric came home he could still get in by guessing it. As Abby punched in the new code, a conversation she'd recently had with Eric came to mind. He'd suddenly insisted on showing her how to program the alarm system a couple of weeks ago. After having her try it, he'd become serious and turned in Abby's direction, taking hold of her shoulders. "Listen. If you ever feel scared, I want you to change the code. Okay?"

His tone of voice had frightened her. "Eric, what are you talking about? Have there been break-ins in our neighborhood? What's going on?"

Suddenly relaxing and taking his hands from her shoulders, he grinned. "I just want to make sure you know how to operate this thing. Okay?"

"Okay." Abby had blown the behavior off, deciding he was just being overdramatic. But she now realized he had anticipated what was around the corner. But if he had known something might be coming, why hadn't he warned her directly?

At the last thought, Abby wanted to scream in exasperation and fury. It was unfair of Eric to put her through this. She didn't know what was happening or how to help him.

Mrs. Johansen was true to her word. Abby received a phone call from the installer, and he was able to come right over and install new locks. In the end Abby only put the electronic keypad locks on the door from the backyard to the garage, and from the garage to the house. Not really liking the looks of the keypad, she decided to simply have a stronger dead bolt installed on the front door.

When her daughters got home from school, Abby asked them about their day and then led them into the kitchen for an after-school snack.

"It was fun, but I told Mrs. Thompson all about the carnival," Susannah said.

"When I told Mr. Phillips I saw him there, he said it couldn't have been him," Tiffany piped in, grabbing a handful of cookies and carrying them over to the table.

Abby stopped in her tracks. Her discomfort concerning Tiffany's teacher intensified. "What did you say then, Tiff?" she asked carefully.

"Nothing. The bell rang and I had to sit in my seat. But I thought it was weird," she said, taking a bite of a cookie.

"I'm almost positive it was him," Abby murmured.

"It was him, Mom," Tiffany said. "I think I know what my teacher looks like." She paused, then added, "Mr. Phillips wanted to know if we had seen Daddy yet."

Abby's eyebrows went up, wondering what his interest in Eric was. "And what did you tell him?"

"I told him no," Tiffany said.

Abby smiled. "All right, then. Let's get started on homework."

While the girls were working on their assignments, Abby began mixing a batch of cookies. The doorbell sounded, and before Abby could stop her, Tiffany raced for the door. As she quickly made her way after Tiffany, she heard commotion coming from the entry. Then she heard a familiar voice and felt immediate anxiety. She watched as Barbara Kincaid entered the room.

"Mom? What are you doing here?" Abby managed to say.

"Is that all I get from you? Aren't you happy to see me, dear?"

"Mom! Mom! Look who's here. It's Grandma," Susannah shouted, making Abby's nerves tingle.

"Yes, I see that," Abby said to her daughter. Then she looked at her mother. "How nice to see you, Mom." She forced a pleasant smile on her face. "I didn't know you were coming."

"No. I decided last night. I thought you could use some company for a while, what with Eric missing and everything." She looked pointedly at Abby's expanded girth. "And I only live up in Sacramento. It's only an hour away."

"How thoughtful," Abby said, swallowing hard. "What about your job?"

"Oh, I took a few days of vacation time."

"I see," Abby said, then turned to her older daughter. "Take Grandma into your room, Tiffany. Strip your bed and bring your sheets down to the laundry room."

"Oh, Abby. Don't make a fuss. I'll take care of it," Barbara said. Then she followed the girls upstairs.

What on earth possessed Mother to come here? I don't need this now.

Abby stopped her negative train of thought. She wanted to have a good relationship with her mother, and she resolved right then to make an effort to get along. After things had gone so well with Jennifer, maybe things would be as positive with Barbara.

Abby heard her mother talking to Tiffany and Susannah as they came downstairs. They went into the laundry room, and Abby heard the washer start up. Pleased that her mother was taking the initiative to help out, Abby's hopes were further raised that this might actually be a pleasant visit. That illusion was swiftly put to rest as the girls went outside to play.

"Abby, I spoke to Jennifer and she told me Eric still has a drug problem," Barbara said, sitting in a kitchen chair. "When are you going to face that?"

Feeling totally betrayed by her younger sister, Abby was too astonished to speak for several moments. Finally she said, "Mother, I know drugs are not the cause of his disappearance." As she said it, she suddenly knew the words were true. But she couldn't ponder the feeling as her mother sat before her—her mere presence challenging Abby's feelings.

Skepticism clear on her face, Barbara shook her head. "When are you going to face up to the reality, dear? Your husband is an addict."

Abby couldn't believe this. "Look, if your purpose in coming here was to try to convince me what a bad person Eric is, you might as well go home." Abby's heart pounded at the confrontational words she'd blurted out.

Barbara's mouth hung open in shock. "What a way to speak to your mother. Well, I guess if I'm not welcome here, I'll go tell my granddaughters good-bye." She stood and walked toward the sliding glass door.

Closing her eyes, Abby thought how happy her girls had been to see their grandmother. With Eric's mother gone, Barbara was the only grandmother they had. "Wait, Mom," Abby said, opening her eyes.

Barbara turned toward her.

"Please, can't we try to have a pleasant visit? The girls are excited to have you here. Let's not talk about Eric, okay?"

Smiling in surrender, Barbara said, "Okay. I'll try." She came back to the chair and sat down. "Now tell me, how have you been feeling?"

"Pretty well. I did have contractions yesterday, but I haven't had any since."

Her mother abruptly came over to Abby's side and began rubbing her back. "Oh, my dear. I hope everything's going well in your pregnancy."

Abby was surprised at how her mother's suddenly loving touch almost made her feel like a little girl again. "Thanks, Mom. I appreciate your concern."

"Let me know how I can help, and I'll do what I can."

Abby smiled, an unexpected feeling of warmth in her heart. "Thank you, Mom. You don't know what that means to me."

That evening, after everyone else had gone to bed, Abby called Jennifer.

"Why did you tell Mom about Eric's drug relapse?"

"What? How do you know that?" Jennifer asked in surprise.

"Guess who showed up today?"

"No. Are you serious? I can't believe Mom would just show up."

"Well, she did. And she told me you told her about Eric." Abby allowed her tone of voice to reveal her displeasure.

"Oh, Abby. I'm sorry. I should never have said anything to her." Jennifer sounded truly repentant.

"Then why did you? You know how she feels about Eric." Abby was bewildered by what her sister had done.

"Really, I don't know what came over me." Jennifer paused. "How did things go with her today otherwise?"

Abby smiled despite herself. "Not bad, actually."

"Well, see? Maybe I was inspired to tell her. It got her to come see you, didn't it?"

"Nice try. But I don't think so. I feel really betrayed by this. How am I ever going to trust you?" Abby paused, giving herself a chance to let the anger subside.

"I give you my word. I will never again divulge to anyone anything you tell me in confidence. Okay?"

"Is there anything else I should know about? Anything else you shared?" Abby pressed, trying to keep her annoyance in check. "Did you tell her about that picture?"

"No. Honestly, no. I only told her about Eric's relapse. And for the life of me, I don't know why I did. Can you ever forgive me?"

As Abby listened to the sorrow in her sister's voice, she knew Jennifer hadn't meant to hurt her or cause her any more difficulties. "Yes. Of course I forgive you." She sighed.

"Good," Jennifer said with relief. "Now, tell me what's been happening."

* * *

A summer pregnancy was new for Abby; Tiffany and Susannah had both been born in the early spring. Consequently, she didn't have maternity clothes suitable for hot weather. In this part of California, the San Joaquin Valley, summer came early and lasted about five months. Abby wasn't looking forward to being pregnant during all that heat, and she knew long-sleeved maternity blouses were out of the question.

She still had seventeen weeks to go in her pregnancy and was already feeling overheated. Barbara had insisted Abby take some time to go shopping and had also insisted on providing the funds to do so. In spite of her embarrassment at accepting the money, Abby was grateful for her mother's willingness to help. That was how she found herself at the mall shopping for a few summer maternity outfits.

Assuming she might not be able to afford any more outfits after this, she wanted to choose carefully. Like most pregnant women, by the time the baby was born she would be sick of every one of her maternity outfits. She wanted to find some she liked in the hope she would enjoy them to the end.

After looking at the maternity clothes in each of the department stores, she made her selections. Feeling pleased with her shopping, she paid for her merchandise and headed to the car.

Glancing at her watch, she was surprised to see she had been shopping for nearly two hours. She popped open the back of the van and placed her items inside. Shutting it firmly, she heard the sound of a car stopping behind her.

"Ma'am? Abby Breuner?"

Abby turned to see who was calling her and saw a flower delivery van blocking her vehicle. "Yes, I'm Abby Breuner," she said, puzzled.

The man seemed uncomfortable. "Delivering flowers in a parking lot is a first for me, but these are for you." He held a bouquet of a dozen long-stemmed pink roses.

She took the flowers. "Who are these from?"

He shrugged his shoulders. "There's a card."

She found the card and began opening it. The man got back in his van. "Wait," Abby said.

"Yeah?"

Abby handed him money for a tip. "Please, when were these flowers ordered?"

He pocketed the money and shrugged. "I don't know when they were ordered, but I know it was a rush."

"How did you know where to find me? I mean, this is a first for me too."

He looked anxious to get going to his next delivery. "Some guy said where you were parked and gave the license plate number, and there was a description of you."

Abby's heart pounded. "Did you see the man who ordered the flowers?"

"Look, lady, I got a lot of deliveries to get to." He started the engine.

"Please. Can't you tell me anything?"

"I told you all I know." He put his van in gear and drove away.

Once he was out of sight, Abby finished opening the card. It read, *Happy Anniversary. My love, Eric.* Abby stared at the card. It wasn't Eric's writing. But, she realized with a stab of pain, it was their anniversary. Their eleventh. She assumed the florist had filled out the card according to Eric's instructions. Eric knew pink roses were her favorite.

Climbing into the minivan and carefully setting the flowers on the seat, Abby wondered how the deliveryman knew how to find her.

Eric must have been watching me, Abby realized with shock. *Was he watching me purchase things?* A combination of joy and sadness coursed through her.

It occurred to her that Eric could still be nearby. Frantically glancing around the parking lot, she tried to see if any of the men in the area looked like him.

None did. Then, pulling out of her parking space, she drove around the parking lot, searching for him. After thirty minutes she gave up and drove home.

CHAPTER TWENTY-TWO

"Can I help you?" Abby asked the large man standing at her door.

"My name is Agent Franklin, ma'am. I'm from the FBI." He held out his identification.

Abby examined it, having no idea what to look for but trying to stall to give her heart time to slow its erratic beating. She handed the ID back with shaking hands.

"I'm sorry to bother you, but I have a few questions about your husband," he said as he took the ID back.

"Do you want to come in?" Abby hoped he would refuse.

"Thank you."

Leading the way to the living room, Abby's thoughts raced wildly.

"Who was at the door, dear?" Barbara asked, coming into the living room. "Oh."

Agent Franklin held out his hand to Abby's mother. "I'm from the FBI, ma'am. I just have a few questions for Mrs. Breuner."

"I'm Abby's mother, Barbara Kincaid. Is it okay if I stay?" she asked, her curiosity obviously piqued.

"What about the girls?" Abby asked.

"Oh, they're fine. They're getting ready for bed. I told them I'd read them a story in a few minutes."

"I'd like you to stay, Mrs. Kincaid. Perhaps you would have something to add," Franklin said.

Abby didn't want her mother there, but it looked like she wouldn't have any say in the matter.

As they all took a seat, Abby felt her palms moisten as Agent Franklin turned to her.

"Mrs. Breuner, I've received two calls from your husband."

Though stunned to hear this, Abby immediately felt better. If Eric was calling them, that seemed a good sign. "What did he say?"

"I'm not at liberty to disclose our conversation, but I need to ask you a few questions."

"Okay." She didn't like the sound of that. She wanted to know what Eric had told this man.

"When did you last hear from your husband?"

"He left a message the day he disappeared."

Franklin nodded. "What did your husband say in that message?"

"Just that he was sorry."

Franklin's eyebrows drew together. "Sorry about what?"

"He didn't say."

"Okay. Have you had any communication since then? Any at all?"

This was the part Abby was afraid of. She didn't want to lie, but Eric had warned her not to tell anyone he had contacted her. "Today is our anniversary. I received a bouquet of flowers with a message from him telling me happy anniversary."

"That's true. I saw the note," Barbara said.

Franklin looked up from his notebook and smiled briefly. "Thank you." He turned back to Abby. "Anything else?"

She shook her head, hoping he couldn't tell she was holding back information and praying this would be done soon.

"Now, can you think of any reason why your husband would steal money from his employer?"

Abby didn't like where this line of questioning was leading. She also didn't like the fact that her mother was hearing these accusations against Eric from an FBI agent. "Look, Mr. Franklin, I'm sure my husband hasn't done anything wrong. Let's leave it at that."

"What about his past drug use? It is in the past, right?"

"It most definitely is," she said.

"Now, Abby. What about that relapse you told Jennifer about?" Barbara piped in.

At that moment Abby would have happily wrung her mother's neck—if an FBI agent wasn't there to witness it. She glanced at Agent Franklin, who appeared to be quite interested in Barbara's comments. "Mom, we've gone over this. That happened many years ago."

"What is she talking about, Mrs. Breuner?" Franklin asked.

Furious at her mother for having mentioned it, Abby briefly explained what happened. "It was a simple case of being with the wrong person at the wrong time. Eric has no intention of allowing that to happen again."

Appearing satisfied with her response, he asked, "Do you have anything else you'd like to tell me?"

She thought about the threatening notes she'd received. This didn't feel like the time to tell him—not with her mother sitting there. Plus, if she told him about the notes, he would certainly dig deeper and she'd have to tell him about the money she'd found. That would only lead him to believe Eric was guilty of embezzlement. "No, I don't have anything else to say."

"All right then," he said as he stood. "That's all I have for now. I'll let you know if I have any more questions." He pulled a card from his pocket and held it out. "Give me a call if you hear from your husband."

"Of course," Abby said, taking the card from his hand.

As soon as she closed the door behind him, she turned to her mother. "Why did you have to mention Eric's relapse?"

"What—did you want me to lie?" Barbara asked.

Pausing while she got her anger under control, Abby silently counted to ten before speaking. "Of course I don't want you to lie. You didn't have to say anything at all. He wasn't even talking to you."

"But if I didn't say anything, that would be dishonesty by omission," Barbara said as if her reasoning were obvious.

"But that happened so long ago. Why do you think it's relevant to what's happening now?"

"Well, I don't know," she sputtered. "I'm going to see if the girls are ready for me to read to them now."

Abby watched her mother head for the stairs, her anger simmering. *Why can't she be on my side?*

* * *

Absently looking through Eric's book on disappearing, Abby waited for her mother to come back downstairs. Her anger had been building ever since her mother had gone to read the girls a story. *Why does she have to stick her nose in where it doesn't belong? Why does she always believe she has a right to say whatever she wants without a thought to how if might affect others?* Abby's thoughts had been going on this way for several minutes, causing her fury to grow to the point where she knew she would have to confront her mother.

She tried to brace herself for the unpleasantness that was sure to follow. As she imagined the potential fallout, she wondered if she should just keep her thoughts to herself. But she knew that wouldn't happen. This moment had been building for years. After all the snide comments Barbara had made about Eric, Abby knew it was time to say something—no matter the consequence.

"I read them three stories and they still wanted more," Barbara said casually as she entered the family room. She was smiling as if nothing unpleasant had happened that evening.

Abby set the book down next to her and pressed her lips together, reconsidering whether she should say anything to her mother.

"You're awfully quiet," Barbara said as she sat on the couch near Abby. "Are you still upset over that FBI visit?"

Taking a deep breath, Abby nodded. "I am upset and I want to talk to you about it."

Her mother immediately went on the defensive. "Abby, you can't expect me to sit by and do nothing when I see things going on. I feel it's my duty to speak up."

Here we go, Abby thought. "What exactly do you feel the need to say?"

"That book for example," Barbara said, picking it up by the cover. "What do you hope to discover . . ."

Abby's gaze followed her mother's and she gasped. The photo of Eric with his other family had slipped out and landed on the couch cushions.

"What's this?" Barbara asked, setting the book down and picking up the picture.

"Let me have that," Abby said in alarm, holding out her hand.

Barbara studied the small photo. "What in the world?" She looked at Abby. "Is this Eric?"

Abby felt tears threaten, humiliated that her mother would discover anything about her personal struggles. Now Barbara not only knew that Eric was a drug user and accused of embezzlement, but that he possibly had a child with another woman as well. She took the picture from her mother's hand. "Please let me have that."

Her mother stared at her. "Abby, what is going on?"

Biting her lip to keep from crying, Abby shook her head.

"That was Eric, wasn't it? And it looked like a recent picture of him. Has he been cheating on you?"

Abby could see her mother was starting to get worked up. "Mother, please don't jump to conclusions. I'm trying not to, and I'd appreciate it if you could wait to pass judgment until I have more information."

Barbara had a look of incredulity on her face. "Abby, what is wrong with you? I've heard of being in denial, but this is ridiculous. It's time you faced the truth. You have the proof right there in your hand. Eric is being unfaithful. He's stolen money—even the FBI thinks so—and it seems drugs aren't only in his past. In fact, it seems that his infidelity isn't short-term, either. It appears he's been with that woman for quite some time, judging by the little boy in that picture."

Hearing her mother voice all her own fears made Abby angrier. "You don't know that! You don't know anything! There you sit, self-righteous and all-knowing, passing judgment on everyone around you. At least Jennifer gave Eric the benefit of the doubt. I'm afraid to tell you much of what's going on for fear of your judgments." Abby paused, watching the expression on her mother's face, wondering if she'd gone too far. Her mother stared at her, wide-eyed and slack-jawed.

"Abby Kincaid! I can't believe you just spoke to me that way!"

Abby's eyes opened wider. "My name is Abby Breuner. I'm married to Eric Breuner, and don't you forget it!" Abby stormed out of the room and ran up to her bedroom, locking the door behind her. She resisted the urge to fling herself onto her bed like a teenager, and instead calmly walked over to the love seat and sat down, curling her feet beneath her.

She wondered why her mother had called her by her maiden name. Had she never accepted Eric as her husband? Today was her anniversary, for heaven's sake! Her anger still fresh, Abby silently prayed to feel calm, then for both her heart and her mother's heart to be softened.

After she heard her mother come up the stairs and close her bedroom door, Abby went downstairs to retrieve the book and picture that had ignited their argument.

As she walked into the family room, the phone rang. In contrast to the hard feelings she had with her mother, Abby was pleased to hear from her father-in-law. When she heard the concern in his voice, she decided it was only right to tell him about the embezzlement accusations against his son.

"Not again," he said.

"What do you mean?" she asked, astonished to hear his response.

"Oh, I guess Eric never told you about that time he took some money from his employer."

"No! This is the first I've heard of this. Please, tell me more."

"This was back when he was just getting started using drugs. Of course, at the time I didn't realize what was going on. He needed money and his job didn't pay much, so one night he helped himself to the cash register. Fortunately for him, his boss was a kind man and he allowed Eric to work off the money he took. He also didn't tell the police."

"Oh my gosh, Harry! Do you really think he's done it again?"

"I surely hope not. What do the police say?"

Abby pictured Agent Franklin. "Well, I haven't heard from the police, but an FBI agent came by earlier today. It was pretty unsettling. I have to tell you, though, I'm glad I didn't know about Eric stealing before or I don't know what I would've said."

"Abby, you just worry about taking care of those beautiful children. Eric will have to deal with the consequences of his choices."

"Thank you, Harry."

When they hung up a few minutes later, Abby was grateful her daughters and mother had already gone to bed. She could only imagine the worry visible on her face.

Turning on the television to try to take her mind off her concerns, Abby felt herself drifting off to sleep when she was startled awake by knocking at the door. Her eyes flew open as she imagined the FBI there to search the house, looking for the stolen money.

Trudging to the door, Abby peeked through the peephole before opening the door to Mr. Phillips. "I've decided not to have you tutor Tiffany," she said as soon as she saw him.

"I'm sorry to stop by so late, but that's not why I'm here."

She could see something was bothering him, but she had no idea what it could be. "Okay."

He sighed. "I just feel bad about what I've done. I felt I needed to apologize to you in person."

"What do you mean?"

"Well, I was approached by someone and told there was a reward for information on your husband's whereabouts. This person knew I taught Tiffany's class and thought I might be able to get information from her. As far as I know it was legal. I just feel bad about it."

Shaken to hear this, Abby stepped back. "What are you saying? Were you spying on my family?"

He looked down at his feet, then back at Abby. "Not exactly. I just asked Tiffany questions from time to time. That sort of thing. But I feel bad because this person paid me to do it. It feels wrong to me, and I apologize."

"That was you at the carnival then?"

"Yes, I'm afraid so."

"Who was this person that paid you? Was it the FBI?"

"It wasn't the FBI, but I don't know that it's my place to name names. I don't want to make things worse than they already are."

"Worse than they are? My husband's been missing for two weeks. Today the FBI stopped by to question me. I think knowing who else is involved would be a good thing." She paused. "Please, Mr. Phillips, if you tell me who is doing this, I think it would redeem you."

He pulled out an envelope. "This might help."

"What is it?" Abby asked as she took it from him.

"The reward money I was paid. It's five hundred dollars." He turned to walk to his car.

"Wait!" she called after him.

He turned back and stopped.

"Please! Tell me who paid you."

"I'm sorry. I can't." He left before Abby could ask again.

Abby closed the door, her mind reeling.

Tiffany's teacher was watching for Eric? Who else might be watching us?

She was suddenly suspicious of everyone she'd had contact with since Eric had disappeared. Then, noticing the card Agent Franklin had left, she wondered if she should call him and have him talk to Mr. Phillips about who was behind the spying.

But what if that just tips the FBI off that people are looking for Eric? Won't that make him look guiltier?

Then she remembered Harry's statement that Eric would have to deal with the consequences of his choices. The idea that people were watching her family was too eerie to leave alone. She decided to call Agent Franklin first thing in the morning—she'd tell him about Mr. Phillips.

The next morning, before her mother had gotten up, Abby tried to call Agent Franklin. She was relieved when he wasn't available and she had to leave a message. She reported the situation with Mr. Phillips, glad she didn't have to endure further questioning.

Abby could hear her mother coming down the stairs and felt her body tense in preparation for the conversation that was sure to come. She had no idea what her mother might say or do, but she decided she would try to be nice.

"Good morning," Abby said.

"Morning," Barbara said, a small smile on her face.

"Did you sleep well?" Abby asked.

"No. As a matter of fact I didn't. You?"

Abby sighed. "Not very well."

Just then the girls came in, and Abby knew she and her mother would have to discuss the issue another time.

Her daughters were in a year-round school, and today was their first day off track. They spent that morning playing games with their grandmother and watching videos.

After lunch, Abby decided to look through Eric's office again for clues as to what might be going on and who might be involved. The first item she picked up was his address book. "What's this?" Abby said, picking up a scrap of paper stuck in the middle of the address book.

She studied the information written on the tiny piece of paper: *515 Buttercup Drive.* The address was circled twice with red ink. The address was unfamiliar to Abby, and she had no idea where the piece of paper had come from or how long it had been there.

Was it here when I looked through the address book before?

She went to the garage to get the map from the minivan.

"Where are you going, Mom?" Susannah asked, jumping up from the floor where she had been watching a video.

"Out to the car for a minute. I'll be right back."

A moment later Abby had the map spread on the counter, searching for the unfamiliar street name. It only took a moment to find it. It was in a part of town she rarely visited.

"Susannah, would you get Tiffany? We need to go somewhere."

"Where are we going?" Tiffany asked, coming down the stairs.

"On a little drive. Hurry, please. Where's your grandma?"

"Taking a nap."

Perfect.

* * *

A few minutes later they were in the minivan headed for the mystery address. With the map in hand it didn't take long to find the house. Abby drove slowly by. The house didn't look particularly special. One house among dozens within a neighborhood. There were no cars parked out front, but that didn't mean no one was home.

Why was this address on a piece of paper in Eric's address book? What's the significance?

She didn't want to approach the house with the girls in tow, so she decided to come back another time when they weren't with her. She wanted to do it soon.

"Mom, is this where we're going?" Susannah asked.

"I, uh, I just wanted to drive around here. Why don't we stop by the store and get a treat?"

The girls shouted their enthusiasm.

* * *

That evening, once the girls had gone to bed, Abby decided to try to clear the air with her mother. She turned on the television and began watching one of the decorating shows her mother liked so well. She hoped her mother would hear it and come join her. Sure enough, a few minutes into the program Barbara came into the family room and joined Abby, sitting on a chair near the couch.

Abby could feel the tension and gathered up her courage before saying, "Mom, we need to talk." She turned toward her mother and was stunned when her mother began to cry.

"I'm so sorry about last night," Barbara interrupted. "I didn't mean to upset you."

Speechless at this display of remorse, Abby just stared at her mother.

"Sometimes I get so caught up in how I want things to be that I forget everyone else may not share the same view of the world that I do. I just want what's best for you." Barbara wiped a tear from her cheek as she spoke. "I've so enjoyed spending time with your children. I want to be a part of your life. Your whole family's life, including Eric, if you work things out."

Abby was touched by her sincerity. "I want you to be a part of our lives too. I know the girls have loved having you here. You're their only grandmother, you know." Abby stood and walked to her mother.

Barbara stood as well, and they enjoyed a warm embrace.

They talked for a while about their years of misunderstanding and why Barbara had struggled to love Eric. Abby realized there was a great deal about her mother she didn't know. Finally, late into the night, and after a measure of resolution had been achieved, Barbara said, "I don't know about you, but I'm exhausted."

Abby agreed and hugged her mother again. "Good night, Mom."

* * *

"We'll be fine, Abby. Just go run your errands," Barbara assured her as Abby walked toward the car the day after finding the address to Buttercup Drive. She hadn't told her mother anything about the address she'd found. She also hadn't heard from Agent Franklin to find out who had been paying Mr. Phillips to spy on them. Maybe today she would do some spying of her own. She was tired of being the victim, always being on the defensive. Today she would be on the offense. It felt good.

Ten minutes later she was parked across the street from the house on Buttercup Drive. Gathering her fading resolve, she stepped out of the minivan and walked toward the house. It was hard to tell if anyone was home. The curtains were drawn and the driveway was empty.

She knocked loudly, then waited several minutes. No one seemed to be home. Abby stepped off the porch and went toward the backyard. She reached for the gate string and hesitated, wondering if there was a dog back there.

Trying to calm the butterflies in her stomach, Abby slowly opened the gate and entered the backyard. She paused, waiting for a dog to jump out at her. All was still. Feeling more confident, she tiptoed toward a window. The curtains were closed there too. She went all the way around the house and found all the blinds and curtains shut tight.

She went back to her car and sat inside, trying to figure out what to do. She didn't have to ponder very long. Five minutes later a car pulled into the driveway at 515 Buttercup Drive.

Abby slid down in her seat, not wanting to be noticed. Sitting up slightly, she peered out the window and watched a woman about her own age go into the house.

Abby waited another five minutes before approaching the house. Her heart pounded as she rang the doorbell. The woman opened the door almost immediately. She was about Abby's height with dyed-black hair swept up into a ponytail. Her pretty features were makeup free, but a little familiar.

"Can I help you?" the woman asked with a Southern drawl.

"Yes. I'm having car trouble and I was wondering if I could use your phone," Abby said, using her planned excuse.

"Certainly." The woman opened the door for Abby to enter. "The phone is in the kitchen."

"Thank you." Abby stepped into the entry hall and surreptitiously glanced around. Nothing seemed unusual about the place. As Abby followed the woman toward the kitchen, she noticed photographs arranged on a piano. Trying not to stare, Abby thought something about the people looked familiar.

"It's right here," the woman said, pointing to the phone and drawing Abby's attention away from the photographs.

Abby lifted the phone and dialed her own cell phone, having turned it off earlier. "Hi, honey. I'm having trouble with the car. Could you come and help?" She paused, as if listening. "The address?" She glanced at the woman, a questioning look on her face.

"It's 515 Buttercup Drive," the woman drawled.

Abby repeated the information. "Okay, hon. I'll see you in a while." Abby hung up the phone and turned to the woman. "Thank you for your help."

"Not a problem," she said. "Can I get you something to drink while you're waiting for your . . . ?"

"Husband," Abby supplied quickly.

"Yes, your husband. How about some lemonade?"

Wanting to spend a few minutes there to try to get information, Abby accepted the offer.

"If you'd like to wait in the living room, I'll grab something to drink."

"Thank you." Abby walked into the living room and immediately went to the piano and the photographs there. Pictured were a woman, a man, and a young boy. As she stared at the photo, she felt the blood drain from her face. It was another picture of Eric, and she suddenly realized that her hostess was a natural blond.

"Cute, isn't he?" The woman had come up behind Abby.

"What?" Abby said, spinning around.

"My son, Alex," she said, handing Abby a glass of lemonade.

Abby took it automatically and turned back toward the picture. "This is your son?"

"Yes," she said with obvious pride. "He turned three last week."

Feeling surreal, Abby turned back toward the woman. "Where is he now?"

"Oh, he's off with his father on some errand or another." The woman looked at Abby with narrowed eyes. "Are you okay? You look pale."

She ignored the question. "When do you expect him back?"

"Oh, Alex should be back anytime now."

Still feeling disbelief, Abby blurted, "Not your son. Your husband."

The friendliness the woman had been showing slowly seeped away as she looked at Abby with mistrust. "Why do you want to know that?" she asked suspiciously.

Suddenly realizing the inappropriateness of the question, Abby felt the color rush to her cheeks. "I'm sorry. I've got to go." Abby handed her glass to the woman and walked quickly to the door.

"But your car!" the woman shouted after Abby.

Ignoring her, Abby ran across the street to her car, which started right up.

CHAPTER TWENTY-THREE

As she drove home, her mind was in turmoil. *This is the same family from the photo I found in that book. There really is another family.* She thought about the slip of paper with the address on it. *Who put it there? Did someone want me to find it? Is this all a setup? Or am I in total denial?*

At the thought, she felt tears pushing their way into her eyes. She blinked rapidly, forcing them back, then pulled over to the side of the road. She couldn't take the insanity anymore and needed someone to tell her she wasn't crazy. She pulled out her cell phone and dialed. Then, as the line picked up, she choked out, "Mary?"

* * *

"You're saying my wife may believe I'm a thief." Eric was using a pay phone at the mall and trying not to speak too loudly. Agent Franklin had finished telling Eric he had questioned Abby and she had been less than helpful. Eric was relieved Abby hadn't mentioned the message he'd given her. If she was following his instructions to not tell anyone about the message, he hoped that meant she trusted him.

"I'm saying I don't know what she believes, but she didn't have any information that helped." Franklin paused. "Except for when she called me the other day." Franklin then told Eric about Mr. Phillips.

Eric finally realized how much danger his family was in. *I need to find the rest of the money and get it to a safe place.*

* * *

"I'm sorry to hear all you've been having to deal with. And all on your own, too," Barbara said as they prepared lunch. Abby and her mother had been discussing the embezzlement accusations. Surprisingly, Barbara had withheld judgment. She had even encouraged Abby to trust Eric. Perhaps Abby's prayers about her mother's heart being softened were paying off.

"Not completely on my own, Mom. I've spoken to my bishop and he's aware of what's happening."

"Well, that's a relief. Have you considered asking for a blessing?"

Abby stopped chopping the fruit she was preparing for lunch. "No, actually. I hadn't considered that. But I think it's a good idea. Maybe I'll do that."

With Barbara's unrelenting reminders, Abby called her home teacher, Brother Shaw, and asked him to give her a blessing. That evening, he, along with Bishop Dunlap, came to the Breuners' home.

As the blessing was being administered, Abby felt peace and comfort. She was assured she and her children would be safe. She also distinctly felt as if she should trust Eric, but she doubted it the moment she felt it. Her emotions weren't steady right now, she told herself. Once the blessing was completed, Abby thanked the men for coming over, then spent some time alone mulling over her feelings.

* * *

"I've had it," the man said, pouring himself another drink. "This lack of respect cannot be ignored."

"I agree," his companion said. "We need to use him as an example."

"I'll leave it in your capable hands."

"It will be my pleasure," he answered, a grin on his face.

* * *

"I'm doing okay," Abby said in response to Mary's question. Abby adjusted the phone against her ear. "How about you? Are you getting by without me at the library?"

"It's not the same without you, of course. But that's not why I'm calling."

Abby drew her brows together at the urgent tone in her friend's voice. "What is it, then?"

"You know how you told me about that picture and that house?" Mary asked.

"Yes," Abby said, feeling a flash of humiliation that her husband might have left her for another woman.

"Do you remember that when you showed me the picture, I thought the woman looked familiar? Well, since she was in profile it took me a little while to place her. But Abby, I remember her coming into the library."

"Well, she doesn't live very far from here," Abby responded.

"She wasn't just visiting the library. She was in our break room."

Mary's words caught Abby's full attention. "What was she doing in there?"

"She told me she was looking for the bathroom. I didn't think much of it until today, when I realized she was the same woman in the picture. I'm so sorry I didn't remember before this."

"It's okay. I wonder what she was up to," Abby mused. "Do you think Eric sent her to check up on me?" The thought upset her, but she had to consider all possibilities.

"I don't know. I couldn't tell what she was doing." Mary paused. "I wish I could do more to help you."

"Just telling me what you remembered is helpful. Thank you."

"Hey, I know," Mary said. "What if I look up that book on disappearing and see if it's something Eric checked out—maybe he used an alternate address or something and we can track him down."

Abby was grateful for her friend's willingness to help, but the idea of confronting Eric was stressful. Still, she had to know so she could move on with her life. She sighed and answered, "Thank you, Mary. You're a true friend."

"No problem, Abby. Look, I'm not at work right now, so I'll check first thing tomorrow . . ."

Abby tried to listen to everything else Mary told her, but she found it hard to concentrate during the rest of the phone call, or, for that matter, during the rest of the day.

* * *

When Abby answered the phone the next day and heard Mary's voice, apprehension washed over her. "Did you find out who checked the book out?"

"Tell me that address again. The one where the woman lived," Mary prompted.

Abby told her, then asked, "Well?"

"The book was checked out by someone named Lauren Douglas. And the address on her file is the Buttercup Drive address."

"Somehow I'm not surprised. I mean, it makes sense that Eric wouldn't want to check it out himself. Why not send someone else?" Even as she thought about it, she imagined Eric and Lauren sitting down one evening and discussing how they would run off and leave Eric's first family behind. A lump formed in Abby's throat at the thought, and she bit her lip to keep from weeping.

"Abby?" Mary asked. "Are you okay?"

Taking a deep breath before speaking, Abby said, "I'm not great, but I'll figure it out."

"Do you want me to come over?"

"No. I need some time alone. But thank you, Mary. You're wonderful."

"Please let me know if I can do anything for you. Promise?"

"I promise."

Abby hung up the phone and wandered over to the couch. Her baby moved inside her, and Abby stroked her abdomen. She felt so betrayed. She didn't know what to believe anymore. Perhaps she had imagined the feeling during the priesthood blessing, the feeling she should trust Eric. She couldn't shake the feeling that he wasn't using drugs, but maybe he was embezzling and had lied to her for years . . . She could hardly believe Eric would do this to her. The more she thought about it, the angrier she became.

How dare he do this to our family. She stood and started pacing before finding herself in the office. She stared at the family picture on the desk before picking it up and hiding it in one of the desk drawers. *If he doesn't want anything to do with us, I don't want any reminders of him.*

She walked around the house and took down any picture with Eric in it, including the large portrait in the entry hall. As she stared at the empty spot where the portrait had hung only moments before, she remembered one other place where she kept Eric's picture.

Going into the bedroom to get her purse, she opened her wallet and flipped to the picture section. Her eyebrows pulled together in puzzlement as she thumbed through all the photographs.

The small family photo she kept in her wallet had vanished.

CHAPTER TWENTY-FOUR

The house on Buttercup Drive looked the same on Monday as it had on Thursday of the previous week, and Abby boldly pulled into the driveway. Breathing deeply to slow her pounding heart, she walked up to the front door and rang the bell. Her heart rate increased when she heard footsteps approaching the door.

"Yes?" a completely different woman asked as she opened the door.

Expecting the door to be answered by the same woman as before, Abby was caught off guard. "Do . . . do you live here?"

"Yes, of course. Can I help you with something?"

"Does anyone else live here?" Abby asked, still trying to comprehend who the woman was.

The woman's eyebrows drew together. "Who are you?"

"I'm sorry. I was here last week and I spoke to someone else. That's why I was wondering if anyone else lived here."

"Oh. Well, my family moved in a couple of days ago. I don't know who lived here before us."

Abby felt foolish for her questions and mumbled something before walking back to the van. She stopped at a nearby park and considered what had happened.

Who was that before? Where did she go? Was it really Eric's other wife and now that I've found him he's back on the run? She remembered the calm feeling of her blessing. Perhaps she had allowed this bizarre turn of events to distract her from listening to the Spirit.

I will be in control of what I believe until I have proof, she told herself. *I have to have faith he loves me and is trying to come home to me, just like he said. Someone's trying to mess with my mind—my missing picture proves it.* She was through being a pawn. She was going to beat whoever it was at their own game.

* * *

Hiding behind a bush, Eric could see his family through the open blinds. They were kneeling in a circle, with him absent. He could also see his mother-in-law there. He knew how she felt about him. Her presence there worried him.

Watching Tiffany's lips move as she said the family prayer made Eric ache inside. He wanted to be with them a great deal, but he also wanted to stay out of jail. "Amen," he whispered in unison with his family as they completed the prayer. He gazed after them as they went upstairs. He knew the bedtime ritual would take at least ten minutes.

He had been surprised to see police cars patrolling his neighborhood, and he'd had to wait for them to drive by before sneaking into the backyard. Now, as he watched his family finally head upstairs, he decided to make his move.

He sprang toward the sliding glass door, but wasn't surprised to find it locked. Next he went to the garage door where he was shocked to find a totally new doorknob. The lock had been replaced by a keypad.

Obviously Abby had been frightened. Guilt flooded Eric as he considered the anguish he had caused his wife. He stared at the keypad and wondered what the code was. First he tried the code he and Abby had chosen—the year of Tiffany's birth. That didn't work. He paused as he considered what else Abby might have used.

The year we married. We almost chose that for the alarm code. He punched it in and was gratified to hear the lock click open. *Abby must still have some trust in me.* He paused as he turned the doorknob, wondering if the alarm would sound. All was silent. He quickly entered the garage and closed the door behind him.

Next was the door to the house. He wasn't sure how much time had passed, but he hoped everyone would still be upstairs. As he reached toward the doorknob, he saw it turning and he jumped back and ran behind the Jeep. Though surprised and momentarily confused, he didn't have long to wonder how his car had even gotten there.

Eric watched Barbara flip on the light and step into the garage. After grabbing something from his workbench, she went back into the house, turning the light off on her way in. He let his breath out and continued kneeling behind the Jeep. He said a silent prayer, asking for help getting in without being seen. He checked his watch and knew his time was about up.

Operating on the assumption that Abby had changed the alarm, he knew if he didn't get in the house before Abby punched in the code, he wouldn't be able to enter the house or leave the garage until she deactivated it.

Creeping up to the door, he listened to discover if anyone was near. It was difficult to hear through the heavy steel. Opening the door slightly, he peered into the kitchen. No one was there. He didn't hear any noise in the adjoining family room. Falling to his hands and knees, he crawled toward the family room and then into the hall closet. The scent of musty coats almost made him cough, and he had to control his breathing.

As he waited in the coat closet, he replayed his decision to come. He had been careful that no one followed him. He knew he was taking a risk in coming here, but he needed to try to find the rest of the money one more time. Not only that, he was desperate to see his family, even if they couldn't see him. If he had to go one more day without being near them, he didn't know what he would do. The intensity of his desire made him fear he would do something foolish.

What do you call what you're doing now?

He shook his head, unable to consider that. He had to be here, just to be close. As much as he would like to speak to Abby, he knew if he did it would be too difficult for him to leave again. And if he stayed he was fairly certain the FBI would arrest him. It was a chance he wasn't going to take.

A while later he heard Abby and her mother come back down the stairs and turn the television on. About an hour later they finally turned it off and headed upstairs.

He pulled down his old wool coat and folded it to make a pillow. Peace flooded his soul as he lay in his home. He felt safe there. Resting his head on the makeshift pillow, he allowed himself to drift off for a while.

* * *

Checking his watch, Eric decided the time was right to search the house for the money. He decided to start in the master bedroom.

Pressing his ear to the closet door and hearing nothing, he carefully twisted the knob. He peered out into the darkened entry hall, then opened the door enough to slide out. He shut the door as quietly as he had opened it and tiptoed up the stairs.

All was still. He reached the landing and immediately headed for the master bedroom. Pausing in the open doorway, he gazed at Abby as she slept. Love for his wife filled his heart as he walked toward the bed.

He stared down at her before reaching his hand out to gently stroke her cheek. She moaned in her sleep and pulled the covers higher. He sat on the edge of the bed and leaned toward her, breathing in the fragrant scent of her hair.

After watching his wife's peaceful face for a moment, his attention shifted to her swollen abdomen. He placed his hand there and soon felt kicking. Tears came to his eyes when he realized it was the first time he had felt his baby kick. He wondered if Abby had found out if it would be a boy.

She began to stir, and he quickly slid down onto the floor and rolled under the bed as best he could. He waited until her quiet snores began again before standing and tiptoeing toward the walk-in closet and shutting the door behind him. He felt along the top shelf until he found the flashlight that they kept there. As he lifted it, he hoped the batteries were still good. He flicked the switch and was rewarded with a bright glow. Shining it around the closet, he looked behind and under everything, but didn't come across any cash.

While in the midst of quietly searching the closet, Eric heard Abby get up and walk across the floor. He quickly flicked off the light, then held his breath. When he heard the bathroom door close, he set the flashlight back in its place and left the closet. Glancing toward the bathroom, he silently left the room and—after visiting Susannah's room, where both she and Tiffany were sleeping—he crept back down the stairs to check the alarm.

As he expected, Abby had set the alarm. He wondered if she had changed the alarm code, considered trying it, then stopped himself. He had to assume she had. With a sigh, he resigned himself to spending the night on the floor of the coat closet.

CHAPTER TWENTY-FIVE

The ringing of the phone woke Eric, and he sat up in the closet. He pressed a button on his watch to light the face and saw it was 8:00 Feds He stretched his arms and yawned, then carefully stood halfway up, working the kinks out of his legs.

He thought he heard someone coming down the stairs. Pressing his ear against the closet door, he listened to footsteps walk past. He wondered if it was Abby and had to control the urge to fling the door open and take her into his arms. He knew if he made such a foolish error it would be impossible to leave, and then everything would fall apart.

He wondered what Abby was thinking after all this time.

Has she gotten the notes? Did she find the rest of the promised money? And if she did, what must she be thinking?

He thought about how he had come into possession of the cash and silently cursed himself. *Why couldn't I just leave it alone?*

Footsteps passing the closet door pulled him out of his musings. He heard the beeping of the alarm and hoped Abby was deactivating it so he could leave his confinement. When the footsteps left again, Eric peered out. On the count of three he ran for the garage. Just as voices sounded in the next room, he pulled the door shut behind him.

* * *

Tess peeked through her window as the large man approached her front door. All these strange goings-on had her a little spooked. When he rang the bell she hesitated before finally opening the door. He looked official in the suit he wore, and she stayed silent, waiting for him to explain what he wanted.

"My name is Agent Franklin," he said before holding out a badge for her inspection. "I'd like to ask you a few questions, if that's all right."

"I've already spoken to your colleague, Agent Webster," she said.

Franklin looked genuinely puzzled. "What are you talking about, ma'am?"

"Don't you people talk to each other?" Tess asked, annoyed she would have to explain everything again.

"I don't know what you're referring to, but wait here a minute, please," Franklin said before walking to his car.

Tess could see him talking on his cell phone. He came back a few minutes later. "Well? Did you talk to him?" she asked, hoping she could get on with what she'd been doing.

"I'm afraid there's been some kind of mistake, ma'am. We don't have an Agent Webster working for the bureau in this area, and the only Agent Webster in the state has never heard of you."

Alarm crept up Tess's spine. "Then who have I been giving this information to?"

"What information have you been giving?" Franklin asked.

Tess peered at the man on her porch more closely. "How can I be sure you're who you say you are?"

He reached into his jacket pocket and pulled out a card. "Call the resident agency office if you'd like."

She took the card from him. "Would you mind waiting here, please?" She locked the front door before getting out the phone book and looking up the FBI's phone number. She called that one instead of the number on his card. The person she spoke to assured her that Agent Franklin was legitimate. She hung up, then went back to her front door and invited the man inside.

He smiled graciously at her embarrassment and, as they sat down, again asked what she had told the "other" FBI agent.

"He wanted me to let him know whenever Abby Breuner left her house or if I ever saw Eric. He also asked me to talk to Abby and see what information I could get from her."

"I see." The look on his face was grave.

Tess suddenly felt terrible about what she'd done. She hoped she hadn't caused more trouble for Abby. They'd had such a good visit over lunch, even if it was under false pretenses, and she felt like a real friendship was beginning. She didn't want to do anything to destroy it.

"What information did Mrs. Breuner give you that you passed on?"

"Nothing, really. She only told me that her husband is missing." Tess sighed and put her head in her hands. "What should I do?"

"How do you contact this person?"

She looked up at Agent Franklin. "The first time I talked to him, he came by the house. But since then we've just communicated through email."

"Do you still have those email messages?" Franklin asked.

"Yes," Tess said, relieved she hadn't deleted them.

"Please forward them to the email address on the card I gave you, and let me know immediately if he contacts you again."

* * *

Barbara finished cleaning the bathrooms and moved on to straighten up each room. She didn't know how long it would be until Abby got back from her errands. She wanted to be helpful, wanted her daughter to be glad she was there.

Tiffany and Susannah had gone to play with friends in the neighborhood, leaving Barbara with time on her hands. Starting in the living room, it took her only a few minutes to arrange the pillows on the couch and make everything look shipshape. Barbara stepped from the living room into the entry and glanced at the closet door. She opened the door and saw several coats lying on the floor.

That's peculiar, she thought, picking them up one by one and hanging them on hangers. She shook her head at the wrinkles that clung to the fabric. *Didn't I teach you anything, Abby?*

Once all the coats had been picked up, she stood back and admired her work. Nodding in self-satisfaction, her gaze fell to the floor and she noticed an object lying there.

Bending to pick it up, she examined the item. It was a key. *I'll give it to Abby later,* she thought, dropping it in her pocket.

Next, she went to the kitchen to scrub the cupboards and forgot all about the key.

But later that evening, as Barbara pulled on her nightgown, she remembered the key. She picked up the pants she had been wearing earlier and took the key out of the pocket. Once she finished her bedtime routine, she took the key and walked toward Abby's room. The door was closed, and she thought she could hear soft snoring coming from inside.

Barbara went back to her room, deciding to give Abby the key the next morning. She set it on the bedside table and then picked up her book. She read until her eyes wouldn't stay open any longer, then absently set her book on top of the key.

* * *

The man in the dark blue shirt rolled the dice again. He grunted, frustrated that he was starting to lose. He'd been so certain things were going to start going his way now. He'd lost enough for ten people—wasn't it his turn to be a winner?

He looked around the casino, feeling like someone was watching him. Seeing no one particularly disturbing, he ignored the feeling and walked away from the table, deciding to try his luck at a game of poker. The game took all his concentration, and he didn't notice the men watching him from the shadows.

* * *

"I found him." A young man in khaki pants and a dress shirt pressed his cell phone to his ear.

"Is he winning?" the voice on the other end asked.

"No, it doesn't look that way." He paused, watching the other people in the casino. "But there's some other guy here watching our man."

"Do you think our accountant owes him money too? Does it look like one of our competitors?"

He shifted his weight to his other leg. "I've never seen him before. What do you want me to do?"

"Make sure he sees the message that you're going to deliver to our friend."

"You got it, boss." He flipped his phone closed and snapped it to his waistband before approaching the poker table and sliding into an empty seat. He smiled at the man in the blue shirt, who suddenly looked terrified.

* * *

A third man watched this interaction with interest and stepped deeper into the shadows to see what would happen. *Khaki Pants and Blue Shirt seem to know each other,* he mused. A moment later the man in the khaki pants stood and motioned for the man in the blue shirt to follow him. They walked outside, where they seemed to be arguing. Khaki Pants grabbed Blue

Shirt and shoved him against the wall. Then he quickly glanced around before twisting the smaller man's arm in an unnatural way.

The man watching from the shadows cringed as the unlucky gambler cried out. He stepped from the shadows and hurried away before anything else happened, suddenly frightened for his own safety.

CHAPTER TWENTY-SIX

Eric thought about the promise he'd just made to Agent Franklin. Franklin had asked him to turn over the cash in his safe-deposit box as a show of good faith.

I might as well get this done, Eric thought, reaching into his pocket for the key to the safe-deposit box. His acceptance of the situation turned to alarm when the key wasn't there. He quickly searched all his pockets, with no success. *Maybe it's in my motel room.* On the drive back he tried to calm himself with the thought that he must have taken it out of his pocket and put it in a drawer.

A short time later he was less calm. *Where is it?* he thought frantically as he yanked out each of the dresser drawers. *It's got to be here somewhere.*

He stood next to the bed and let his stare probe the entire room. He had looked everywhere.

He collapsed on the bed, forcing himself to relax, if only for a minute. Then it came to him. The closet at his house. It had probably fallen out of his pocket when he had slept there.

* * *

That night Eric watched his family from the shadows. When Abby, her mother, and the girls headed upstairs to get ready for bed, Eric made his move. He sprinted to the sliding glass door and was both thankful to find it still unlocked and concerned at how dangerous that was. Taking advantage of the opportunity, he quietly went to the closet and opened the door.

The closet had been cleaned up. The coats he had used for his bed had been neatly hung up. He paused, listening for the sound of someone's approach. Soft voices floated his way from upstairs, but all was quiet where he was. He quickly searched the closet floor for the key. It wasn't there.

I know I lost it here. Someone must have cleaned up and found it. Now what?

He searched the coat pockets hoping the key had been put in one of them. Nothing. Panic rose in him as he considered the promise he'd made Agent Franklin to give over the money. His heart beat erratically with anticipation as he considered one option.

He would search the master bedroom, and if that didn't turn up the key, he would wake Abby.

* * *

Tess absently flipped through the television channels, thinking about her conversation with Agent Franklin. *If Franklin is really an FBI agent, then who's that guy I've been emailing, and why is he so interested in the Breuners?* She thought about the questions he'd had concerning the family, and how she'd freely shared what she knew.

Rubbing her fingers against her forehead, she tried to figure out what was going on. She'd heard some rumors at work about missing money, and she wondered if Eric was involved with that. *Is that why the*

FBI was asking questions? Has Eric committed a crime? The idea shocked her. *To think, one of my own neighbors might be a criminal.*

But what about Abby? She seemed so nice at lunch. I hope I'm wrong about Eric. Her thoughts went back to her first question: who'd sent that fake agent to get her to spy on the Breuners? She racked her brain trying to figure out who might care about what her neighbors did.

Every time she thought about Abby, Tess was flooded with guilt. Abby had never done anything to her, yet she may have inadvertently hurt her. She wondered if she should tell Abby about the imposter agent. *She'll hate me if I tell her I've been spying on her family. Besides, the real FBI is keeping an eye on her—I don't want to get in the middle of that.* The reasoning assuaged her guilt, but only a little.

* * *

"Good night, sweetheart," Abby said as she tucked the blanket around Susannah. "I'll see you in the morning."

"Do you want to watch TV?" Abby asked her mother as they finished tucking the girls into bed.

"Sure."

"Let's watch one of those decorating shows. I'm not sure which ones are on tonight, though."

"I can tell you which ones are on tonight," Barbara said as she led the way down the stairs and into the family room.

As Abby listened to her mother, she wondered if Barbara was lonely. *I need to make more of an effort with her. Jennifer and I are probably all she has.*

An hour later Abby found herself falling asleep on the couch. "Mom, I'm going up to bed. What about you?"

"Not yet. My favorite show is on in a while. I'll see you in the morning."

"Good night," she said as she went up to her room. She fell asleep as soon as her head hit the pillow.

* * *

Eric sat on the closet floor, leaned against the wall, and listened to the television. He wondered when Barbara was going to go upstairs. Abby had gone to bed over an hour before. He wondered if Barbara was awake. *I can't take the chance she'll see me.* But he knew that he couldn't stay there all night again—it was just too dangerous. Counting on the TV to distract his mother-in-law, Eric slipped from his hiding place.

His pulse quickened as he approached his bedroom, silently turned the knob, and entered. His gaze immediately went to his wife, who was sound asleep. He went to her bedside and stared down at her, wanting to touch her but not wanting to wake her yet. If he could find the key without her knowledge, that would be best. He knew it would be difficult to leave if Abby found him there.

He searched both nightstands, but came up empty-handed. Next he looked on the dressers and in the drawers. Again, nothing. As he gazed around the room, using the moon as his light source, he wondered where the key might be.

It could be anywhere. I have to get that money to show the FBI I mean what I say.

He stepped toward the bed, adrenaline pulsing through his veins. His hand reached toward Abby but froze when he heard one of the girls cry out. Abby stirred, and Eric rushed to conceal himself in their walk-in closet.

* * *

Abby rolled over, wakened by Susannah's cry. Groaning, she pushed herself to a sitting position and went to her daughter. "What's wrong?" she asked a moment later.

"I had a bad dream," Susannah said, tears in her eyes. "Daddy was hurt and no one would help him."

Abby's heart wrenched as she pictured what her daughter described. "It was only a dream. Try to think of happy things, okay?"

"Okay, Mommy."

Abby tucked Susannah back in bed and left the room, trudging back to her own bed. She quickly fell asleep again and began to have a bad dream of her own. Someone was walking around her room, and she was all alone, defenseless.

The dream woke her.

Without opening her eyes, she strongly felt the presence of someone in her room. Her heart pounded and terror flooded her body.

Warm breath surged past her ear, and she froze in place. Then a hand clamped over her mouth. She tried to scream as her eyes flew open.

"It's me, Abby. Eric," he whispered.

Relief and joy swept through her as she looked at her husband kneeling next to the bed.

"Shhh," Eric said, removing his hand from her mouth.

"Eric," she whispered, throwing her arms around him. "I can't believe you're here." Her racing heart began to slow. "You scared me half to death. I could feel someone in the room and I was terrified."

He lay down next to her and wrapped his arms around her. "I'm so sorry. You don't need to be frightened."

She laid her head against his chest, reveling in the warmth of his presence, and began crying with relief. "Eric, I've missed you so much."

"I've missed you too. You can't imagine how much."

Then all the frustration she had been feeling for the past several weeks boiled up, and she pushed away from him. "Where have you been? What's going on?"

He frowned. "I can't explain everything right now."

"Please try," she said in anger. "I mean, how can you be gone for weeks and then just show up without any explanation? I think I have the right to know."

"Yes, you do, but there's just not time to explain it all right now. Please understand." He paused. "I can tell you that I'm working with the FBI to make everything right."

Abby sat up against the pillows and tried to control her frustration. Eric moved next to her.

"The FBI?" she asked. "Someone came to see me from the FBI. His name was Agent Franklin."

"Yes. That's the guy I'm working with."

"What do you mean, 'working with'?" Disappointment shot through her as she considered what Eric could mean. Was he working out a deal to escape going to jail for embezzlement?

"I don't want to get into it all right now. Your mom could come upstairs any minute, and it's unsafe for you to have information. I need to know if you found a small key."

Her disappointment in her husband was strong, but Abby shook her head in resignation. "No, I haven't found a key."

"Are you the one who cleaned up the front hall closet today?"

"I guess Mom did. Why?"

Eric bit his lip, hesitating. "I was here last night, looking for something, and I think a key fell out of my pocket when I was hiding in the closet."

Abby pulled back. "You were here last night? And you didn't wake me up?" Fresh anger mixed with her feelings of relief. "Do you have any idea how horrible it's been not knowing where you are or what's been going on? How could you not wake me up when you were right here?"

"I wanted to. You have no idea how badly I wanted to."

"I don't understand. What's going on? Does this have anything to do with Tim Meher?"

"Tim?" Eric said, surprise on his face. "What has he said to you?"

"Lots of things." She turned away briefly. "He said you stole money from the company."

"Do you believe him?" Eric said, visibly hurt by the thought that she did.

"I don't know what to believe anymore." She paused. "I found money in our closet."

"You did?" He paused. "How much?"

"Fifteen thousand dollars," Abby said, wondering if there was more to be found.

"I didn't steal it," Eric said, seeing the doubt on Abby's face. "You have to believe me."

"I can't help but remember when you had that drug relapse. I'm having trouble knowing what to believe. And your father told me you stole money from past employers."

"Drugs are not the issue here. Not at all," Eric said defensively. "I promised you I wouldn't touch them. And I only stole money once. I repented of it, Abby."

"What is the issue? Please, Eric. You have to tell me what's going on." She reached for the nightstand and picked up the book about disappearing. "I found this too."

Eric took it from her, his expression one of puzzlement. "What's this?"

"It was in your dresser drawer."

He held it out to Abby. "It's not mine. I've never seen it before."

Abby wasn't sure if she should believe him or not. "Then what was it doing in your dresser? It has a picture of you in it." Abby pulled out the picture.

Eric seemed to be in genuine shock. "Abby, I've never seen this woman in my life. It must've been planted just like the money—to make me look guilty."

Suddenly they heard the TV shut off and footsteps coming up the stairs. "Look," Eric whispered. "We'll have to figure this out later."

Abby sighed, frustrated at not knowing the facts but recognizing that Eric wasn't going to tell her anything more now. "Fine," she surrendered, not certain what to believe. "So what about this key? What's it for?"

"What did you do with the money you found?"

"I put it in a safe place. In the bank. Why?"

"Okay. That's good," he said, thinking. "Keep it there and don't touch it. We'll have to give it back soon." He glanced around the darkened room. "I need you to ask your mother if she found the key. If you find it, put it under the front doormat tomorrow. I'll come and get it."

"What's the key for?"

"A safe-deposit box."

"What's in it?" Abby asked, wondering how much she wanted to know.

"It's the money that was planted on me." He tried to smile. "Just try to get the key for me."

"Didn't the bank give you a backup key?"

"No. Why? Were they supposed to?"

"When I got a safe-deposit box, I was given two keys."

Eric shook his head in annoyance. "Well, I guess someone screwed up then, because I was only given one key."

"Isn't there another way to get into that box?" Abby asked, wanting the ordeal to be over with.

"I don't know. I never asked. I didn't think I'd be dumb enough to lose the key."

"Do you want me to get my mother right now and ask her?"

Eric considered the idea. "No. She would wonder why you need it during the night. I don't want her to know anything."

"What about the money I found? Do you want to give that to Franklin?"

"I will eventually. But right now I need to get into my safe-deposit box," he said, picturing the note that was with the money.

"The girls miss you terribly, you know."

He sighed. "I know. I miss them too. But I can't do anything about that right now."

"I talked to your father. He knows you're missing. I think you'd better let him know you're okay."

"I'll talk to him when I can." He paused. "Did he sound like he wanted to talk to me?"

"He's worried about you. He's your father, Eric."

"I know." Eric glanced around the room, then looked at Abby. "He probably thinks I'm using drugs again, doesn't he?"

Abby sighed, afraid to admit she had thought the same thing. "Just let him know you're safe."

Eric grimaced. "Did you change the code on the burglar alarm too?"

"Yes," she said. "I also changed all the locks. You obviously figured out the code, and it's the same for the alarm."

"Thank you for trusting me," he said, "and for being so clever."

Abby paused a moment, her feelings stronger—she did trust him. But before she could respond, she was interrupted by a nearby sound; it was her mother checking on the girls. It sounded like Tiffany was awake.

"I hate to tell you this, but I have to leave now," Eric said.

"No, Eric. Please don't go." Abby grabbed his shirt.

"Don't make this harder than it has to be. I promise I'll be home again soon." He pulled her into his arms and held her tight for several moments. "I love you, Abby," he whispered fiercely.

She sobbed as he left.

* * *

Abby had prayed herself to sleep and awoke feeling better than she had in a long, long time. Though she had been devastated when Eric left, she'd treasured the time she'd had with him and was grateful to have some idea of what was going on. Her feelings to trust Eric had been reconfirmed during the night, and she walked around the house enjoying the feeling before stopping in front of the bookcase.

The origami bird was still perched on the shelf, and Abby suddenly realized that in all the excitement of seeing each other, she had forgotten to have them unfold the bird together. It felt like a bad omen as she realized they might never get the chance—Eric was still in danger, she still couldn't contact him, and she didn't know who was harassing her or why.

CHAPTER TWENTY-SEVEN

"Oh, yes. I'd forgotten all about it," Barbara said after Abby asked her about the key. "I left it in my room. I'll go get it."

Abby followed her mother up the stairs into Tiffany's room, relief cascading over her. Barbara walked over to the dresser and perused the top of it.

"I thought I left it right here." She turned to Abby and smiled wryly. "You know, old age can be a hard thing on one's memory."

"Well, it's not there. Where else might you have put it?" Abby said, anxious to get the key to Eric.

"I'm thinking, I'm thinking. Oh, yes. I remember now. I set it on the bedside table." Barbara stepped over to the bed and stared at the tabletop. She reached for the book she had set there earlier. There was nothing beneath it. She smiled at Abby apologetically. "I'm sorry. I know I left it on the table."

That's what you said about the dresser, Abby thought, feeling more panicky by the second. "Could it be in the dresser among your things? It's really important I find it."

"What's it for?" Barbara asked as she walked to the dresser.

Abby wasn't about to mention Eric's visit. "It's for something I need, that's all." Abby stood next to Barbara at the dresser. "Here, let me help you look."

They searched the drawers together but couldn't find the key.

After a few frustrating minutes, Abby said, "Thanks anyway, Mom."

"I'm sure it will turn up," Barbara consoled her.

Abby went down the hall to her bedroom and sat on the love seat in her alcove. Anxiety at not finding the key made it difficult to relax. She knew it was critical that Eric get into the safe-deposit box, so she decided to leave a note under the mat to let him know she couldn't find the key, but would keep looking.

* * *

Under cover of darkness Eric lifted the porch mat. Instead of finding the precious key, he found a note from Abby. He read it quickly, then went back to his motel to try to think of another plan. He'd just have to meet with Franklin and tell his story. Maybe the Feds would have the authority to get into the box.

* * *

The next day it was time for Barbara to go back to work. As Abby hugged her mother good-bye, she was surprised to realize she was going to miss her. It was the first time she could recall truly enjoying spending time with her mother. Having Eric missing was the worst thing that had ever happened to her, but along with that challenge had been the blessing of drawing closer to her mother and sister. For that she would always be grateful.

"Bye, girls. I'm going to miss you," Barbara said as she gathered Tiffany and Susannah in a big hug.

"Good-bye, Grandma. I'll miss you too," Susannah said, wiping a tear from her cheek.

"Now, don't get all teary eyed on me. If nothing else, I'll be back when that new baby brother or sister arrives." Barbara looked at Abby for her agreement.

"Yes, of course. Grandma will be back before you know it. Now give her one last hug before she goes," Abby said before waving good-bye and shutting the door.

The house seemed emptier with her mother gone. Abby went into Tiffany's room to strip her bed in preparation for her daughter to reclaim her room. As she pulled the fitted sheet from the bed, she thought about the key. Her mother had found it in the closet and brought it to the room, but where could it have gone?

Impulsively Abby lifted the corner of the mattress. It wasn't too heavy and she was able to peek underneath. Her heart beat hard in hopes of finding the key, but it wasn't there. She dropped the mattress back in place and, with a heavy heart, brought the laundry downstairs.

* * *

As Eric compared the two papers in his hands while waiting outside the door of Agent Franklin's office, he thought back to when he had come into possession of one of them.

Just a month before, when he had been doing the books at Central Valley Construction, he had noticed payments to a supplier he had never heard of. The amounts weren't huge, only ten to fifteen thousand dollars each time, but enough that he decided to investigate. When he hadn't found that supplier on the approved list, he had gone to Tim, the senior accountant, and asked if he knew anything about it.

"I think something might be going on," Eric had said to Tim as he showed him an invoice for the unknown supplier.

Tim looked puzzled for a moment, then relieved. "No, no, no. This is a new supplier. Didn't you get the memo with the new list?" Tim clicked his mouse, pulling up a document listing their current suppliers. "Look," he said, motioning for Eric to come around and look at his monitor. "It says right here they're one of our suppliers now."

Eric looked at the monitor, surprised to see the name of the company from the invoice. "That's weird, because they're not on my list, and I'm sure my list is current."

"I don't know what to tell you. I guess Brock forgot to email you the latest list," Tim said. "I'll forward it to you."

"I guess you're right. Thanks."

Once back in his office, Eric had gone through the invoices and purchase orders and was stunned to find his signature scrawled across the bottom of each PO. He had no memory of signing those purchase orders; he could only conclude his signature must have been forged. Then he added up the invoices and was alarmed to see they totaled at least sixty thousand dollars. The checks had been mailed to a post-office box.

The realization hit him. *I'm being set up!*

He had been caught completely off guard, and when he'd gotten home he'd quickly discovered five thousand dollars stashed in his home office. In a panic, he had locked all of it in his desk drawer. Later, he'd taken the money and the few purchase orders and invoices he had found and put them in a safe-deposit box at the bank. That evening he'd gone online, searching for information on embezzlement and trying to decide what to do.

That night he had tossed and turned, arguing with himself about a course of action. Obviously someone had the ability to get into his house and hide incriminating evidence there. What if the authorities were called and they found more evidence against him? Would he be arrested? Would he go to jail? Before the night was over he'd decided to go on the run until he could prove his innocence.

And then, under the driver's seat in his Jeep, he'd discovered more money along with the note implying he had asked for the cash. Obviously it was meant for the authorities to find. Fortunately, Eric had found it first and was able to keep it locked up with the cash in the safe-deposit box.

Cursing his past life choices, Eric had realized he couldn't go to the authorities until he had evidence he wasn't behind the embezzlement. He knew they would investigate his past, and since he had a drug arrest on his record, they would immediately suspect him. Such an investigation would not go well for him unless he had irrefutable evidence he was being set up.

So, while in hiding, he'd done some research on the Internet. He'd found a legitimate company with the same name that was used for the bogus company, but not at the address the checks had been sent. He had the PO box number where the checks had been sent, but he needed to verify it wasn't a PO box the legitimate company used.

He had tried to call them several times but had continued to get an answering machine. Finally he had obtained a new Hotmail account under an assumed name and had emailed the company. He'd finally gotten a response saying they weren't a supplier for Central Valley Construction. He'd done everything he could to track down evidence that he wasn't the embezzler, but the only good thing he had was what he'd witnessed at the casino. There was more to this story than he had originally realized. It was obvious now why the embezzler had felt the need to steal. He was pulled from his thoughts as Agent Franklin opened the door and ushered him in.

"I don't have all the money yet, but I can explain," Eric began, holding out the note from his car.

CHAPTER TWENTY-EIGHT

"It's for you, Mom. It's Grandma," Tiffany said, handing Abby the cordless phone.

"Hi, Mom. Everything all right?" She had been sitting on the couch reading a magazine, her feet tucked underneath her.

"Of course, dear. I thought you'd like to know I found that key we were searching for."

"Oh." Abby swung her feet to the floor. "You have it now?"

"Yes, right here in my hand. What do you want me to do with it?"

"The girls and I will come up and get it right now." Abby leaned forward intently, pleased to have the key found. When she hung up, she loaded the girls in the car.

As Abby and her daughters made the hour drive to Sacramento, she wondered how she could get the key to Eric. *Maybe I can access the safe-deposit box myself,* she thought. *He said it was at our bank, so I know where to go.* Feeling closer to accomplishing what was necessary to bring Eric home lifted Abby's spirits, and once back home, she found someone to watch Tiffany and Susannah so she could go to the bank.

She knew from her experience of getting her own safe-deposit box that her signature had to be on the safe-deposit box lease agreement in order to open it. She knew her name wouldn't be on the slip for Eric's lease. She was hopeful they would allow her to open her husband's box anyway.

All I can do is try, she thought, saying a silent prayer as she entered the bank.

Abby approached someone at a nearby desk. "Excuse me. I . . . uh . . . I need to get into my husband's box."

The woman was all business. "I'm afraid I can't allow that. If he's the only one authorized to open it, then I can't let you access it."

"I have the key right here, though," Abby said, holding out the key to prove it. "And my husband's not able to come himself. It's extremely urgent that I get in that box."

The woman smiled sympathetically. "I'm sorry. There's nothing I can do."

* * *

After picking up her children, Abby drove home, dejected at her failure to help her husband. She wished she had a way to get the key to him.

The girls were excited after being at their friends' house, but Abby wasn't in the mood for noise. "Who wants to watch a DVD and eat popcorn?" she suggested.

"Me! Me!" they both shouted.

"Mom, can we eat the popcorn in the family room?" Susannah asked.

"Sure, why not?" Abby said, putting the bag in the microwave.

A few minutes later a knock sounded at the front door.

Before Abby could stop her, Susannah yanked the door open.

"Susannah!" Abby said, pushing her aside, not wanting her to open the door to a stranger.

Susannah looked at her mother in surprise and stomped away, angry at being reprimanded. "There's nobody here anyway," she grumbled, as she rejoined her sister in front of the television.

Abby stepped onto the porch glancing right and left, trying to discover who had doorbell-ditched her house. She shook her head, irritated. Then, as she looked at Pumpkin's bowl to see if it needed filling, she noticed a small slip of paper tucked under the edge. She picked it up, her stomach clenching in worry. She prayed it was from Eric. "This is your last chance," Abby whispered as she read the message. "Give us the money now and your family will be safe—" She stopped, then stared at the last line in confusion and mounting fear: *Cat got your tongue?*

"What did they do?" Abby gasped, fear crowding out all other emotion. She looked around the bushes lining the house, then froze as her eyes locked on Pumpkin's collar lying on the ground. The cat was nowhere to be seen. She slammed the door shut and bolted it with shaking hands.

We have to get out of here, she thought frantically. *We've got to get away somewhere.*

Looking at her daughters' happy faces as they were immersed in the movie, Abby knew she had to do whatever it took to protect them from danger. She crossed the family room and went into the office, pulling out a map of California. She ran her finger along the map looking for a safe place to take her children—a place she had been before but a place at least a hundred miles away.

Then she spotted it. *Carmel.* She and Eric had gone there for one of their anniversaries. It was a quaint little village but full of tourists. They could hide out there, but it would still seem like an adventure to the girls.

Abby ran out of the office and went out to the garage. She chose two medium-size suitcases and took them upstairs. First she packed her own, trying to remember all she would need.

She dragged the first suitcase down the stairs and through the family room.

"Mom, what are you doing?" Tiffany asked, looking at her mother like she was crazy.

"Tiffany, turn off the movie and you and Susannah go to the bathroom. We're going on a trip."

"Yes!" Susannah shouted, remembering the last trip they had taken.

Tiffany didn't seem as sure. "Why, Mom? Where are we going?"

"I don't have time to explain." She paused halfway across the room. "Susannah, would you go grab the map off of the desk, please?" Abby watched her run into the office as she continued dragging the suitcase toward the garage.

* * *

Tess carried a stack of papers toward Tim Meher's office. As she approached his partly open door, she paused, not wanting to interrupt his phone call. She tried not to eavesdrop, but he sounded angry, which made his voice louder. Then she heard her name mentioned, and her curiosity got the better of her.

"Tess hasn't given me anything new lately. I think that avenue of information has been lost," Tim was saying. He paused, apparently listening to someone on the other end. "No, I appreciate your help. You did what you could . . . I'm going to head over there myself to take care of this once and for all . . . Abby's had all the chances I'm willing to give. I need to get that money and I need it now. You know what they did to me. If she won't give me the money willingly, I'll just have to take it by force."

Tess couldn't believe what she was hearing. She began backing away from Tim's office, stunned to realize that he must have been the one behind the phony FBI agent. He was the one who was keeping an eye on Abby.

Just as she began to gain her composure, Tim stormed out of his office. When he saw her, he stopped, a look of suspicion on his face.

"How long have you been there?" he asked.

"I . . . I just got here." She held out the papers she had in her arms, willing herself to act normal. "I have some papers for you to sign. Would you like me to put them on your desk?" She offered him a tentative smile.

He narrowed his eyes at her, seeming to decide whether he believed she had just arrived. Then he smiled, though it didn't reach his eyes. "Yes, please put them on my desk. And there are some files I need you to take care of right away. I'll be back in a while."

Tess watched him go before hurrying into his office. She set the papers down on his desk and picked up his phone. She dialed Abby's number, hoping to warn her neighbor before Tim got there. With shaking hands she punched in Abby's number, but the phone just rang and rang.

CHAPTER TWENTY-NINE

Just as the garage door slid open and Abby began pulling the luggage toward the back of the minivan, a door-to-door salesman approached her. She tried to ignore him as she opened the rear door on the van.

"Excuse me, ma'am," he said as he walked up to her. "Do you have a dirty carpet I can clean?" He held up a bottle of solution. "This will get out any stain you may have on your carpet."

"I'm sorry, but I don't have time right now," Abby said, lifting the first suitcase into the back of her open van.

"I can see you're busy, but this will only take five minutes."

Susannah came out of the house and held the map out to Abby. "Here, Mom."

Abby glanced at her daughter. "Thank you." Then she turned toward the salesman. "This really isn't a good time."

"What time would be good for you?" he asked.

Abby felt trapped. The salesman was standing right behind her van.

"Your turn, Susannah," Tiffany said as she slammed the door to the house.

"But Mom, I don't have to go to the bathroom," Susannah whined.

Abby knew they would be on the road for at least two hours, and she didn't want to stop once they got going. "Please try. We won't be stopping for a while."

"Ma'am? When would you like me to come back?"

"I don't know," Abby said, exasperated that she wasn't on the road yet.

"Mom? Where's Pumpkin?" Tiffany asked. "Don't you want him to be in the garage while we're gone?"

Abby turned toward her daughter, suddenly remembering the reason she had felt so frightened in the first place. "Don't worry about Pumpkin. I'm sure he'll be fine."

"But Mom, what if he gets hungry? Or if it rains or something? He should be in the garage where he'll be safe."

"Can I put you down for next Tuesday?" the salesman asked, his notebook in hand.

"I'm going to go look for him," Tiffany announced as she trotted toward the back gate.

Abby looked from her daughter to the salesman. "No, you can't put me down for next Tuesday. I don't want my carpets cleaned."

"Oh. Sorry to bother you, ma'am. Have a nice day," he said as he quickly made his way down the driveway and toward the neighbor's house.

As Abby lifted the last suitcase into the car, Susannah came running out of the house. "Tiffany's playing on the swing in the backyard! If she can play, so can I!"

"Susannah, please get in the car. I'll go get your sister," Abby said as she went back into the house. *I'd*

*better check if I left anything in the bathroom before we
head out,* she thought as she walked down the hall. As
she passed the office, the phone began to ring.

Wanting to be on the road, Abby almost ignored
the call, but then decided to answer it. As she said
hello, she looked out the window into the backyard
and saw both her daughters playing on the swing.
Darn it. They should be waiting in the car.

"Abby?" the person on the phone asked.

"Can you hang on for a minute?" Abby said before
bothering to ask who it was.

"Wait!"

Abby wondered who could be so insistent. She
didn't exactly recognize the voice. "Who is this?"

"It's Tess. I have to tell you something."

Abby sighed, wondering what Tess was so excited
about. "I'm on my way out the door. Can I give you a
call back when I get home?"

"It's Tim, Abby. You have to watch out for Tim!"

As Abby registered the frantic tone in Tess's voice,
she felt panic welling up. "What are you talking
about?"

"There's no time to explain. Just get out!"

Abby dropped the phone, intending to grab her
daughters and run. As she pushed open the sliding
glass door, she froze. Tim was using one arm to push
Susannah on the swing. Curiously, his other arm was
in a cast.

"Hi, Abby. Do you want to join us? We're having a
good time, aren't we, girls?"

When Tiffany saw Abby, she jumped off the swing.
But Tim grabbed her arm. "Where are you going,
sweetheart?"

Tiffany looked up at him and hesitated, then looked in her mother's direction. Tim's gaze followed Tiffany's, and his eyes met Abby's. He shook his head.

"Mom?" Tiffany said, unsure what was expected of her. Terrified for her daughters, Abby couldn't move.

"Come over here and join us," Tim said, motioning to Abby.

"I'm coming," Abby said to Tiffany as she began walking in their direction. As she reached Tim's side, he let go of Tiffany and grabbed her instead. Relieved he had let her daughter go, Abby was now frightened for herself.

"Let's go inside," Tim said, pulling Abby toward the open door. When Tiffany and Susannah began to follow, Tim said, "You girls stay out here while I talk to your mommy. Okay?"

When Abby opened her mouth to speak, Tim squeezed her arm.

"I'll be fine. You stay out here," Abby said, trying to put a reassuring smile on her face.

"Okay," Tiffany said, looking uncertain.

"Come on," Tim said, yanking Abby into the house.

"What do you want?" she hissed when they were alone.

"I'm here to collect what's mine. I know you have some money. I need it now."

"It's not here," she said, glancing toward the backyard, hoping her daughters would run to the neighbor's and call the police.

Tim's gaze followed Abby's. "You have beautiful children, and I'm sure you wouldn't want anything to happen to them." He looked at her swollen abdomen. "*Any* of them."

Feeling more terrified by the second, Abby tried to think of a way to get Tim away from her children. "I have the money. But it's at the bank."

He let go of her and smiled. "How much do you have?"

"Fifteen thousand."

Tim frowned. "Eric had more than that. Where's the rest? Did you spend it?"

"No. I only had fifteen."

"Eric must have the rest," Tim muttered to himself.

"He turned over what he had to the FBI," Abby said, wondering how Tim would react to this bit of information.

"The FBI, huh? So he's the one who told them I was involved. I figured as much." He glanced toward the back-yard again. "Well, then, there's no time to lose. Let's go."

"I need to tell my children I'm leaving," Abby begged.

He considered this. "Okay, but I'll be listening, so be careful what you say."

Abby walked toward the sliding glass door. She didn't care if Tim got the money she'd been holding onto. It wasn't hers. It certainly wasn't worth the risk of getting herself or her children hurt. She would coop-erate with Tim and give him what he wanted.

"Tiffany, Susannah," Abby called from the door. "Would you come here, please?"

"Careful, now," Tim reminded as the girls ran toward her.

"I have to go somewhere for a few minutes. I'm going to leave you here by yourselves, so you need to be very good."

"Okay, Mom," Tiffany said, glancing behind her at Tim.

"I don't want you to go," Susannah whined.

Abby hugged her. "I know, but you'll be fine. I'll be back soon. I promise. I want you to come in the house and watch television now. Okay?"

"Okay," Tiffany said, glancing at Tim as she walked past him into the family room.

Susannah followed her and said, "It's my turn to pick the show we watch."

Abby watched her daughters turn on the television, thankful Tim wasn't insisting they come along. Her first goal had been met. Now she had to figure out a way to make sure she and her unborn child stayed safe.

"Let's go," Tim said, pushing Abby toward the front door. "You'll drive my car."

She followed him to his car and climbed in the driver's seat. He got in the other side. "Don't try anything clever." He opened the glove box and pulled out a gun.

Trying to stay calm, Abby backed out of the driveway and started driving. She had a bad feeling that once Tim had the money he would hurt her. Not only that, if he got away she was afraid he might come after Eric or her children. Frantically, she tried to think of a way to get out of this. First she tried to appeal to Tim's conscience. "I don't care about the money, Tim. I'll give it to you. Just don't hurt me."

He laughed while glancing at the cast on his arm. "Yeah, no one will get hurt."

"What happened to your arm?" Abby asked, attempting to take the attention from herself.

"This is what they do when you get behind on your payments. That's why I need that money."

"Oh." Discussing his broken arm probably wasn't a good idea, she realized, trying to think of another subject. "Are you the one who set up the house on Buttercup Drive?"

He smiled. "Did you like that?"

"That was pretty smart," Abby said, trying to make him feel less angry. "How did you do it?"

"Well, that woman was a friend of mine." He seemed to relax as he spoke. "She was going to be moving, so I asked her to find a book at the library and a picture of Eric. She's also a graphic designer. Pretty handy with digital photo enhancement." He paused, staring at Abby. "I was afraid you wouldn't find that slip of paper until after she'd already moved. But it ended up working perfectly. I'll bet you were pretty shocked to see that picture, weren't you?"

"Yes, I was," Abby laughed, trying to keep things light.

"Why are you going so slow?" Tim asked, suddenly angry. "Step on it, already. But don't get pulled over."

Abby glanced at Tim as she bit her inner lip, an idea brewing in her mind.

* * *

Eric tried to relax as he leaned back in the chair. He was sitting across from Agent Franklin at the resident agency office, listening to Franklin explain how they had found proof that Tim was behind the embezzlement. Relief swept through Eric as he realized he was no longer a suspect.

"We verified that Tim's behind the phony company," Franklin was saying.

Breathing out slowly, Eric smiled. "What now?"

"We need to speak to him again. We're trying to find him. Before we can clear you, though, we need to get the funds you mentioned."

"Sure. I just need to go home and get my wife." At the words, Eric felt immense happiness. He could hardly wait to tell Abby it was all over.

"That's fine. Bring it in today."

"Of course," Eric said, ready to agree to whatever they demanded. As he went to shake the agent's hand, a man opened the door and said the agent had an urgent phone call. Eric felt bad for whoever was calling, relishing the freedom from his own dire situation.

A short time later he was still having trouble containing his elation as he pulled up to his house. He nearly ran to the front door. When he turned the knob he was surprised to find it unlocked. His eyebrows drew together. "That's funny. Abby usually keeps the door locked."

The first thing he heard was the sound of the television. When he walked into the family room, he found his daughters engrossed in a cartoon.

"Hi," he said, nearly shouting to be heard over the sound of the television.

"Daddy!" they screamed, flinging themselves into his arms.

He hugged them close, warmth flooding his heart. "Where's Mom?" he asked, pulling back.

"She's not here," Tiffany said.

"Where is she?" Eric asked, alarmed. He knew she had never left the girls home alone before.

"She went somewhere with a man," Susannah said.

"Who was it, honey?" Eric asked.

"I don't know."

"Tiff? Do you know who it was?" Eric asked, turning to his older daughter.

"No, but he had a broken arm, and Mommy looked scared."

Adrenaline pulsed through his veins as he grabbed his cell phone to call Franklin, picked up the girls, and ran them over to a neighbor's.

* * *

Abby pulled into the bank parking lot and turned off the engine. She watched as Tim put the gun into his jacket pocket.

"That's right," he said, catching her watching him. "Don't try anything foolish. You'll walk next to me and pretend everything's fine." He reached into the backseat and picked up a briefcase.

Abby nodded, praying she wasn't about to make a mistake.

They exited the car, and Tim handed her the briefcase. "You carry this."

As they walked toward the bank, Abby thought over her plan. She needed to stall. Maybe Tess had called the police too, although she wouldn't know Tim had forced Abby to go to the bank.

"Open the door, Abby," Tim said, keeping his good hand in his pocket with the gun.

Abby complied and they got in line behind an older woman. When it was their turn, Abby set the briefcase on the floor, then opened her purse, pulled out her wallet, and set it on the counter. Tim watched her every move.

"How can I help you folks?" the teller asked them.

"I, uh, I'd like to make a withdrawal," Abby said.

"Okay. What's the account number?" the teller asked.

As Abby fumbled with her wallet, she could sense Tim's nervousness. "Let me see. I have it here somewhere."

Abby pulled out a business card and flipped it over before Tim could see what was on it. "Let me just jot it down for you." Quickly scrawling her account number on the card, Abby handed it to the teller and tried to convey with her eyes that something was wrong.

The teller didn't seem to notice anything out of the ordinary as she asked, "How much would you like to withdraw?"

"Fifteen thousand dollars," Abby said, her heart pounding. She ventured a quick glance in Tim's direction and saw him grin.

"I'll need to see some ID, ma'am," the teller said.

"Oh, sure." Abby held her wallet out to the woman, her license facing up.

"Thank you." The teller barely looked in Abby's direction as she typed the numbers into her computer.

Abby held her breath, waiting to see what would happen.

The teller looked at Abby and Tim, puzzled. "I'm sorry, ma'am. Your account doesn't have the funds to cover that withdrawal."

Tim stepped forward. "How much is in there?"

Startled at Tim's sudden movement, the teller's gaze jerked in Tim's direction, then back at the screen. "It says you have $548.63."

"What the—?" Tim sputtered.

Abby's heart raced as she looked at Tim. He clenched his jaw, and his eyes bored holes into her face. Without looking away from her, Tim said, "We'll take it all."

Inhaling sharply, Abby tried to calm herself. She hadn't foreseen Tim emptying her bank account when she'd thought of this diversion.

"Ma'am?" the teller asked.

Turning back to face the teller, Abby again tried to convey her concern.

"Sign here, please," the teller said.

Unsure what else to do, Abby signed the withdrawal slip and passed it back to the teller.

"Do you want that in twenties?"

She felt Tim step closer, his arm going around her shoulders.

"That would be fine," he said, smiling.

The teller looked at Abby, hesitating. When Abby didn't respond, the woman began counting out the money.

Not taking his arm from Abby's shoulders, Tim motioned with his chin toward the cash. "Go ahead, honey."

Abby slowly scooped it up, placing it in her purse along with her wallet.

"Don't forget the briefcase, sweetheart."

Tim's arm still on her shoulder, Abby picked up the briefcase. Pressing Abby close to his side, Tim walked with her away from the teller's window.

"Ma'am! You forgot this," the teller called after them, holding up the business card.

Barely able to turn her head in the teller's direction, Abby called out, "It's fine." She prayed the woman would turn the card over and come to the right conclusion.

Once Abby and Tim had cleared the bank's doors, Tim released Abby's shoulders and gripped her arm, nearly dragging her to the car. She could hear him swearing violently under his breath.

When they got to the car, he spun her around so she faced him, making her drop the briefcase.

"Where's the money?" he said through gritted teeth.

Abby trembled at the fury in his face.

He squeezed her arm harder.

"You're hurting me. Let go." She tried to pull away, but his hand was like a vise.

"If you think you're hurting now, just wait until we're no longer in public." He moved his face within inches of hers, then spoke very slowly. "I don't like being tricked."

"I'm sorry," Abby whispered, trying to back up a few inches, frightened to see there were no other people around. "I wasn't tricking you. The money was there."

"Where's the money now? Or should we go back to your house and see what your daughters are up to?"

Abby's eyes shot open, fear making speech difficult. "Eric—Eric must have needed it. But I have more."

Without lessening his grip, Tim pulled back slightly. "That teller didn't seem to think so."

"It's in a safe-deposit box."

Tim spoke with barely controlled rage. "Then why didn't we ask for that?"

Abby shrugged slightly. "I'm sorry. I guess I was just scared and not thinking clearly."

"Take the money in your purse and put it in my glove box," Tim said, never letting go of her arm.

"Let go of me first."

"Fine. But don't forget who has the gun," Tim said as his grip slackened.

Nodding, Abby opened her purse and pulled out the cash. She opened the car door and slid into the seat, then opened the glove box and placed the money inside.

"Okay," she said, standing next to the car once more. "Now what?"

"Now we go back inside and get my money. All of it." He looked around at the parking lot, a determined expression on his face, then turned back to Abby. "I have to warn you. I've had all I can take of you. I don't even think I care that we're in a public place. If you do anything stupid, I think I just might shoot you in front of everyone. Got it?"

Seeing the expression on his face, Abby believed him. "Yes, I understand."

"Get the briefcase."

Abby picked it up and allowed Tim to lead her back to the doors of the bank.

As soon as they entered, Abby looked over to the teller's window to see if the woman who had helped them earlier noticed them. Her window was closed. Abby stared numbly ahead as Tim got someone to help them with her safe-deposit box.

* * *

"Do you think it could be Tim?" Eric said into his cell phone as he drove toward the city center.

Agent Franklin was clearly also in transit as he answered, a car's horn interrupting him. "Now, don't panic, but I just received a call from the manager at your wife's bank. He said a man and woman came in a few minutes ago trying to make a withdrawal. He said the pair were acting strange, and the woman had written her account number on the back of one of my business cards." Franklin paused. "He asked if I knew a woman named Abby Breuner."

A ball of anger began working its way up Eric's throat. "Then it must be Tim."

"I agree." Franklin paused again. "Eric, I want you to stay home with your children. Let us handle this."

"No way. This is my wife we're talking about. I'm already on my way."

"You'll just get in the way. Look, I'll call you as soon as she's safe."

* * *

With shaking hands, Abby loaded the briefcase with the bills from the safe-deposit box. As she approached Tim, she tried to act normal and not reveal her terror. She held the briefcase out to Tim.

"You carry it," he whispered. "I need to keep my good hand free to make sure you don't do anything stupid."

She nodded and followed Tim toward the front door of the bank. He pushed it open and allowed Abby to go first. She kept walking, not wanting to give Tim a reason to get angry.

"I want you to put the briefcase in my trunk," he said, pulling out his car keys. He unlocked the trunk and it popped open. "Nice and easy now."

Abby followed his instructions and watched as he closed the trunk. "Okay. I did what you asked. Let me go now."

"Patience, patience." Keeping his hand inside his jacket, he jerked his head toward the passenger door. "Get in."

Abby had always heard that once you got in the car with your kidnapper, your chances of survival decreased. She hadn't balked before, because she had wanted to get Tim away from her children. Now, however, she couldn't see how going with him could be beneficial. Her hesitation agitated him.

"What are you waiting for? Let's go." He pushed her toward the door. "Open it."

"No," Abby said as she tried to bolt away. Her pregnant shape made her slow and awkward. Tim caught her easily and pulled her toward the door. As panic welled up inside her, a thought came clearly to her mind. *Pretend you're in labor.* Suddenly she bent over and held her abdomen. "I think I'm going into labor."

That caught Tim's attention and he let go. "What?"

Abby forced a moan and slid to the ground. "Help! Help me!"

Tim knelt next to her. "Shut up and get in the car."

He tried to pull her up, but she made herself limp. He squeezed her arm hard and wrenched her up, forcing her to stand.

"Stop it!" she screamed. "You're hurting me!"

Abby watched him form his hand into a fist and pull it back. She closed her eyes, preparing for the impact, then heard a thud and felt Tim's hand drop from her arm. Her eyes opened to see Eric on top of Tim, pummeling him.

Shocked to see her husband there when she needed him most, she stared at the scene unfolding before her. Then, realizing Eric might hurt Tim badly enough to cause them all more problems, Abby reached for Eric. "Stop, stop!" she screamed. "You're going to kill him!" Eric looked in her direction, seeming surprised to see her standing there, then let his hands fall to his sides.

Eric stood and faced Abby, exhaustion and relief on his face. Abby smiled and held out her arms. As Eric stepped in her direction, she heard the sickening sound of a gun being cocked, and her eyes widened as she saw Tim point his gun at Eric.

Eric pushed Abby behind him, using himself as a shield. "You're only making things worse, Tim. The police are on their way. Let us go."

"No," Tim said, his eyes filled with rage. "I'm not the only one who's going to suffer."

"You brought this all on yourself," Eric said.

"It doesn't matter." Tim stood up, holding the gun steady. "If I go down, you're going down with me."

"He's got a gun!" a woman coming out of the bank screamed. Tim turned his head. Taking advantage of the distraction, Eric dove into Tim, knocking him to the ground. The gun shot one bullet into the air, and Eric grabbed Tim's wrist, slamming his hand into the ground until the gun was free. Eric grabbed it and held it against Tim's forehead.

"Freeze! FBI!" a voice shouted.

Abby watched in horror as several men pointed their weapons at Eric.

"Drop the gun!" the commander yelled.

Eric dropped the gun and was immediately thrown to the ground.

"You have the wrong man," Abby yelled, trying to make herself heard above the chaos. "Tim's the one you want." She pointed at Tim, who lay on the ground, watching. As soon as eyes turned away from him he tried to roll over.

"Stay back, ma'am," one of the men said to Abby, gently pushing her out of the way.

"But you've got the wrong man," she shouted, nearly hysterical. She was terrified that Tim would get away.

"The lady's right. Let that man go," a familiar voice said.

Abby turned to see Agent Franklin walking toward them.

She watched as he approached Tim and, after searching him, placed handcuffs on his wrists as best he could with the cast on Tim's arm.

A moment later Eric grabbed Abby and pulled her close.

"Oh, Eric," she sobbed.

"It's over now," he murmured into her ear.

"Really?" she choked out.

"Yes, and I'll never leave you again." He loosened his arms and looked at her. "Everything's going to be okay now. Agent Franklin spoke with the assistant U.S. attorney, and since I'm cooperating, he let me go. He said because I came forward and am turning in the money, they won't press charges even though I held onto the money for a while. They understand I was being framed."

Abby put her hands on his face. "Does that mean you get to come home now? For good?"

Eric grinned. "Yes. Are you ready?"

Abby nodded, too overcome with emotion to speak.

"Excuse me," Franklin said as he approached them. "Are you okay, Mrs. Breuner?"

"I'll be fine, I think."

"Good. Uh, we need to get a statement from you."

"Now?" Eric asked.

"I'd like to do it as soon as possible."

"Right now I'm taking my wife home. She's been through enough today. We'll come to your office tomorrow and take care of this."

"Wait," Abby said. "There's a briefcase in the trunk with the money that was stolen, and I have the key to your safe-deposit box, too. There's also money in the glove box that belongs to us."

After the FBI took the briefcase and gave the Breuners their money, Eric led Abby to his Jeep and they headed home.

* * *

Late that night, after the girls had been tucked in bed, Abby and Eric settled down together on the couch in the family room. They had called family and concerned friends and had been trying to avoid the media all day.

"I still don't understand," Abby began. "Why did Tim steal the money and then try to blame you?"

"It seems he's addicted to gambling and had to borrow money from some pretty bad people to pay off his gambling debts. Apparently he paid them off, but decided to set me up so there was an explanation for the missing funds. The only problem was that he kept gambling and losing. He had to borrow more from them, but then he couldn't keep stealing because he'd already set me up to take the fall, but I'd left."

"I see," Abby said, petting Pumpkin as he lay on her lap. The cat had turned up at the house that evening, collarless but apparently unharmed. "He couldn't very well continue to embezzle from the company when you weren't there to be blamed."

"Exactly. So he needed to get back the money he'd planted on me so he could start paying these guys back. I guess it wasn't fast enough for them, though."

"Why didn't you just go to the police right away?"

"I wanted to. But you know about my past mistakes. I knew if the authorities checked my record they would have reason to doubt me."

Inwardly Abby winced, vividly remembering her own doubt in her husband. She took his hand. "I'm just glad no one was hurt. When Tim pulled out that gun today, I thought that was it." She shuddered at the memory and pulled closer to Eric.

Eric stroked Abby's cheek. "I would have given my life to protect you."

As she imagined all that could have gone wrong, she felt a lump form in her throat. She said a silent prayer of thanks that none of them had been injured. "What did your dad say when you told him everything?" Abby asked, trying to turn her thoughts away from what could have happened.

"We had a good talk. I think we understand each other better now." He paused. "What about your mother? Does she still think I'm not good enough for you?"

Abby cringed, saddened to realize her husband knew what her mother thought about him. "She's coming around. She wasn't thrilled when I told the whole story, but she was heartened to know you were innocent. Her feelings are just something she'll have to work out. Besides, Jennifer said she'd put in a good word for you." She turned to face him directly. "The important thing is how I feel about you, and I love—"

Suddenly Abby's eyes lit up. She got up and went to the bookshelf, taking down the origami bird and holding it out to Eric.

"What's this?" he asked.

"Open it," Abby said, smiling, thrilled to have her husband home with her again.

He did, staring at the words inside. "Is this what I think it is?"

"I got it the day you disappeared. I've been waiting for you to come home to see what it says." Abby sat on the couch next to Eric and snuggled up to him. "So?"

EPILOGUE

Eric brought their new baby boy to Abby, settling him into her arms. She ran her fingers through the soft fuzz on her son's head.

They had come home from the hospital earlier that day and were enjoying a peaceful moment. Brock had kindly given Eric the week off to spend time with Abby and the new baby.

"It feels good to be home," she said, tucking the blanket around the little bundle.

Eric smiled at his wife and sat on the bed next to her.

Just then Tiffany and Susannah ran into the room.

"Can I hold him, Mom?" Tiffany asked.

Abby placed the baby into Tiffany's arms and watched as Susannah crowded close to her siblings. Her heart warmed with joy as she watched her children. Taking Eric's hand, she said a silent prayer of gratitude for all of her blessings.

"He's so tiny," Susannah whispered as she watched her baby brother sleep. "Do we really get to keep him?"

"Forever and ever," Eric said as he gazed into Abby's eyes.

ABOUT THE AUTHOR

Christine has always loved to read and has recently discovered a love for writing. She grew up in San Jose, California, but now makes her home in Utah. She is married and has four children. Christine earned a bachelor's degree in information technology, and she now works in the IT field. In her spare hours, she enjoys spending time with her family, reading, and watching movies.

Christine would love to hear from you and can be contacted through Covenant Communications, PO box 416, American Fork, UT 84003-0416, or through email at info@Covenant-lds.com.